THE GREAT WESTERN RAILWAY GIRLS DO THEIR BIT

JANE LARK

First published in Great Britain in 2025 by Boldwood Books Ltd.

Copyright © Jane Lark, 2025

Cover Design by Colin Thomas

Cover Images: Colin Thomas and iStock

The moral right of Jane Lark to be identified as the author of this work has been asserted in accordance with the Copyright, Designs and Patents Act 1988.

All rights reserved. No part of this book may be reproduced in any form or by any electronic or mechanical means, including information storage and retrieval systems, without written permission from the author, except for the use of brief quotations in a book review. This book is a work of fiction and, except in the case of historical fact, any resemblance to actual persons, living or dead, is purely coincidental.

Every effort has been made to obtain the necessary permissions with reference to copyright material, both illustrative and quoted. We apologise for any omissions in this respect and will be pleased to make the appropriate acknowledgements in any future edition.

A CIP catalogue record for this book is available from the British Library.

Paperback ISBN 978-1-83656-568-0

Large Print ISBN 978-1-83656-567-3

Hardback ISBN 978-1-83656-566-6

Trade Paperback ISBN 978-1-80635-298-2

Ebook ISBN 978-1-83656-569-7

Kindle ISBN 978-1-83656-570-3

Audio CD ISBN 978-1-83656-561-1

MP3 CD ISBN 978-1-83656-562-8

Digital audio download ISBN 978-1-83656-563-5

This book is printed on certified sustainable paper. Boldwood Books is dedicated to putting sustainability at the heart of our business. For more information please visit https://www.boldwoodbooks.com/about-us/sustainability/

Boldwood Books Ltd, 23 Bowerdean Street, London, SW6 3TN

www.boldwoodbooks.com

In memory of Geoff Smith
September 1940–July 2025

AUTHOR NOTE

Thank you to the volunteers who give their time, knowledge and commitment to support the **Swindon Heritage Preservation Charity** and work in the **Railway Village Museum**. This charity is doing an amazing job preserving and restoring the buildings and community spaces that are Swindon's heritage. If you visit the **Steam Museum** in Swindon, don't forget to take the time to walk through the subway to the Railway Village and take a look at the purpose-built Victorian Town where the real Great Western Railway workers lived.

You can find out more about the Railway Village Museum, the cottage at 34 Faringdon Road here, https://mechanics-trust.org.uk/MUSEUM.

1940

1940

1

CATHERINE PEARCE

Saturday 11 May

Mr Pearce reached forward and switched off the radio. 'Damnit,' he cursed.

Catherine's father never usually swore, but the invasion of France by Hitler's forces on the previous day would compel a swearword past anyone's lips. Britain and its Allies had done so much to stop the Nazis, and they had failed.

Catherine's lips pursed, she had no idea what to think, let alone say – Charles, her fiancé, was fighting on the European continent, so were her brothers and some of her friends.

What did this mean for them?

'Dear God, protect our men,' she whispered the prayer.

The Polish refugees who'd arrived on trains into Swindon a few months ago, brought with them terrible stories of destruction and cruelty. Right now, as she sat here in the comfort of her parents' parlour, the French people may be experiencing the same. It was a contrast that was difficult to imagine.

'It's awful,' Violet said. 'Have we lost?'

'No,' Catherine's father answered in a firm voice.

Catherine looked across the crescent-moon of her railway sisters, who were sitting on the carpet around the wireless. A *rally* of Great Western Railway,

GWR, machine shop girls, she had come up with the collective noun for them not long after she met them.

Her friends had walked up the hill from Swindon's new town to her home in the older part of the town to share a meal. Catherine hadn't dared venture out very far since her accident with a pressing machine at work. Her hand had been too badly damaged to be saved, and she was still coming to terms with the amputation wound. In the meantime, her friends endeavoured to walk up the hill every couple of days to see her. She had no idea what she would do without this group of women. They had met the month the war began and eight months later they were the closest friends she'd ever had – other than Charles.

They'd each kindly contributed to their lunch, with cheese, bread and a tin of spam. If they had not, Catherine and her parents would have eaten pickles and eggs all week until next week's ration tokens came into date. There were jars and jars of pickled vegetables and stewed fruit in the cupboards, and eggs that were plentiful with all the chickens they kept in the garden busy laying.

Cooking was becoming an imaginative event for her mother, who had newly discovered the art from their housekeeper when the war began.

Meanwhile, in comparison to her mother's creative productivity in the kitchen, Catherine was doing nothing beyond sitting in the comfort of her parents' home being mollycoddled. No – hiding was what she was doing. Or rather, hiding the stump where her missing hand used to be. She was sulking, she would not admit it to others, but she'd admit it to herself.

She was struggling to accept the stump at the end of her arm because she needed help with so many things – she could not dress herself or use a knife or a pen. She'd been telling herself everyone suffered self-pity sometimes, so it was alright to sulk. But that was until the Nazis invaded France and then no one, in a lovely home in England anyway, should feel sorry for themselves! She needed to pull her socks up, as her grandmother used to love to say, and get on with life. People were dying, their lives were being destroyed; all she had lost was a hand.

Her friends looked at one another. Catherine knew them well enough to understand their expressions. They all wanted to act immediately, to get up and do something to stop this war, but there was nothing they could do... Except, they could, and did, make 25-pounder bombshells to help the forces obliterate the Nazi army.

Lily twirled the engagement ring on her left ring finger around and around, no doubt silently praying for her fiancé, Lenny. If Catherine had a right hand she would have touched her engagement ring too, she used to habitually spin hers like that when she thought of Charles.

'The only thing for it,' Maggie declared, 'is for us to make the bombshells quicker than ever. The military need our bombs.'

'They do indeed.' Catherine's father rubbed his temple a couple of times as he spoke. Then his hand fell.

She knew her father's expressions too, his mind was troubling over sourcing the materials to make the amount of bomb cases and other equipment Britain required to win this war. As chief clerk he had the overall responsibility for many aspects of anything the Great Western Railway company manufactured in Swindon, and everything they were making now was for the war effort, for use abroad or at home. Britain depended on the work they did more than ever now. There was so much at stake, lives, livelihoods, freedom to do and think as they pleased. GWR had to keep production going, but her father juggled acquiring all the resources that were growing scarcer amid all the industries with competing priorities. She knew he was constantly on the phone with the Ministry of Supply, bargaining for deliveries of metals, wood and other goods, balancing GWR's need with the needs of other supply chains.

She should not know, but she had overheard her father speaking with a man who came to the house late one evening. She'd guessed he worked for a different firm, and she knew, because she'd shamelessly stood outside the closed door of her father's study and eavesdropped, whoever the man worked for was making Spitfires and other aircraft. She'd also heard GWR had workshops in Swindon that were making aircraft parts to deliver to the other factory. Her father and the other man had been talking about unblocking a delay in the distribution of coal and iron ore, to keep the furnaces burning and steel in production.

Last year she saw giant camouflaged aircraft hangars being built on the hills behind the Old Town. From the conversation she'd heard, the Royal Air Force, the RAF, were storing the aeroplanes built in Swindon up there.

There were so many workshops on the GWR three-hundred-acre site, and so many other factories around Swindon that had tapped into GWR's skilled workforce, the people of Swindon were probably making thousands of parts and items for the Government's ministries of transport and supply.

Catherine's father smiled and she knew the smile was for Maggie's sake, to give her friend confidence that the war would be won.

He had mellowed in character since her accident. Before she lost her hand, she hid her true identity from her friends because of her father's position in the company. She'd feared they would treat her differently and not include her. Now they knew and they were all here anyway. Feeling at home in her home, as much a part of her family as she was of theirs.

At the very beginning of the war, she predicted it would become a leveller of society and rank, and for her, and her father and mother, that had been true.

Her next breath ended in a sigh; thinking of all the activity in Swindon reminded her again that she'd stopped contributing – sitting here happily letting everyone run around her, while she did absolutely nothing to help win the war.

'Cath...?' The tone in Naomi's voice asked her if something was wrong.

The others had not heard her sigh, they were speaking to her father about how to speed up the production of bombshells. Catherine's house was a rare safe space for open conversation outside the factory, there was no risk of information being overheard or accidentally passed on to spies here.

Unless her father considered Catherine's nosy earwigging spying.

When she studied her arm while the dressings were changed, she thought it looked more like something in an H.G. Wells novel than the arm that belonged to her, but there would be something she could do one-handed. The stump had healed over. She could press the buttons on the machinery, or tick off lists.

The GWR clerks must manage the logistics of transporting the bombshells to sites to be filled with explosives and wired up for ignition. Trains must transport them to airfields and the frontlines in Europe too. Everything that was made for the military, the aeroplane parts and other items all had to be moved, so, there must be plenty of lists to tick off. If she could get back into the machine shop, though, pressing buttons, she would much prefer to be with her friends. But, whatever she did, as long as she was doing something to support the fight, she would be happy.

'Cath...' Naomi nudged her, asking what was wrong again.

'I must pull up my socks, Naomi, and get on with things,' she whispered. 'I cannot sit in this house doing nothing any longer. It isn't right. I am not usually the sort of woman to let life knock her down and not get back up. I've been letting everyone down, including myself.'

'Nonsense. You've let no one down. You have been recovering from an injury that nearly killed you. But I know you, so I am not at all surprised that the first minute you feel better you are itching to get going again.'

Last year, Naomi was the first person Catherine told about her desire to fight. They'd signed up to work with the heavy machinery at the same time. Working the machinery to make bombshells had fulfilled Catherine's desire. She'd become an important part of the fight through the supply chain.

In the weeks since her hand had been removed, while she shut herself off to give the amputation wound a chance to heal, and her head a chance to accept it, she'd denied the outside world and the war. But Hitler was not waiting for people to recover, he took advantage of every weakness.

Catherine's right arm lifted to interrupt her friends and her father, her mind expecting her hand to rise and move where her arm abruptly ended. 'I must go back to work,' she declared loudly.

'You must not,' her father replied, rising from his chair. His words as blunt as her arm. 'What could you do?'

'I can press the buttons to move the cranes and start and stop the large machinery,' she told him.

The room became silent as her friends heard the risk of a row. So silent, if there were not a carpet on the floor, she might hear a pin drop. They knew her father had attempted to stop her working before the accident, because the machines were dangerous. He was proven right. But even so she had made dozens of bombshells before it happened, and those shells must have saved the Allied forces' lives in Poland and other countries.

He came to stand in front of the chair she was sitting in. Breathing in and out quickly, then he suddenly huffed out a breath – expressing his annoyance and frustration. She held his gaze, she knew he could see what was on her mind. It was not his choice, it was hers and nothing he said or did would make a difference. They had been in this standoff before, last September when the war began. Then, she'd moved into her friends' parents' home, to avoid the arguments, the home of Lily's fiancé, where Lily lived, with Mr and Mrs Faraday, the Great Western Railway's chief gardener and his wife.

Their house, Park Lodge, was situated in GWR's park, a recreation area for the Railway Village, beside the factory. A recreation area that was now a source of vegetables, a parade ground and the site of GWR's air raid shelters.

She raised her eyebrows as she waited for his forefinger to rise and point accusingly at her. He always expressed his anger while pointing. But his hand stayed by his side, and his temper did not rise. He huffed out another breath. 'We all have to make sacrifices to win this war,' he said in a quieter voice. 'I suppose I must accept that. I have work to do, I am going to my office.' He turned away and left the room.

'Would you like another drink, anyone?' Her mother stood too, as she made the offer to Catherine's friends.

'No, thank you, Mrs Pearce.'

'No, thank you.'

'Thank you, I'm fine, Mrs Pearce.'

'Well, I am going to treat myself to a cup of proper tea, as we have some, and the grocer had plenty more.'

A moment later, when the door closed behind Catherine's mother, Naomi looked at Catherine. 'When do you think you will come back to the workshop?'

'As soon as they will let me. Though, it may take me a while to remember to use my left hand and not my right.' It was a joke, but none of her friends laughed.

When she joked about her hand, or rather the lack of it, the atmosphere always became awkward. She was only trying to be cheery. Her jokes upset Charles too. When he'd come home for a few days' compassionate leave, at the point the accident happened, he grimaced every time she mentioned her missing hand. *'It's not anything to laugh about,'* he'd said. *'I see injuries all the time, they are not funny.'*

No, she agreed, losing her hand was not funny. But equally she had two options. One was to miss it and moan about it forever, the other was to accept the change and get on with it. This was her choice – to get on with it.

'I think the wound is healed enough for me to work safely,' she clarified. 'If the doctor and the foreman agree, I could come back any day now.'

'Good.' Lily smiled. 'Because we miss you on the shopfloor.'

'I miss spending from dawn until dusk with all of you, or the other way around dusk 'til dawn, depending on whether it's a day shift or a night shift.' Catherine smiled.

'Everyone needs to do what they can,' Maggie said. 'Your Charles, Cath, and Lenny, Lily, need our bombs if they are going to push the bloody Nazis back.' Maggie used the swearword pointedly. They all swore occasionally these days. The Nazis' behaviour drew anger and swearing from everyone's mouths, as her father had proved when he listened to the radio earlier.

'I can't believe the Nazis are in France...' Lily's voice expressed the cloud of shock that hovered over Catherine too. 'What do you think will appen? Can they take France?' she asked as though any of them might know the answer.

Silence fell across the women again, for a different reason, as Catherine presumed they all imagined the worst of what might happen. She found it impossible to picture the awful things Poland had faced from the very beginning of the war.

'Thank God, the Government saw sense and kicked Chamberlain out of the prime minister's office yesterday,' Naomi said. 'He was obsessed with trying to bargain with Hitler. Bargaining with the Devil is never going to achieve peace. Hitler doesn't want peace, he wants to rule the world, and destroy it.'

'Well, I'm looking on the bright side and I'm glad Churchill is the new prime minister, he'll lead us in a good fight,' Violet responded.

'Do you think the Government knew itler was about to invade France?' Lily asked another question that none of them could answer.

Maggie laughed, suddenly changing the mood. 'I do love the way you say Hitler, Lily, with your Wiltshire accent way of dropping the aitch. Itler. It makes him sound stupid. Itler...'

'I would bet the Government knew that the Nazis were on the French border, Lily,' Catherine answered Lily's question. Her hands, including the one that was no longer there, became fists as they rested in her lap. 'I bet that's why the Government kicked Chamberlain out. After all, he was happy to betray Czechoslovakia, signing away that country to Hitler as if he had any right to do so, and as though giving in to a bully would stop him.' She would fight by working, no matter what Charles said, because her fiancé was even more likely to disagree than her father.

'The article on the front page of the newspaper this morning said Hitler's U-boats have sunk enough British ships containing food to feed the British Isles for six months,' Maggie contributed. 'And quarter of a million tons of petrol.'

'Blimey,' Violet exclaimed.

'I'm scared for France,' Naomi commented. 'Hitler is trying to stop us from supplying our army and he must be succeeding to some extent if he's sunk that many ships. He's won Poland, Denmark and nine tenths of Norway and the Allies haven't been able to stop him.'

'Our bombs will stop them!' Lily declared. 'They aint killin my Lenny,' she added, tipping up her chin defiantly.

'Nor my Charles, or my brothers,' Catherine agreed.

'Nor my brothers,' Naomi added.

They shared smiles.

Catherine's desire to work became as strong as it had been at the beginning of the war, like a flooding river current pressing up against a dam, driving her to do more. It felt good. The determination made her feel like her old self, the woman who had two hands.

'Naomi, when you have time, would you help me remove the cuffs from my blouses and dresses to shorten my right sleeves and sew the sleeves closed?' All her friends could sew, but Naomi was the seamstress, she would make the best job of it. 'I think it will look smarter if I do not have to pin up my sleeves.'

Naomi nodded. 'Of course. Shall I come on Monday? I am working a night shift so I can come in the day.'

'Oh, Monday is the Whitsun Bank Holiday, isn't it? I forgot. Yes, please. Thank you.'

'It's not an oliday any more,' Lily said. 'Churchill was only in office a few hours when ee decreed the Whitsun oliday is cancelled. Production's too important. The factory's workin on Monday, like any other day. The military need our bombs, Cath.'

Catherine smiled. 'Papa didn't say. It goes to show that Churchill means business, though.'

'I forget your dad knows everything,' Maggie answered.

Catherine laughed. 'Not everything, and do not let it put you off telling me things either, because he chooses to keep some things a secret from me.'

'Anyway, I best be goin. I said I would elp Mrs Faraday with the cleanin.' Lily got to her feet, walked over to Catherine, leaned and embraced her firmly. 'I miss you,' she whispered in Catherine's ear. 'I liked it when you stayed with Lenny's parents.'

'Me too.'

Lily was hounded by the guilt of causing the accident that took Catherine's hand. But her ring had fallen off, she had not dropped it deliberately, it was not her fault Catherine had reached out at the wrong moment and her hand had been trapped.

'You know,' Catherine said to them all, 'we must not let Hitler make us glum. We must keep laughing. In the future, I think laughter is going to be as important as making bombs if we are going to win this war.'

Maggie stood and brushed the creases from her skirt. 'There's no if about it, we will win the war and the bombs we have a hand in will ensure it.'

'As if we are the only people makin bombs,' Lily said, rolling her eyes.

The friends laughed.

Catherine stood to walk to the front door with the others.

She hugged each of them. Maggie clutched her tight. Violet kissed the air beside her ear. Naomi held Catherine's left hand and squeezed it gently as they kissed each other's cheeks. Then Lily opened the door, blew Catherine a kiss from her fingers and they left.

Catherine's right arm rose to wave goodbye. She exchanged it for her left hand.

All her friends looked across their shoulders, almost at the same time, smiled and waved too.

When Catherine closed the door, immediately her heart hung as heavy as lead in her chest. Now the Nazis were in France – Charles must be caught up in the combat. As much as Lily felt guilty for the accident, Catherine now felt awful for being idle for so long. There were things she could have and should have done before now. She'd let her parents treat her like an invalid, fetching and carrying for her. There were many things it was hard to do, but she could walk, and she had a left hand, and the rest she was going to have to learn again.

She could not even pretend she hadn't known how serious the situation was on the Continent. Her father had known the invasion of France was likely. Chamberlain had been ready to surrender. Her father had mentioned it to her mother one night, when he'd thought Catherine could not hear. He'd said the fighting was becoming fiercer, and that GWR's hospital ships were running across the Channel daily and bringing back wounded soldiers.

When she overheard that conversation, that was the moment she should have gone back to work.

She could not prevent anything that Charles, her brothers and friends faced – what she could, and must, do was not spend any longer in a chair with her perfectly capable feet up.

2

MAGGIE ABBOT

'How's Cath?' Maggie's sister Dot asked before Maggie had even shut the door. Her other sisters, Edith and Marjorie, were working a shift in the factory. Dot worked last night.

'She's doing as well as you'd expect, getting on with things with a smile.'

'Good for her,' Dot answered, her voice a little bitter for what was meant to be a nice sentiment.

Her tone of voice made the statement sound ingenuine, but Maggie understood. Dot was glad for Catherine, but sad for herself. She had been struggling to smile for months. Dot's situation was different, though, as well as grieving for their dad, she grieved for the child she'd felt forced to abort.

Life had been throwing awful things at them left, right and centre since the war began. Maggie felt worn to the bone with putting a cheerful face on and she had not gone through what Dot had, but she missed her father and she missed the old, lively, Dot.

'Did you pack up the kitchen things?' she asked Dot.

'Yes. Everything that needs to be stored in Mr Faraday's sheds is in the sealed crates, everything else is packed in the crates over there, and I've put all the things from the drawers upstairs into pillowcases or tied them in sheets.'

Maggie nodded.

They were moving out of their GWR cottage in the Railway Village tomorrow.

The cottage had been let to their father by the firm, the letting agreement ending when he died. The Great Western Railway clerks had given them several weeks to find somewhere to move to, but the time had come to go. Their end terraced cottage was for a foreman. It was larger than most properties in the Railway Village's terraced rows – they had three bedrooms, most cottages had two.

Sadly, none of the other smaller cottages were empty. So, although Maggie and her sisters worked for GWR they had to move elsewhere.

When they were looking for a place to live, Maggie had trawled through the property and rooms to rent listings in Swindon's *Evening Advertiser*. Nowhere for four women to live together had been available, unless at least two of them were willing to sleep on the floor. They would compromise on some things in order to stay together, but none of them were willing to sleep on the floor every night. A night or two wouldn't matter, but night after night when they needed their sleep after a shift at the factory, a bed was the only thing they really did want.

Their future home had been decided two weeks ago, when Maggie was telling Lily how hard it was to find anywhere, while sitting at Mr and Mrs Faraday's kitchen table. Lily and Mrs Faraday were sewing shirts to send to soldiers and Maggie had offered to help.

Her needle left planted in the flannel fabric, Mrs Faraday had looked up from the task. 'I can't believe I have not already said this to you, Maggie. You and your sisters must move in with us. We have Leonard's room and the room Catherine was using spare. Plus two small rooms in the attic we can make good enough, especially if you have furniture you can bring.'

'I...' Maggie hadn't known what to say, the kindness had struck her firmly in the chest, with a good punch to the heart. It spoke to her grief and left her in tears, sobbing like a baby, tears dripping onto the cloth of the shirt she was sewing. She'd rubbed a hand beneath her nose to catch the drips of tears that found another path and apologised. 'Sorry. That is kind of you to offer, but wouldn't Mr Faraday mind? It would be a big imposition, an invasion really, having the four of us sharing the house with you.'

'Whatever I say, Hector will support me. He prefers a full house anyway. You'll be very welcome, and it is not kindness, the more rations we pool together the better meals we'll have. It's selfishness really,' she had joked.

A laugh had hiccupped from Maggie's throat, to spite the tears still trickling down her cheeks. 'Thank you,' she'd answered with her whole heart. 'I will ask my sisters, but I bet they agree.'

'Tell your sisters to walk along and come in for a drink if they would like to get to know us better beforehand,' Mrs Faraday had offered.

Of course, Maggie's sisters had said yes. It was the best offer they had. They would all have a room to themselves and still be close to the railway works.

'It's a grand solution,' Edith had declared, when Maggie had presented the idea during dinner.

So, tomorrow, they were moving into the chief gardener's lodge in the GWR Park with the Faradays and Lily.

Because it was supposed to be the Whitsun Bank Holiday Monday tomorrow, they had expected to make the move together on a day off. But as Churchill – or Hitler really, because he was the one waging war and making them fight – had chosen to cancel the holiday, now they were packing and managing the move around their shifts at the factory.

Maggie walked into the parlour, the room where she'd spent so many happy days in her life. Dot had packed everything away. The framed photographs of her father and mother and her mother's porcelain must be wrapped up in newspaper pages in the crates.

Maggie liked imagining when her mother first placed those ornaments on the corner shelves, and stood back to admire them. That would have been before Maggie was born. In her mind's eye, her mother flicked a feather duster across the shelves, brushing the dust off her precious things. Because Maggie was so young when her mother died, she was never sure if images like this were imagination or memories. It didn't matter which, though, not really, every image of her mother remembered or imagined, of mundane days or holiday days, were precious. It felt as though, because she was leaving the cottage, she would be leaving the memories and her father behind.

She sighed and wiped tears off her cheeks. Who knew when she would see her mother's ornaments again. Mr Faraday had offered to store what they would have no use for in their rooms in his sheds, but when would she have a chance to take them out?

Of course, the ornaments were not her mother and father, nor was the house for that matter. They were not being left behind or shut away in the crates – but it still felt to her heart like they were packing up and walking away from every memory.

Her dad would not want Maggie to feel like this, he must be happier than ever in heaven with her mother, knowing his girls were old enough to look after themselves, and though they did not have him any more, they had each other. Yes, she did have Dot, Edith and Marjorie, but she still missed him, probably as much as Catherine missed her hand. Sometimes it felt as though she couldn't live without him.

Heartsore and bone-tired, Maggie collapsed into the armchair her father had always used. The scent of his tobacco in the upholstery embraced her.

'Maggie...' Dot stood in the doorway. 'Edith managed to buy some cocoa at the store, do you fancy a cup of warm milk with cocoa?'

Maggie sat up straight and wiped her cheeks with her sleeve again. 'Yes, please, then I think I'll go up to bed. It will be a long day tomorrow and I am knackered.' She was working the night shift after they moved everything tomorrow too. These days, there was no pattern to days and nights, she just grasped any and every moment there was to sleep.

When Dot left her to heat the milk, Maggie leaned back in the chair and closed her eyes as tiredness rested heavily on her shoulders.

When she opened her eyes a mug of cocoa stood on the nest of tables beside her. 'Dot!' she called. There was no answer. She reached out, and her fingers curled around the mug. The cocoa was stone cold. Maggie looked at the clock. She'd slept for over two hours. Dot must have left for her night shift.

Even cold, the cocoa tasted good, smooth and sweet – and it reminded her of the nights her father read bedtime stories while they sat around him with cups of cocoa in their hands. Tears tumbled onto her cheeks as she drank; she'd spent so many wonderful hours in this room, in this house. Tomorrow it would be Joe Marsh's home, not theirs. It didn't feel right. Losing their home was another cruel kick in the teeth from fate.

'At least I like Joe,' she said aloud, silencing her internal voice.

Joe was a carpentry foreman and a friend of the man she used to have her eye on for a husband. The man she'd fancied was a carpenter too, Ron Smith, Violet's lodger. Dietrich, the Jewish German refugee Naomi's family had taken in, was a carpentry apprentice and knew Joe too. Those connections meant Maggie had met Joe a few times and he was nice, he would respect the house. He had encouraged her to visit after her family moved out.

Joe needed the cottage, it would have a new person who needed shelter. He had been renting a private property on the top of the hill in Old Town, and he had a limp that made it awkward for him to walk longer distances. Now, with the shortage of petrol he couldn't use his car to get up and down the hill. He had been using the buses, but it made more sense for him to live in the Railway Village, right by the factory.

He'd said they could stay in the cottage as lodgers, in the rooms they shared now. 'After all, I only need the one bedroom,' he'd said.

But it wouldn't have been right for single women to lodge with a single man. War or no war, people were still people and they loved a good reason to gossip about their neighbours.

3

MAGGIE ABBOT

Whit Monday 13 May

When Maggie woke in her bed for the last time in her family home, she lay still, looking at every mark on the wall, where she or Dot had bumped or scratched it. The cobweb in the far corner of the ceiling where she and Dot had left their pet spider, Stan, to catch the moths and flies. She committed every single item and mark to memory, stretching out her last moments in this room for as long as she could.

Dot wasn't in her bed. She probably came in from her shift and decided not to bother coming upstairs, she would have only had an hour or so before needing to wake up. A year ago, Maggie would have felt guilty that Dot worked last night, but life was like this now, everyone in the factory worked as hard. Because she was working tonight, Maggie wouldn't be able to sleep properly until tomorrow; unless there was a spare couple of hours in the day after they'd moved everything.

Maggie threw the blanket and sheet aside, to get up. There was no getting around it, they had to leave.

It could be worse, she reminded herself.

It was a lot worse for people in Europe.

Her clothes lay across the end of the bed. She'd put them there last night so she could dress quickly.

As she walked down the steep twisting stairs, her last descent before she would be carrying things to move out, she sniffed away tears.

Dot was sitting at the kitchen table, embracing a mug of tea in both hands. She looked up at Maggie. 'Good morning.'

'Good morning.' They shared half-hearted smiles.

'I made a pot if you want a cuppa, it's real tea, the grocers had some in yesterday.'

'It's good to know something made it past the U-boats,' Maggie joked, rather pathetically. 'Where are the cornflakes? I'm hungry.'

'In that crate, and there's bowls and spoons, I thought it would be the easiest thing if anyone wanted breakfast.'

'Thank you,' Maggie acknowledged. 'Do you want some?'

'No, I'm fine.'

'You're still too thin,' Maggie told Dot, in a nagging tone.

Dot's eating habits had been awful after the abortion. She was eating now, but she was still stick-thin, she could do with a lot more flesh on her bones.

'Alright then, pour me out some cornflakes,' she grumbled, but in an amused voice. 'I know you, if I don't eat them, you'll keep moaning at me all morning and I'm in no mood to listen to it.'

A heavy knock struck the front door a few minutes after seven thirty, while Maggie was tucking their washed and dried mugs and bowls back into the crate.

Dot answered it.

Maggie looked into the hall from the kitchen.

'Good morning, Ron!' she called through as Dot let him in. The temperature of her skin rose – how could that man still make her blush, without even saying a word? 'Hello, Asher!' she shouted towards his friend, who was also Naomi's boyfriend. Asher followed Ron inside.

The country could not spare petrol to run their things in a van a couple of hundred yards up the road, so, Maggie had asked Ron if he could borrow a handcart from the railway works. He'd immediately volunteered himself and his friend to help. *'I will get you one, and Asher and me can help you load up and carry everything.'*

On the night her father died, he'd asked her to go for a drink with him. Of course she hadn't gone, not after losing Dad, and he hadn't asked her again. She wasn't even sure she was interested in having a fella any more. Her heart didn't leap when she saw him, not like it used to. She just felt embarrassed.

'Vi's on her way,' Ron said. 'She'll be here in a minute. Where do you want us to start?' He looked at Dot as he asked the question, his lips parting into that charming smile of his. Dot responded with a brief but relaxed rise of her lips.

Because Dot had refused to tell Maggie who the father of the baby she'd aborted was, every man in the Railway Village was a suspect in Maggie's mind. She'd considered Ron at one point. Especially as around Christmas time, when Dot was pregnant, he was in an off mood. But the look they shared held no hostility or discomfort and it would have done, on Dot's side anyway, if he was the father. No, Ron was definitely off the list of the men who might have hurt Dot and left her broken-hearted.

When Maggie worked out who the man was, there was going to be hell to pay.

'You might as well move the things that need to go into storage in Mr Faraday's sheds first,' Dot said. 'It's the furniture and most of the crates. They'll be easier to move on the cart. Can you start in the front room? Maggie and I can carry the cases and full pillowcases and sheets. Edith and Marjorie will help us whenever they bother to get up.'

'Fair enough,' Ron agreed.

'What do you want us to take first, the furniture or the crates?' Asher asked.

'The crates,' Maggie said. 'They can stand in a pile at the back of a shed, the furniture is more awkward, it will fit in afterwards.'

The narrow hall became a lot larger once the two men moved into the parlour.

Maggie's gaze trailed after Ron, her eyes following broad shoulders and falling to look at the firm pair of nicely curved buttocks his trousers alluded to as he bent over to lift a crate.

'Let's take the kitchen things that Mrs Faraday said she'd like for the house,' Dot touched Maggie's elbow, to get her attention. 'Then we won't muddle things up or be in the men's way.'

The solid heels of Edith's boots hammered heavily down the stairs. 'Are the men here?' she asked in a quiet voice, although the house was too small to say anything without it being overheard when the doors were open.

'We are indeed!' Ron shouted. 'Good morning, Edith!'

'Good morning!'

'Shall we bring the things down from upstairs?' Marjorie called from the top of the stairs.

'Bring what you can carry over now,' Dot called back up. 'We'll walk them over, then come back for the next lot.'

'Good morning, Marj!' Ron shouted.

'Morning, Ron!'

Maggie returned to the kitchen, as they all set to the task of leaving their lovely little family cottage.

Another tear rolled down Maggie's cheek as she picked up what she could carry. Ron would think she was a watering can. She didn't look at Dot as she walked along the hall, so Dot wouldn't see, otherwise she'd set Dot off too.

4

CATHERINE PEARCE

Catherine's breath left her lungs on a sigh as she walked along the hall to the kitchen. She'd been sighing an awful lot lately. Her left hand rested on her right forearm. The gesture was becoming a habit. She was forever embracing her injured arm, as though her mind continually comforted it.

'You're mourning the loss of your pretty hand,' Charles had phrased it.

She reached to turn the door handle with her missing right hand, then, instead used her left. She did that all the time. But her mind would learn eventually.

She had got up and dressed herself early this morning, then snuck out of the house quietly. She'd visited the family doctor who had treated her since she was born. She had gone early, because if he said she was well enough to work she would start today.

The doctor had looked at the wound and confirmed that although the new skin covering the stump was still tender and red, it would not harm her to work if she kept the wound clean and cared for.

The glorious smell of stewing rhubarb crept about the kitchen door as she opened it now. There was a sweet scent to it. Honey. Her mother must have added a few spoonfuls of honey to the sour rhubarb.

'Hello, darling.'

Catherine shared a smile with her mother, who was stirring the steaming saucepan.

Mrs Fletcher, her mother's housekeeper, and as Catherine's brothers fondly described her – her general dogsbody – would usually cook on a Monday. But because it was supposed to be a bank holiday her mother had insisted Mrs Fletcher still took the day as leave; the factory workers may have been asked to continue but it didn't mean everyone else had to. Not changing the sheets on a bed or stewing rhubarb for a day wouldn't change anything for the war effort.

'What are you making?' Catherine asked.

'The bread is stale, and I didn't like to waste it, so, I'm turning it into breadcrumbs and mixing it with some stewed rhubarb. This will do for a pudding and last a couple more days. It will be nice with the cream from the top of the milk.'

Catherine smiled at this new mother of hers. Before the war she hardly ever entered the kitchen, and here she was inventing dishes to make the most of their food.

'Good morning,' Catherine acknowledged her father who was seated at the kitchen table, with the morning paper spread open in front of him. Beside his elbow was a small plate containing a piece of half-eaten toast. More toast stood in a rack on the table. She imagined that was not the stale bread, but from a fresh loaf.

He looked up and smiled. 'Good morning.' Then looked back at the paper.

Catherine walked over to her mother and took in a deep breath through her nose, drawing in the smell of the rhubarb and honey.

The rhubarb was growing in their garden. Her mother must have broken off these stems this morning. As a child, Catherine had broken off stems and eaten them raw, peeling back the pink skin and eating those strips then chewing on the bitter green centre. She'd enjoyed the sour taste.

'I think rhubarb is nice in chutneys, Mama.'

'Is it? I might try that. I'll ask Mrs Fletcher if she has a recipe we can use.'

Last autumn, Mrs Fletcher taught her mother how to make bramble jam with blackberries and chutney with apples, green beans, onions and other vegetables. They had pickled lots of things too. Everything it was not possible to eat or keep was turned into jam, chutney, or pickled and preserved for the future. Like the rest of the country, her mother had been afraid of having no food. The kitchen cupboards were full of jars. The Government had introduced rations to prevent people hoarding essential things, but it didn't stop everyone hoarding in other ways. It was for peace of mind's sake, they knew they had things to eat for months now, if necessary.

'It's only natural,' Charles said in a letter. 'It's human instinct to keep food just as it's human instinct to defend ourselves. We all do unexpected things under pressure.'

Everyone traded jars, though, a jar of pickled onions for a few eggs from someone who had chickens, or a straight swap, a jar of chutney for one of honey from a beekeeper.

Catherine had never seen herself in her mother before the war, her mother liked to call herself a homemaker not a housewife, which she thought was too 1920s. It was the same thing really. Charles pictured Catherine as a homemaker when they married. But Catherine would have to do something outside the house, she could cook, organise, wash and clean and do other things as well.

Mrs Faraday led and participated in local committees and charities. She led GWR's Helping Hand Fund and sat on Swindon's Civil Defence Committee. She was much more like Catherine imagined she would be as a married woman. But in recent months, her mother had shown just how resourceful she could be too, and Catherine could see she had acquired some of her personality from this woman. Her mother was stalwart.

It was probably because Catherine was as staunch as her mother that since her accident, she had been mostly chipper. She may have been idle, but she'd kept a determined smile since the day she woke and realised her hand was missing.

In a moment when the frustration of not being able to do things made her irritable – which then annoyed her as she'd felt guilty for not good-humouredly getting on with it – her mother had said, *'Of course it's frustrating. Permit yourself that. You would be a very odd person if you were not upset.'*

Catherine had answered sulkily, *'But I hate making a fuss about this when I read, daily, about the men who are far more severely wounded.'*

'Your life changed absolutely. You are not making a fuss about needing to become accustomed to it. It is natural, darling.'

Perhaps, but she had been indulging self-pity too often and now she must just get on with whatever her new life would be. She would be much better off, following what her mother was doing than listening to what she said. Working would help take Catherine's mind off her problems anyway, and when the Allies thrashed the Nazis, she wanted to know she had played a part.

'Can I help?' Catherine offered. 'I can grate the bread into crumbs.'

Her mother looked across her shoulder, her expression saying she was about to mention Catherine's one hand… She did not. 'Yes, please, if you think you can manage.'

'I must learn how to do things,' she answered, seeding the conversation to what she wished to discuss. She'd deliberately not thrown the information of the doctor's verdict on her capability at them. Even though her father agreed to her working yesterday, they would still be unhappy.

She lifted the lid off the bread bin, then lifted out the bread, then put the lid back on, in the same way she opened the cupboard, took out the grater then closed the drawer. Everything took a moment longer with one hand to use, every action was a single task, but she could still do it. She steadied the grater on the tabletop with her blunt right arm and held the bread with her left. It worked. But she needed her mother's help to be able to tip it into the stewed rhubarb.

'Papa,' she said, when they had spooned the mixture into a pie dish to go into the refrigerator.

His presence in the kitchen was another change brought about by the war. Like her mother, a year ago, he'd rarely stepped through the kitchen door but in the winter the kitchen was the best place to keep warm with the limited amount of coal. It was also easier in the large town house, to just leave the blackout sheet nailed across the windows day and night. The kitchen window was left clear, they drew the curtain across at night and kept the lights low, but it left them with this one room with natural light to enjoy in the day, and her father preferred it.

He looked up from his perusal of the columns in the newspaper.

'I saw Dr Morgan this morning,' she said.

Her mother looked at her, her neatly plucked eyebrows lifting, querying the sound in Catherine's voice.

'Already?' her father said, his eyebrows rising too.

'Yes, he had time to see me before breakfast. He said the wound is healing as it should, and I am able to work.' It was a statement that did not encourage any comment. She did not want to argue.

'Surely that is too soon,' her mother rushed in.

Catherine shook her head quickly. 'He said it will be fine as long as I protect the new skin and keep it clean.'

'But, my darling—' Catherine's mother deserted the saucepan she had been scrubbing in the sink.

'There are no buts, Mama.' Catherine stopped her mother's words with a raised right arm. In her head her hand was there and her palm faced her mother saying she would not listen to any more. 'My mind is made up.' The reality was her forearm waved the loose end of her emerald blouse, that she'd haphazardly pinned with an awkward left hand.

She could not help it, she smiled, and bit her lip, holding back absurd laughter as a thought flew through her head – *she'd have to be careful, or she would become known in her family for her angry stump*. Like all her missing hand jokes, her father and mother would not find her humour funny, so she kept the joke to herself, and swallowed her laughter. 'There can be no buts because we are at war,' she said. 'In the current circumstances, it is shameful to do nothing.'

Between the stubborn streak she had inherited from her father and the unwavering commitment it seemed she may have inherited from her mother, they had no chance of persuading her against it.

His gaze held hers. She saw him thinking – logically questioning his own concerns without any anger in his eyes. This was another thing that had changed since war broke out and even more so since her accident. It was not only that he had mellowed – he had become more liberal. Perhaps because no one knew what tomorrow would bring so decisions could only be about what was right today. If Hitler reached Britain, it would not matter what she had not done. But if they stopped him, it would matter what she had done.

He took a deep breath then huffed it out. 'Very well. At least I will know what you are up to if you work for GWR.'

Perhaps, also, he had learned how deep the stubborn vein ran from him to her. Or he agreed that everyone should be doing something because the threat was so high.

'Thank you.' She rushed forward, leaned and embraced him firmly, forgetting that her father was a man who disliked physical expressions of emotion. She was about to release him and step back, but then his arms wrapped around her and held her too.

'All I want is for you to be safe,' he said quietly.

'I know.' She kissed his cheek and relished the feel of his hug for the moments until he released her.

Clunk. Clunk.

The heavy double strike of the door-knocker had them all looking towards the hall.

'I'll go.' Catherine left them and closed the kitchen door behind her.

There were no further knocks. Whoever stood on the other side of the front door understood the house was large and it may take time for someone to respond.

Only Naomi was expected and Naomi would not have struck the door-knocker that heavily. Catherine would guess that was done by a male hand.

When she opened the front door, Joe Marsh was the person on the other side.

'Hello, Joe. How kind of you to come,' she said, automatically polite, hiding her surprise as her mind questioned his reason for being here.

'Good morning, Cath. I hope it's not too early for you?'

'No, we're all up. Come in.'

'Are you sure? I would not like to inconvenience anyone.'

'You will not. Come inside.'

'How are you feeling?' he asked as he stepped across the threshold.

She had befriended Joe when she worked as a clerk, before she met her female friends in GWR. But he had only visited her at home once before and that was immediately after the accident to see how she was faring.

'Well enough, thank you.' She closed the door behind him. 'We are in the kitchen. Come through?'

Before the war, inviting a guest of any class into their kitchen would have horrified her mother, but that was before.

'I brought you a gift.' He lifted a shoebox-shaped and sized parcel, wrapped in sacking and secured with string. The sacking smelt of the sap of freshly cut and crafted wood and the string was tied in a bow.

'That's kind of you. Thank you.' She reached out to accept the parcel, then was unsure how to navigate it one-handed.

'I'll carry it to the kitchen,' he said. 'You can open it there.'

'Papa is here,' she warned him, just in case he might feel uncomfortable having such a superior GWR manager around.

He nodded. He was much further down the GWR management chain than her father, but Joe had never appeared nervous of authority.

'Mr Marsh is here!' she called as she led him through the hall to the kitchen.

Her father looked up. 'Good morning, Mr Marsh.'

'Hello, Mr Marsh,' her mother acknowledged.

Catherine smiled at him. 'Would you like a cup of tea, Joe?' she offered.

'Yes, thank you. That would be very kind.' Joe put her present on the table, removed his flat cap, folded it in half and pushed it into his jacket pocket.

She lifted the kettle off the gas hob, stood it in the sink and turned on the tap to refill it, then turned off the tap and carried the kettle back to the stove. Everything was going to be double the work and double the time, but that was not too much to endure. Her mother had picked up the box of matches and struck one on the side of the box as Catherine turned on the gas – lighting the gas would be harder to do one-handed. The gas caught alight with a long lick of flames about the kettle, then settled down.

'Do sit down, Joe,' Catherine encouraged.

He withdrew a chair opposite where her father was seated. 'I brought Catherine a gift,' he explained to her father who was staring at the parcel.

'That is kind of you,' her father answered.

'I'll admit something before Catherine opens it, Mr Pearce, this is a foreigner. I made it on site. On my own time, mind. Not company time, sir. For a very good reason, obviously. I hope you won't think badly of me.' Joe nudged the parcel across the table towards Catherine. 'Open it up then, I'm itching to know what you make of it.'

Catherine left the kettle to boil, glancing at her father, looking at his reaction. A foreigner was what the working men called something they had used company materials and equipment to make for their own use; she hoped Joe would not be in trouble for her sake.

Her father's forehead crinkled into a frown. He had acquired more wrinkles and significantly more grey hairs in the last nine months. His gaze dropped, watching as she pulled a loose end with her left hand, unravelled the bow and unwrapped the package from the sacking.

She couldn't imagine what Joe would break company rules to make for her. Especially as materials and equipment were so precious for the war effort.

Beneath the sacking was a beautiful wooden box. Her fingers stroked across the top. It was perfectly smooth and the grain rubbed with wax so the wood shone. It was not decorative, the finish was plain apart from the pretty letters carved in the centre of the top. Her forefinger traced the word he'd carved out.

Cath

She looked into his hazel eyes. The light brown flecks in his irises caught the morning light that shone through the kitchen window. He had nice eyes, but today, the expression in them held wariness, telling her he was concerned about her reaction to his gift. It was unlike Joe. He was usually a take me as I am, like it or lump it type of man.

'Thank you,' she said.

'The box isn't the gift,' he answered in a hoarse voice. He coughed, clearing a throat that sounded dry. He really was nervous. 'Open it,' he encouraged, 'see what's inside.'

Her fingers found a leather carrying handle that he had attached with small brass tacks on the front side, then she found the brass catch beneath it that held the box closed. The brass was just the tiniest waste of the precious metals her father battled to obtain. She freed the catch and lifted the lid.

Her lips parted, her jaw dropping and her mouth gaping. 'Oh.'

She opened the lid fully and let it fall back on its leather hinges, unable to breathe for a moment.

She touched it. 'It's beautiful.'

What lay nestled on a bed of rusty brown velvet was an inanimate but beautifully crafted wooden hand. 'Oh.' The sound escaped again, as her fingers explored it. It looked so realistic, each finger was slightly curved and the joints looked as though they would change their positions. It was perfectly shaped and sized for a woman's hand, just like her own hand. She held her left hand beside it, palm upwards. It was the same size, the fingers the same length and width.

She looked at Joe. 'How...?'

Her mother leaned across Catherine's shoulder to see. 'Oh, my gosh. That is beautiful, Mr Marsh. How kind.'

The kettle whistled as steam spewed from its spout. Her mother turned to attend to it.

Her father stood, and leaned forward across the table, peering into the wooden box. 'Good Lord. That is genius, Mr Marsh. Just the ticket.'

A single tear trailed from Catherine's right eye, her eyes swimming, as her fingertips stroked across a silky-smooth wooden forefinger. It was so perfect it was a piece of art. The fingers even had the shape of fingernails, and each joint did move, stiffly, but that meant the fingers would hold position so she could hold things with the hand. She looked at her left hand again. It was as though he'd fashioned the wooden hand in a mirror.

She wiped away more tears and looked at Joe. 'Thank you.' Her voice had no strength as overwhelming emotions tried to choke her. 'I can't tell you...' Her emotions strangled any further words from her throat.

'You don't need to thank me. I know it is hard to learn how to do things when you lose a limb, at least with a false hand you may balance things easier if you want to pick things up. The brace which secures the hand on your arm will let you attach other tools. There is a pen holder attachment beneath the velvet. If you find any task too difficult I'll try to make another attachment to help you.'

'Thank you.' Her father walked around the table and held out a hand, to shake Joe's. Joe stood and they shook for a few moments, as Catherine's mother lifted the skirt of her apron and wiped away the tears from her cheeks.

Nausea rolled Catherine's stomach over, like a boulder tumbling down hill. She'd never felt sick with joy before but... it was the relief... the hope this hand presented. It was being able to see a future in which she could do the things she thought would be impossible. She could write to Charles.

When her father released Joe's hand, without thought, she embraced Joe, wrapping her arms around his neck. She held him so close her tears smeared across his cheek.

He did not hold her in return. He tensed. He was more muscular than she had imagined. His physique was solid.

She hung onto him for a few brief moments, expressing her utter joy. Then released him. 'Thank you.'

'While I drink my tea, shall I show you how to fit it and use it?' he offered. 'You can practise holding a cup.'

'I will make the tea,' her mother said. 'You sit down and learn how to fit your new hand.'

'You are so kind, Joe, and so clever,' Catherine said as she sat down and lifted the hand off its bed of velvet. She knew how much effort he must have put into making this. Like everyone else, he was working around-the-clock shifts, so he must have lost valuable sleep to make this. 'I will be saying thank you at least five times a day for the rest of my life.'

5

MAGGIE ABBOT

Maggie carried a knotted pillowcase that contained some of their bedroom items, brushes, combs, the old iron curling tongs that had been her mother's, and her dad's favourite table lamp from the parlour. She was going to put the lamp in her bedroom.

A year ago, her arms would have ached from all the packing and lifting, but since she'd started working in the machine shop, she'd developed muscles where she didn't know it was even possible to have muscles.

Ron walked on the road beside her, his strong hands gripping the shafts of the borrowed handcart, bearing the weight of their first load.

Violet walked ahead of them with Asher, followed by a ginger cat that had jumped down from a wall and trailed after them. Maggie had seen it before, it had begun walking in the shadow of everyone in the Railway Village.

Violet held the heavy teak wooden box containing their best silver cutlery. Asher carried a crate of heavy crockery and kitchenware, including the china they only used on Sundays and holidays.

'After we've moved you out, we're helping Joe move in,' Ron told her.

'It is kind of you to help. We all appreciate it.' Maggie's voice came out stiff – sounding stoically polite – as she firmly restrained the emotions screaming for her dad and the happy life she'd known in the house they were leaving behind.

'It is the least we can do for you all. I know this must be hard.'

She did not want him to be kind today, because if any of her friends were nice to her, she would drown in a puddle of tears.

Violet and Asher were walking faster than them. With heavier loads they probably wanted to get to the Faradays' sooner.

Maggie walked at the pace the cart dictated for Ron. It would be rude to leave him walking behind her.

'With all that's been going on, we've never had chance for that drink, Maggie. I would like to take you out, when you feel up to it.'

She was still sweet on Ron Smith, despite his up and down ways with her. She had liked him an awful lot until she thought he didn't like her at all. That was when he ignored or avoided her for a few weeks. Maybe going for a drink with him would help lift her mood a bit. 'I would like that, thank you. A night out would be good. All I'm doing is working or sleeping.' *Or crying.*

'If you're nervous about coming on your own, invite Dot. I'm sure Dot can find a chap to accompany her.'

Maggie's head spun, pivoting to look at him. The question in her thoughts was one she had asked before and less than an hour ago dismissed – *are you the father of Dot's baby?*

It is not Ron, she assured herself. She had never heard of him walking out with a woman, and if he got a woman with child, he was the sort of man who would marry her. Also, Dot had smiled at him this morning, she wouldn't smile if he was the father. Unless she was acting nice… If it was him, though, Dot would have resisted his help with the move. Or maybe she would have let him help because he owed her.

'I've lost you,' Ron said. 'Where have you wandered off to in your head?'

'Sorry. Something made me think. There's a lot going on.'

'I know,' he said as they walked. 'What with your dad dying, losing the house and working all the hours God sends to fight a war, you're allowed to be a bit scatty.'

'I feel a lot more than scatty,' she answered. 'But in the current circumstances, it feels selfish to speak about my grief.'

'It isn't selfish. You do what you need to do to cope. But that's why I thought you probably need that drink, to get out and pretend nothing else is going on for an evening.'

'I won't be able to pretend Dad is here, even for a minute.'

'He is here, though, you're talking about him, so he's still in your heart, walking along this road with us.' His lips lifted into a smile.

His smile still made her stomach topple over in a fainting fit and her soft spot for him glow. She used to daydream about marrying him. These days, she couldn't contemplate marrying anyone, the only future she thought about was what would happen today. But a couple of hours in his company was not going to kill her, and she would probably enjoy it.

'Dot won't want to come. Naomi and Asher could come,' she said. She would prefer it if one of her friends was there, in case she needed a safety net.

His eyebrows lifted and at the same time his skin blanched.

'Is the cart getting too heavy? Put the handles down for a moment,' she suggested. He had worked the night shift to be able to help them, they had all swapped shifts to achieve this move. Like Dot, he would be shattered today. Maggie's tired hours would be tonight.

'No, I'm fine, it's just a few more yards. I am not sure Asher would want to come out with us either. I don't think he's taken Naomi to a pub. But I will ask him.'

'Come on, lad!'

The shout drew Maggie's gaze to the end of the road.

Mr Faraday stood at the open park gates, waving Ron forward. Asher and Violet had already walked past him.

'Do you need a hand?' Mr Faraday offered as they reached him.

Maggie walked ahead as Mr Faraday took one shaft and left Ron to hold the other, and they steered the cart on the paths to Park Lodge.

'Maggie!' Lily squealed, as Maggie walked towards the front door of the lodge. Lily was definitely the most excited about their move. 'Let me elp.' She took the lamp from Maggie's overloaded arms as Maggie entered the house.

'Tell me what needs to go where?' Violet came into the hall, having deposited her first load in the dining room.

If life had to be hard, at least Maggie had her friends as well as her sisters to travel through it with.

'Let's get this lot unloaded then we can head back for the next cartful,' Mr Faraday said to Ron, as Maggie was drawn into her new home by the women.

'These are for my room,' Maggie said. 'If you take them up, I'll go back and—'

'No.' Lily refused. 'I'll show you your rooms first,' she said as Marjorie and

Edith arrived. 'Leave your things there an then I'll walk back with you for another load.'

'Have you heard from Lenny?' Maggie asked Lily as they climbed the stairs.

'No, I avent ad a letter for days.'

'You don't know if he's upset about us using his room, then?' she said.

'Ee won't mind.' Lily shook her head, but the smile fell from her lips. 'I'm startin to worry. I usually get letters all the time, and Betsy said she aint eard a word from Art either. Nor as Cath eard from Charles. Somethin is goin on.'

'Yes, there's something going on, alright! They're busy fighting!' Asher called up the stairs as he followed Mr Faraday towards a downstairs room with a crate in his arms.

'They've always been fightin! That's not different!' Lily glanced back and shouted. 'Maybe itler's U-boats sunk a ship full of letters,' she said to Maggie and Violet. 'Anyway, we can't do anythin but wait to ear from them, an worryin won't get anyone anywhere. I'd end up like a dog chasin my tail an drivin myself mad.' Lily shrugged off her concern as they reached the top of the stairs.

'It is odd, though – if all the letters from the soldiers have stopped,' Violet said, 'and more and more ships are being sunk. The newspaper's named at least ten Swindon men killed in the U-boat attacks.'

None of them knew the men who had died, which was a blessing, but the war felt real when local people were killed. In Maggie's experience, war was the men leaving, the aeroplanes frequently flying overhead, rationing and working all the hours God sent. In September she'd expected Swindon to be bombed. Like everywhere else in the country, Swindon had prepared to be pounded with a blitzkrieg, but the German aeroplanes never came. The Germans had struck the British in the sea not from the air.

'Which room do you want?' Lily asked Maggie. 'The one Catherine used, Lenny's or an attic room?'

'Marj and me have already bagsied the attic rooms,' Edith shouted up from downstairs, having just arrived with a load.

Maggie's middle sisters were as close as she was with Dot. The attic rooms meant they could be closer to each other.

'Dot and I will be happy on this floor,' Maggie answered. 'I said I'd use Lenny's room, if that's alright. I can move in with Dot when he's home.'

'I told you ee won't care. It's next to mine, so if you can't sleep you can sneak over to my room. I found it strange at first to av my own bed, let alone an ole room to myself.'

Maggie could understand why Lily had felt strange in this large house – Lily had a family double the size of Maggie's, who lived in one of the smallest Railway Village cottages, and a father who was too heavy with his hands; that was why she had left home.

Lily opened a door. Maggie and then Violet followed her into the room, as Edith and Marjorie hurried past and climbed the stairs to the garret rooms on the top floor.

'I put all Lenny's clothes in the bottom three drawers of the chest,' Lily said. 'You can use the top two an the wardrobe.'

'Thank you. I'll put everything on the bed for now. Then we'll fetch another load.'

'Alright,' Lily answered.

Maggie wasn't sure if Lily expected a more enthusiastic response to her new room, but she didn't have the heart to fake happiness today.

As they crossed the landing, Lily pointed out the doors for the bathroom and indoor toilet.

Violet shared a look with Maggie and smiled. They'd been such close friends for so long, she knew Violet's thoughts. She was thinking about how Maggie had fallen on her feet with an indoor toilet – in the terraced cottages the lavatories were still in the yards.

Lily ran down the stairs ahead of them, light on her feet. Behind her, Maggie's heavier steps reflected her heavier heart.

It was lovely that Lily obviously felt so at ease here. It was a good sign that Maggie would eventually feel this was home too. But at the moment, Lily's happiness just highlighted Maggie's miserable, grieving, mood.

Even seeing Ron standing outside waiting for her, looking ridiculously handsome, as he took a long drag on a cigarette, his free hand casually resting in his pocket, did not lift her spirits.

Violet's arm threaded around Maggie's.

'I'll pull the cart,' Lily said.

'You don't have to, lass,' Ron returned.

'I wanna. Well, while it's empty anyway. You can av it when it's full.'

Asher, who stood beside Ron, choked out a laugh.

Maggie freed her arm from Violet's and gave Lily a brief hug. 'I love you,' she said in Lily's ear. 'I'm so glad we'll be together here.' Lily would certainly make Maggie's days brighter. 'Come on, you take one shaft, and I'll take the other and we'll pull the cart together.'

When she turned to take hold of the shaft, Maggie saw Ron looking at her. He'd been staring, studying her. She smiled and nodded, then as Lily held the other side, rolled the small cart forward, a quiver trembling in her heart. The sensation was annoying, but Ron had made her feel like this for years.

'Let me pull the cart,' Violet said, lifting the shaft out of Maggie's hand, giving her no chance to reject the idea.

It left Maggie free to walk beside Ron – which may have been what Violet intended because she knew Maggie liked him.

She and Ron walked on ahead, a little faster than the cart bearers, as Asher hung back talking to Lily and Violet. He looked across at her and there was that gut-melting shallow smile, and a nod that stirred the curls on his forehead.

She did like him, so, she plucked up her courage. 'Ron,' she dared. 'I would like to go out with you. It would be nice to go out and do something other than work.'

What happened after that would be up to fate, and if it led nowhere, she did not care at the moment.

'That would be great. Later on, I'll let you know my shifts, and we can work out a night,' he said, as his skin coloured a rosy pink.

6

NAOMI ISAACS

Naomi rapped the lion head knocker against the brass plate on Catherine's parents' front door. The grandfather clock in the hall on the other side of the door chimed. It rang out ten times, announcing the hour. Her other hand clutched the handle of her wicker sewing box. She'd brought lots of different coloured reels of cotton because she wasn't sure how many dresses and blouses she needed to sew.

Catherine opened the door, smiling from ear to ear. Naomi hadn't seen her smile this fully since the accident.

'Good morning, come in. Thank you so much for coming.' Catherine's jolly smile transmitted into her voice.

'Good morning to you too.' Naomi laughed as she stepped over the threshold. She wiped the soles of her shoes on the mat and lifted the sewing box. 'I brought my things.'

'Wonderful, but you won't need them.' Catherine's eyebrows lifted, the broadest of smiles continuing to part her lips. 'I have something to show you. Go through to the kitchen.'

Her damaged arm was tucked behind her back and Catherine was moving in a way that prevented Naomi from seeing it. Naomi wasn't sure if that was deliberate, but what could Catherine have done with her arm to prevent her needing to change her cuffs?

Naomi walked ahead as Catherine closed the front door. 'Are your parents at home?' she asked.

'No. Papa went to the factory. He said he can hardly not work when everyone else is, and Mama went to a Staff Association meeting.' The note in Catherine's voice expressed her surprise that her mother had gone.

'You probably shamed her into doing more yesterday when you said you could not sit by and do nothing.'

Naomi walked through the open kitchen door and put her sewing basket on the table.

'Possibly. I was only thinking earlier that she's changed since the war began, and I heard her telling Papa she must do something to help the war effort.'

'Was he cross? He seemed quite cross when you said you were going back to work.'

Catherine grinned, a little cheekily, still appearing excessively happy. 'He was cross, yes. But he cannot deny what the war requires of all of us now the Germans are in France.' Even the mention of the war did not wipe the smile from Catherine's face.

'Now, come along, show me whatever it is that's making you smile like that.' Naomi smiled too. She'd never seen Catherine this excited, not even when her fiancé came home on leave.

'This.' Catherine lifted her right arm from behind her back.

'You have a hand!' Naomi stepped forward and touched it, awe opening her eyes wider. It was a work of art, wooden, sanded and oiled to a smoothness that was like skin. Naomi couldn't take her eyes off it. 'Do the joints move?'

'They do.' Catherine showed her, by moving the fingers with her left hand. 'The joints are stiff, but that's so they stay in place. I can hold things, and it's strong enough to carry things. Joe made it for me. It slides onto a metal staff and twists to stay in place. There are other tools I can attach to the brace too. There's a pen holder I've tried, I can write. Not as fast or as tidily, yet. But I began a letter to Charles this morning and I am sure after a while I will get the knack of it and be able to write as I used to.'

Naomi's hand closed around Catherine's wooden one, as if it were real. 'Joe Marsh made it?'

'Yes. It's beautiful, isn't it?'

'It's wonderful.' Naomi reached for Catherine's other hand and held it beside the wooden one, comparing them. 'It looks just like your other hand. How did he do that?'

'I don't know, but it is as good as any artist's work, isn't it? So now you see why I won't need my sleeves shortened, because I have a pretty hand that I don't want to hide.'

Naomi released Catherine's hands and instead her arms surrounded Catherine's neck as she hugged her firmly. 'I am so happy for you, it's gorgeous.' The solid feel of the wooden hand rested against Naomi's back as Catherine returned the embrace.

'Shall I make a pot of tea?' Catherine offered as she released Naomi and stepped back.

'Yes, please. Have you heard from Charles?' Naomi asked as Catherine turned to the kettle.

'No. Not yet. I am still patiently waiting. Because I can't write to him, perhaps he thinks it's less important that he writes to me.' Catherine picked up the kettle with her wooden hand, looping the thumb underneath the handle. 'But, then again, I know no one has heard anything. None of my brothers' wives have had letters recently. Everyone at church yesterday was asking if anyone had heard from the men over there. No one's received letters in recent days. As the saying goes, *"it's all quiet on the western front".*'

She said that as a joke. Naomi didn't laugh. Sometimes Catherine's sense of humour was a little macabre.

'When I said that to Papa, he said *"it most certainly is not quiet at the front".*' She mimicked her father's voice. 'Of course, he did not tell me what he knew about the front on Sunday morning, but later the minister of information told us the Germans had invaded France. I presume, therefore, the truth is the men, including Charles, are too busy to write. I won't let my mind dwell on the reasons why, though.'

'We haven't heard from Samuel or Nathan either. I pray to God daily that they're safe.' Naomi withdrew a chair and sat down at the table.

'I pray for everyone involved,' Catherine answered.

'I worry about Hitler.'

'Hitler is a sly, evil bigot,' Catherine declared, then lifted her wooden hand. 'I think a wooden hand will be an advantage. Steam from the kettle can no longer scald me.'

Naomi laughed. 'Just do not put it close to the flaming gas.'

When Catherine had made the tea, they sat at the table, and Catherine excitedly explored what her wooden hand could achieve, successfully pouring the tea from the pot. Then she set the first two fingers into a curved, hook-like, shape, and slipped them through the narrow handle of the teacup so she could pick it up.

Naomi smiled. 'It is clever, isn't it.'

'It's taking some concentration, but it's a wonderful gift. I feel very normal, and I will get used to it.' She raised the cup and tapped the rim against Naomi's. The fine china chimed. 'Cheers,' Catherine said.

'Cheers.'

'So, tell me.' Catherine leaned closer. 'Have you decided whether you will accept Asher's marriage proposal?'

The warmth of a blush raced across Naomi's skin. 'The answer is not yet, but he keeps asking me. I told him if he does not stop trying to persuade me, I will say no to shut him up.'

Catherine's slim eyebrows lifted. 'Then I would say, if you can turn him down, you do not love him and you should say no.'

'I do love him. I know that much. But I love my job too and I won't leave GWR. They will lay me off if I marry, so he must wait.'

Catherine's left hand reached out and lay on Naomi's forearm. 'You know, if you leave the factory, you will never lose your friends, we are in your life forever. I think we will still be close in our dotage.'

Naomi's smile rose. 'I know. But I like working. I told him he must wait until the war is over. Even your father can't change the no married women policy.'

Catherine's eyebrows lifted. 'No, but the war might. We have no idea how long it will go on. So, yes, wait. They need women, and now we are skilled, I think they will have to change the policy to keep the factory running. We can't be the only women who want to marry.'

'Churchill said the war would take a year or so...'

Catherine shook her head. 'Yet, the Germans are winning ground, I cannot see us winning the war this year.'

Naomi sighed. The war made her fret constantly – about her brothers and Dietrich's missing family, and for every Jew. She could quite easily spend all day being sick with worry.

'Tell me some gossip. Take our minds off the war. What has been happening in the Railway Village?'

'Catherine! Catherine!'

The shout came from the hall before Catherine had a chance to reply.

Catherine looked towards the closed kitchen door and got up. 'Here, Papa!'

His footsteps came quickly along the hall.

Naomi stood up too, as Catherine opened the kitchen door.

'Thank the Lord,' he said, one hand gesticulating as he breathed heavily.

He was obviously agitated and rushing. He had not removed his top hat, and his cheeks glowed red.

'What is it?' Catherine asked. 'Why are you here?'

'I could not call you on the phone in case the operator listened to the call. The Government are evacuating the children from the east coast, the Germans —' He stopped mid-sentence, his eyes looking beyond Catherine and seeing Naomi behind her.

'Good morning, Mr Pearce,' Naomi said.

'Good morning, Naomi.'

Whatever he had been going to say was withheld. So, it must be bad news. If the Government were evacuating people from the coast on this side of the English Channel, they must be preparing for a German attack on England.

'Will you help the clerks plan and organise everything, Catherine?' was all he said beyond his initial outburst.

'I can't write quickly or tidily enough yet, Papa.'

'But you can speak to the Parish Councils and help rally them to find homes for the children and families who will be brought into Wiltshire.'

'How? Is there diesel in the car?'

'Darling, ride a bicycle or catch a bus,' he snapped, impatience and urgency pressing through every word.

Naomi's stomach toppled over, tumbling like a heavy pile of bricks. Whatever was happening on the Continent was serious and her brothers were there…

'Yes, I can help for a few days,' Catherine agreed. 'Then, I will go back to the machine shop.'

'Can you come to the factory with me now?' He glanced at the clock on the kitchen wall. 'The bus runs back down the hill in fifteen minutes.'

'Yes, of course.' She looked at Naomi, her eyebrows lifting again, this time apologising for her hurried exit. 'I'm sorry to abandon you.'

'It does not matter at all. I will get out of your way.' She picked up her sewing basket, then, unable to hold her tongue, looked at Catherine's father. 'Should I contact the parents of the girls we homed for a few weeks when London was evacuated last year? Is there a real risk to London now too?'

He nodded, confirming what he could not say. 'Possibly.'

Did Churchill really think the Germans were coming? That they would come over the English Channel?

Naomi's heartbeat thundered as Catherine walked through the hall with her, to show Naomi out.

How long would it be before England was under attack? And if the Germans were that close, what had stopped the soldiers writing? She closed her eyes and prayed to Yahweh quickly. *Protect Samuel and Nathan from evil, and care for Dietrich's family. Please save them and watch over all those who mean good.*

Her thoughts reeled as she walked back home, and when she reached home, she could not tell anyone what she knew.

7

LILY FRANKLIN

Dinner, eaten around the Faradays' pine kitchen table, was a lot noisier than normal. Even in her family home, with all her half-brothers and half-sisters around the table in the kitchen of their small railway cottage, their meals had been quiet. Her father shouted if anyone was noisy, and he'd wallop Lily around the ear if she spoke.

Maggie and her sisters must have never been told to be quiet at the table.

Among their friends Maggie was the loudest, but among her sisters she was the quietest. She sat at the table with her eyes focused on her plate, letting the other women talk to Mr and Mrs Faraday, asking and answering questions. She communicated with Lily only through occasional shallow smiles. Effortful smiles that expressed sadness and grief.

Later, *it must be so difficult, losing her father and now her home...* Lily wrote in her letter to Lenny.

Lily was the only one left in the kitchen. Edith, Marjorie, Dot and Maggie had gone up to their rooms and Mr and Mrs Faraday had sought privacy in the parlour. Lily stayed to write her letter at the table. The evening was chilly, and it was warmer in the kitchen.

The last sunlight of late evening illuminated the table and her words on the paper.

I know she loved her father very much, so she must miss him lots. The house is going to be—

Bang. Bang.

The back door rattled against its frame as someone thumped hard on the outside, the knock was dull so they must be using the side of a closed fist.

Bang. Bang. Bang.

The quick heavy strikes transmitted their urgency through the door.

'Who is it?' Lily called as she got up, her heart pulsing hard, the chair legs scraping back on the stone flags of the floor.

'Lily! Is that you? Let me in!'

The desperate voice belonged to her sister Polly.

On a surge of terror, Lily rushed to the back door, slid back the thick bolt, threw the latch and pulled the door open. 'What is it? As Dad it you?'

'No.' Polly's chest heaved as she filled her lungs, fighting to catch her breath, showing how fast she had run to get here. 'It's not me who needs you. It's Betsy. She's avin the baby. Mam is at her sister's ouse in Faringdon an I can't find the midwife or the doctor. Will you elp? I don't know what to do!'

'Where's Dad?'

'At the Glue Pot, drinkin. Ee doesn't care about Betsy, does ee? Please, Lily. She's screamin like the baby is rippin er in alf.'

'I'll come. I'll just tell Mrs Faraday where I'm goin an fetch some towels to put on the bed an I'll come. I'll only be ten minutes or so. Go on, go back, she'll be needin you. And put some water on to eat. We'll need warm water to wash the baby when it's born an to clean Betsy up.'

Polly nodded, already looking calmer. Lily reached for her hand, pulled her close and kissed her cheek quickly. 'You did the right thing, comin for me. She'll be fine. I'll be there soon.' She let Polly leave and turned to find Mrs Faraday.

When Lily hurried along the path towards the home she had run away from, her heart felt as if it pulsed in the back of her throat, a large lump of fear. If her dad came back from the pub, she'd be in for it.

Hopefully Mrs Faraday would find the midwife soon; she had left Park Lodge to look for her. But if the woman was attending another birth she could not be in two places at once.

The baby would be Lily's nephew or niece. It was her brother Art's, and it would now sadly be born a bastard. Poor Betsy. Betsy had desperately hoped Art would be given some leave before the baby was born so they could be married. He'd not been that lucky. Really, they ought to call the fathers the bastards, for leaving their girlfriends pregnant – it wasn't the children's fault. And Art should have married Betsy before he went off to fight. Even if they married now, officially the child would have been born to an unmarried mother, and people would stick their noses up in the air when Betsy or her child walked past. The best chance Lily's nephew or niece had was if Art and Betsy moved away from the Railway Village so no one would know the date the baby was born or the date they married.

Lily hammered on the front door as hard as Polly had hammered on the Faradays' door.

Her little brother Jimmy opened it. 'Ello, Lily.'

'Where's Betsy?'

She needn't have asked, a scream from upstairs told her where Betsy was.

'In our room,' he answered bluntly.

Lily rushed past him and raced upstairs.

The sight and the smell of her old bedroom hit her as she reached the small square landing. The door on the right led to her parents' room, the door on the left led into the children's room. Betsy was lying flat on the single bed the older girls shared, the bed that used to be Lily's too. Betsy's hands clutched her belly as it contracted.

Lily dropped the towels she'd brought on the end of the bed.

Jimmy had followed her upstairs and stood at the open door, and Ken and Bert stood beside the bunk bed they slept in – they all stared at Betsy wide-eyed with fascination rather than concern.

'Out,' Lily said, sharply. 'All of you. Go downstairs an make yourselves scarce, that's the best thing for you lot.'

'Should I go?' Her young sister Pen stood with Polly at the head of the bed.

'Yes, darlin, sorry, but it's best we give Betsy some privacy. If I need your elp, I'll shout.'

The children drifted away as Betsy's contraction wore off.

'Thanks for comin, Lily,' Betsy said through a grimace. Drying tear marks drew lines on her cheeks. 'It kills. If feels like it's gunna split me in alf.'

'I'm sure you're fine, we'll get you sorted. I am by no means as good as a midwife, but I've elped my stepmam a few times an watched the midwives. Av your waters broken?' she asked.

'Yes, all over the back yard when I was hangin the washin on the line.'

'Well, better there than in the ouse.' Lily laughed briefly. 'Do you know ow far apart your contractions are, av you counted the minutes?'

'A few minutes,' Polly answered for Betsy. 'Maybe five.'

'I've ad backache all day,' Betsy said in a voice that expressed the agony of it. 'I thought it was because the babe as got so eavy. I'm uge. I didn't know it was the baby comin.'

'Shall we see ow close you are to birthin? Close the door, Pol, an let's get your knickers off, Betsy, an these towels beneath you.'

Betsy screamed, reached out and grasped Lily's forearm. She held on so tight Lily felt her fingernails cut into her skin. Betsy gritted her teeth, and Lily saw her belly tightening, like someone had pulled a thick strap around it. It was the muscles instinctively working to push the baby out.

'Breathe,' Lily said, to stop Betsy shouting. That was what she'd heard the midwives say. 'Slowly, in through your nose an out through your mouth. Let your body do what it as to do because this baby is comin out whether you like it or not.'

When the contraction subsided, Lily helped Betsy get her knickers off.

'The baby is crownin already,' she said, a bit shocked by the sight of the top of the baby's head pushing through between Betsy's legs.

When Polly looked at the sticky dark hair on the crown of the baby's head, she turned as pale as the bedsheets.

'What does that mean?' Betsy asked, before groaning. 'Fetch me a pot, Pol, I'm gunna be sick.'

'It means the top of the baby's ed is showin. You're stretched about this far apart.' Lily showed Betsy with her thumb and forefinger, a gap of about an inch and a half. 'The babe's got a shock of hair as black as mine and Art's.'

'It's slimy,' Polly declared as she bent to pick the chamber pot up from beneath the bed.

Betsy's mouth dropped open. She looked horrified by the word 'slimy'. Her mouth snapped shut and she used a hand to help prevent herself puking before Polly handed her the pot.

Betsy grasped it and threw up.

'Go get a wooden spoon, would you, Pol,' Lily said to her sister. Then to

Betsy she said, 'Babies always come out slimy. That's why you need ot water to wash them after. Lenny's mum's lookin for the midwife, an opefully she'll be ere before the baby comes, but sometimes they're quick once they've crowned. I know what to do, though, so don't be scared, I've elped birth nearly all the young ones.'

Betsy screamed again.

Lily caught hold of her hand. 'Breathe,' she said. 'It's alright.' She looked between Betsy's legs.

When the contraction ended, Lily rolled up the sleeves of her blouse. She didn't bother asking for something to cover it up, if it got stained, she'd soak it in brine. Part of the reason why she didn't want babies herself was because she'd seen how bloody and messy birthing was. In the end, most of her brothers and sisters had torn their way out.

When the contraction ended, Lily moved the pillows over from the boys' bunk beds and shoved them behind Betsy's back to make her more comfortable.

'It really urts, Lily,' Betsy complained.

'I know, but you'll forget about the pain fast enough when the baby is in your arms.' Lily parroted the words she'd heard the midwives say, she didn't know if it was true.

The next contraction came quickly, clasping at Betsy's belly like a demon had a hold of her. She retched too, just as Polly ran back into the room with the spoon. Polly held the chamber pot as Betsy puked yellowy-green bile into it.

'Get out of me, you little bugger!' Betsy swore as the contraction persisted.

Lily looked between Betsy's parted legs. More of the top of the child's head was showing. She thought it was going to be quick from here on.

'Pol, do you think you can keep old of Betsy's and, no matter ow ard she olds you, while I elp the baby come out?'

Polly nodded, in a way that said she was too shocked by it all to speak.

'Lift your knees,' Lily told Betsy. 'An take some deep breaths before the next contraction comes. I av a feelin the baby isn't gonna be long before it comes out. Put the andle of that wooden spoon between your teeth an bite on it when the pain comes. The ed's the worst bit, once that's through I need you to stop pushin for a moment so I can check the cord isn't around the baby's neck. But then it'll be out quick.'

Lily leaned a knee on the end of the bed, watching as the next contraction came, and Betsy's body eased a little further open to allow the baby the space to come out. Lily had seen this before, but even so, she still wondered at how a woman's body could achieve this.

'Bite the spoon an breathe through your nose!' she yelled at Betsy.

Betsy did as she was told, trusting Lily completely. Art would be proud of them both when he heard about his child's birth.

There came the moment when Betsy's body tore apart and then, in a slither, the baby's head came through, and Lily braced it in her palm. The child had a full head of short black hair, and its skin was the colour of Tate and Lyle's golden syrup – lighter than Art's and hers. 'Don't push for a minute!' she shouted at Betsy. 'It's ere! I av the ed!' She ran her fingertips about the baby's neck, feeling for the umbilical cord. The cord wasn't there. 'It's alright. Push!' she shouted at Betsy.

Betsy's belly automatically pushed for her, the muscles squashing down, as she bore down, biting the spoon and turning puce as she pushed hard. A moment later the warm slimy body of Art's son slid into Lily's waiting hands.

'Oh!' Polly said in awe.

Lily swallowed, her heart pulsing in the back of her throat not from fear, from happiness. No, it was beyond happiness – amazement, pride, awe. She felt like crying with joy. Her nephew was beautiful, even though he was a little green and slimy. She wished Art was here to see him.

'Is it alright?' Betsy asked urgently as she did her best to sit up. 'What is it? A boy or a girl? Why isn't it makin a noise? Why isn't it movin?'

'It's a boy. I'll slap im, that'll get im breathin.' Lily lifted her hand and slapped the child's bottom, perhaps too hard, but she had never had to smack the babies before.

The boy gulped in a breath, then cried out in annoyance. Betsy reached out, and Lily handed him over, the rope-like umbilical cord still attached at his tummy and between Betsy's legs. 'Give im your breast,' she told Betsy. 'Ee'll want the comfort of it, an your body will learn ow to feed im.' Or so the midwives said.

'Pol, go down an dampen a towel in the water you eated, but make sure it's not too ot. Then we'll clean im up.'

The soles of more than one person's boots raced upstairs, and a tap knocked on the bedroom door. It was not noisy enough to be the hand of one of her brothers.

Lily lifted the sheet and covered Betsy to make her decent to some degree. 'Who is it?' she called.

'Lily, I've brought the midwife.' It was Mrs Faraday.

'Come in!' Betsy shouted. 'But ee's ere now! Lily birthed im.'

* * *

When Lily returned to Park Lodge with Mrs Faraday, the letter Lily had been writing to Lenny lay on the kitchen table where she'd left it.

'Would you like a cup of hot milk and honey, dear?' Mrs Faraday offered. 'You must be exhausted.'

'I'm not tired at all. My nerves are ummin. I won't be able to sleep,' Lily said.

'Then a cup of warm milk may help you settle. I'll put a pan on. You sit down and finish writing your letter.'

Lily's trembling legs carried her to the chair she'd left a couple of hours ago, then collapsed.

As Mrs Faraday opened the refrigerator, Lily looked down at the letter, picked up the fountain pen and removed the lid. She put the three dots of an ellipsis at the end of her last words, then below wrote.

Since the last sentence and this, I became Auntie Lily. Betsy had the baby – and I birthed it! The midwife didn't make it in time, so Pol came to get me, and there was only me and Pol in the room with Betsy when he came slithering into the world.

He's beautiful. He is 7lbs 3oz. He's long, though, he's 23 inches. He has long legs and arms. He'll be tall when he's grown, just like Art. He had a full head of curly black hair too. And he has some lungs on him, that boy can scream when he wants his mum.

She smiled, remembering him as she described him. The love already in her heart said she would have a special bond with her first nephew.

I hope Art can take leave soon, to meet his son. He'll love him.

When Lily had finished the letter, and finished the mug of milk, she went upstairs to tell Maggie the news.

8

MAGGIE ABBOT

Saturday 18 May

Tap.

The single light knock woke Maggie and brought her quickly into consciousness. She yawned and stretched her arms. It was early, the birds were still singing their dawn chorus on the other side of the window.

Tap. 'Maggie, are you awake?' Dot whispered through the door.

Last night, Lily had come in and spent a couple of hours sitting on the bed beside Maggie, talking about her new nephew and how she had helped with the birth and sharing memories of her childhood with her brother. Lily had been too excited to sleep. Maggie had sat there yawning, listening more than she spoke, being a good friend despite being tired. While internally she'd wept over her childhood memories that contained her dad.

Lily had left the room when the clock downstairs chimed once.

Maggie was going to be dead on her feet in the factory today, without Dot waking her up early too.

'Yes, come in,' she called back quietly, being as a good a sister as she was a friend.

The doorknob turned and the door opened. Dot was barefoot, still wearing her nightdress but with a cardigan pulled on over it. She closed the door behind her, then hurried across the carpet. Maggie pulled the sheet and blanket back, and shuffled across, making room so Dot could get into bed beside her.

Dot smiled. It was a shallow smile, but it glowed in her eyes displaying happiness as brightly as a Christmas window display in McIlroys department store. An expression Maggie had not seen in her sister's eyes for months. Maggie smiled too.

'Good morning,' Dot said quietly.

'Morning. Why are you here?' She would have asked 'what's wrong', but obviously nothing was wrong.

They lay facing one another, scarcely inches apart, their heads on the one pillow.

Dot's cold hand held Maggie's beneath the covers. 'I have something important to tell you. I made a decision last night, and I want to tell you before anyone else.' The happiness that glowed in Dot's eyes warmed her voice. 'I am going to become a nun, Maggie.'

'A *nun*?' Maggie heard her horror in her voice. 'Why?'

'Because I have been called by God. Perhaps that is even why I had to give up my child, for Him. He asks Abraham to give up his child, in the Bible... I don't know if He is the reason I had to do the same, but I am happiest when I pray. I love God and Christ, and I feel solace in the Holy Spirit.'

'Where has this come from? Where would you go? You can't leave me.'

'Since I spoke about the abortion to Father Arnold in the confessional, he's been helping me, advising and supporting me to explore my faith. It doesn't matter that I sinned, he says God has forgiven me and if I want to dedicate my life to Him then God would welcome my devotion. My life will have a purpose too, I'll be doing charitable works.'

'You can do charity work without being a nun,' Maggie protested, her voice now sulky and irritated. 'You would make an awful nun. You're the loudest of us, and silly and...' She stopped because that had been the old Dot. That had been what Dot was like before the abortion – then she'd been the most vibrant, joyful person Maggie knew. The old Dot had always made people laugh with a sharp quip, or a rude joke.

'That woman made a mistake,' Dot said. 'I can't be her any more. I don't want to be. I am happiest when I pray, and when I'm in church. I know God is calling me. But don't say a word to Marjorie and Edith yet, Maggie, nor to anyone else. I want everything to be agreed before I tell the others.'

Maggie didn't know what to say. She thought she might go mad if she lost Dot now. 'Don't leave me...'

'You'll still see me sometimes and you can write to me.'

But she would leave home, and Maggie might only see her once or twice a year. She couldn't cope with another goodbye. Maggie hated the man who made Dot pregnant even more intensely. If he hadn't gotten her pregnant and buggered off, Dot would not want to be a nun. This was not about her faith, it was about her guilt.

'Promise you won't tell a soul,' Dot said quietly.

'I promise.'

* * *

Maggie followed Ron into The Oxford public house, only to face a sign on the door in front of them.

NO LADIES SERVED IN THIS ROOM.

Women did sometimes go into the public bars, but if they did it was assumed they were prostitutes looking for business.

Ron turned to the left instead and pushed open the door marked, LOUNGE BAR. There were quite a few men and women together in that room. Ron held the door for Maggie and then for Naomi, so she and Asher could follow.

'Thank you,' Naomi said.

'You're welcome,' Ron replied.

They had watched *The Shop Around the Corner*, starring James Stewart and Margaret Sullavan at the cinema before coming here. Maggie had not been able to follow the film, her thoughts were trapped in the heavy emotions in her heart. It did not feel right to be doing normal things, as if her dad had not died and Dot hadn't said she was going to become a nun. *I mean, a nun!* her internal voice screamed. It was an absurd idea, from Maggie's perspective.

Ron touched her arm. 'What do you want to drink?'

'A shandy, please, if they have lemonade. If not, just a half an ale will do. Thanks.'

He and Asher walked to the bar. Maggie saw Joe Marsh perched on a stool, sitting with an elbow on the bar top – the new occupier of their cottage.

'Joe.' She raised a hand to catch his attention and walked over. Naomi followed. 'How are you?' she asked as she neared him.

'Fine, thanks, Maggie.' He nodded towards Naomi. 'But if you're really asking about the house, that is fine too,' he said more gently.

'The hand you made for Catherine is gorgeous,' Naomi said.

'Thank you, but my aim is that it's practical. It needs to help her do things she wants to do.'

'It is,' Maggie and Naomi said in unison.

'She is testing what she can do with it all the time,' Naomi added.

'That's good then. Then I am happy with it,' he said, as though he was talking about something that was equipment for the railways.

Naomi glanced over her shoulder. 'There's only one table free, we'd better grab it.' She looked back at Joe. 'It was nice to bump into you.'

'You too, love, and you, Maggie.' He nodded again, then raised his pint glass in a sort of salute as they turned away.

Naomi sat at the free table near the darts board, where several women stood playing, and chalking up their scores on a blackboard beside it.

'I hope they're good,' Maggie commented, as she sat beside Naomi. 'I don't fancy an arrow in my ear. Maybe no one is sitting here because they know they're bad at throwing.'

Naomi laughed, then glanced beyond Maggie, looking at their men at the bar.

'You like Asher a lot, don't you?' Maggie said. Naomi had spent the duration of the film holding hands with him and half of it with her head resting on his shoulder.

She nodded. Then smiled, a blush adding colour to her cheeks. 'I love him. I'm not marrying him yet, but I will do. When I'm ready.'

Maggie nodded, an image appearing in her mind of her and Ron, and Naomi and Asher walking up the aisle for a joint wedding. Which was utter nonsense because Naomi and Asher were Jewish, and Maggie was only on her first date – a marriage offer was a million miles away. And, these days, she was not even sure she would accept if he asked, even though it was all she'd wanted in the past.

Naomi leaned forward. 'You don't seem that keen on Ron.' She spoke quietly, even though the chatter in the pub would have made it hard for Ron to hear from the bar.

While Naomi had been holding Asher's hand, Maggie's hands had been clasped tightly in her lap as she'd stared at the wide picture screen, trying hard not to cry.

'I'm just out of sorts, with everything that's gone on lately.'

'Sorry, that was tactless. Of course you're not feeling happy, you lost your dad.'

'No. It's alright. I do like Ron, it's just not the best time for me to be dating. He asked, though, and I thought it would be nice to get out at least.' *Then Dot told me she was leaving...* She had nearly cried off, but she didn't like to let Ron down at the last minute.

Naomi looked towards the bar again. Maggie looked too and sighed. It was strange, remembering how she looked at him last year – with naïve adoration. So much had happened since the war began, she had an entirely different perspective today – the rose tint had faded. He was still handsome, though, and polite, kind – most of the time. Hardworking – he definitely was that. And the scents of wood sap embedded in his skin and clothing did make him smell nicer than most of the working men. But now, instead of noticing those things with a softening heart, she listed them like any woman might notice them.

He turned, a pint glass and a half-pint glass in his hands.

The women using the dartboard cheered a bullseye while he walked back to the table. Ron smiled, looking towards the cheering women. Then he looked at Maggie and realised she was watching him. Her gaze seemed to knock him backwards for a moment, as his step hesitated, then recommenced.

She smiled, a genuine emotion of pleasure rising, because she was with him, sitting here as someone he chose to be with. A year ago, he would not have bothered talking to her in a pub, beyond a quick hello. She'd been elbowing her way into his circle for years, trying to catch his attention. Now she'd stopped trying, she'd won it.

She sighed again. Was it too late for them now?

His lips lifted in a quick smile as he put her glass down. 'They didn't have lemonade, it's beer, and they didn't have any choices, they only had one tap on.'

'Thanks.' She appreciated anything and everything these days, since the start of rationing and the imports of food stuffs had slowed. Alcohol wasn't rationed, though, it was just low in supply and heavily taxed.

'Shove over then,' he encouraged as he put his pint glass down on the table.

She hopped her bottom along a seat to make room for him as Asher sat opposite, beside Naomi.

Asher took a sip from his pint, then wiped the foam from his top lip with the side of his hand. 'How do you like living at Park Lodge, Maggie?'

'It's alright, but it's not home. If you know what I mean. And Mr and Mrs Faraday talk about the war a lot; with Mrs Faraday being a member of the Civil Defence Committee and Mr Faraday running the Great Western Gardeners' Society, dig for Britain and all that...'

Ron coughed out a laugh, covering his mouth to stop himself spitting out his beer.

'It's not funny,' Asher responded.

'It was just the way Maggie said it, in a – this is boring voice. Dig for Britain and all that...' Ron mimicked her.

Maggie rolled her eyes at Ron.

He grinned.

'The Nazis are dangerous not funny,' Asher complained. 'The Dutch Government fled this week, did you hear that?'

Yes, Maggie knew that. Talk of the war was constant at the moment. Like it used to be when the war began. Yet as Catherine said the other day, laughter was going to help them get through the war as much as fighting. Since Christmas, most people had just got on with things. But after the invasion of France, everyone was nervous. If anyone said one word about the war, conversations instantly switched to any war news.

Maggie felt swamped by it. She had too much to worry about anyway. When she lay in bed at night – the grief and worry were overwhelming. Now Dot had added to that... If Dot left, Maggie didn't know what she would do.

'Yes,' Ron answered Asher. 'And with Italy joining Germany, it's spreading outside Europe. Civilians are being evacuated along Egypt's Libyan border now, because of the Italian forces in Libya,' Ron shared what he must have read in a newspaper. 'But you can still laugh, mate, because you can't spend every second afraid.'

Naomi's eyes had widened, though, showing shock not amusement. 'I didn't know the war was affecting North Africa.' She took a sip of what looked like cordial, something that wasn't alcoholic anyway, then smiled as she caught Maggie watching her. 'Golda and Esther, the twins who were billeted with us in the autumn, during the first evacuation. You know, the girls who came from

London and returned when the bombing didn't happen. They are coming back to us. The Government are offering the London children evacuation again, they're running two more trains, one tomorrow and one on 2 June. The twins are arriving on the train tomorrow. My mother is collecting them from the station. I'm looking forward to seeing them, though I'm sure they would rather stay at home. I suppose the Government must think there really is likely to be bombing again.'

Ron lowered his glass, having taken a sip. 'Did you hear what the BBC did?'

Asher and Naomi shook their heads, saying no, as they leaned forward to hear what he had to say over the noise of the women around the darts board.

Maggie remained sitting back in the chair, she didn't care what the BBC had done, it wouldn't solve any problems or make her life feel any better.

'They only put out a false call for all the reservist air force pilots to report to their stations,' Ron said dramatically. 'The next day they apologised for the error. I couldn't see how that could be an error. I reckon the error was they didn't want the Germans to know.'

Naomi bit her lower lip, pinning it between her teeth as though she restrained a thought or a comment, stopping herself from saying something she wanted to keep secret.

Ron didn't appear to notice, he carried on talking, leaning further forward, his voice lowering. 'They must have realised they'd told the Nazis what we were doing. They must be listening to our radio announcements. If the Nazis are breaking across the border of France, we must be using more aircraft to stop them.'

Maggie thought of Edith's boyfriend, who she only knew as The Pilot. She'd never met him. Edith hadn't seen him for a few days. He would know if they were being asked to do more. But if what Ron was saying was true... 'Then if the Government is trying to keep it a secret, we should talk about something else,' Maggie snapped. 'There could be German spies in here as much as anywhere else.' She pressed a finger to her lips, and widened her eyes at Ron, telling him to shut up.

Maybe that was what Naomi had wanted to do a minute ago.

'I'm just glad we're responding,' Naomi said. 'I worry about my brothers all the time. If they need help, then I'm glad they're sending the aeroplanes.'

Asher stared into his tankard of beer.

He knew the most about the Nazis because he had experienced the Nazi way of life before he left Austria.

The women around the darts board applauded, and one of the women raised both her hands in a victory pose, clearly the winner of their game.

'Do you fancy a game of darts?' Maggie asked, looking at Ron then Naomi. 'Can you play darts? Shall we play women against men?' She was not in the right mood to sit and talk about anything, let alone the war. So, if a game of darts distracted them, all the better.

'I have never played,' Naomi said. 'But I'm a quick learner.'

They left the pub at just after half past eight. Not late, but Maggie was happy to get home, and Naomi and Asher were working a shift on the Sunday.

The sun was lowering towards the west of Swindon, as Maggie embraced Naomi with a firm hug.

'Goodnight,' Maggie said as they separated.

'Goodnight,' Naomi replied. She lifted her hand and waved as she turned away then reached for Asher's hand and they walked on hand in hand, in the opposite direction from Maggie and Ron.

Maggie kept her hands to herself as she and Ron turned to walk to the Railway Village.

She gave her hands a task, to feel less awkward, moving the cardigan she'd lain over her shoulders like a shawl, to stop it sliding off.

'Are you cold?' Ron asked.

'Only a little. But I can put my cardigan on properly if I get too cold.' The sky was darkening by the minute, and as the sun lowered, so did the warmth in the air.

'Would you like my jacket?'

'I'll manage as I am.' She did not want to be enveloped in the smell of him. A year ago, she would have fainted for joy over the offer.

'Does Lily know how Betsy is? No one's seen her since the birth,' he said in a conversational tone. 'Has Lily seen her and the baby?'

Of course, everyone in the Railway Village knew about the bastard born in the Franklins' cottage. No one had any secrets in the Railway Village. The houses were too close, everyone was on top of one another and saw what went on in other houses, from the front across the streets and the back across the yards and alleyways.

'Not since the birth,' Maggie answered. 'Her dad won't let her go in the house, and now her stepmother is back at home, she can't call round when he's out.'

'Has she heard anything then?'

'I don't think so. She is hoping to have a chance to speak to her sister at church tomorrow and I'm sure she'll ask then.'

He nodded.

She took the questions about Betsy as more evidence that he was not the one who had impregnated Dot. It implied he asked after everyone. But that took her back to another of the thoughts that plagued her sad mood – no other man had asked about Dot's health in the six months since she had stopped going out to the pubs or dancing. So, whoever the dad was, he was horrible, and if he was horrible, she could not imagine Dot willingly having sex in the first place.

Maggie's fingers rubbed her forehead; she spent her life with a constant headache these days.

'Are you not feeling well?'

She shook her head as her hand fell.

'I know it must be hard, Maggie. Losing your dad. If you need to talk to me about it, I'm a good listener.'

'There is not a lot to say. I miss him like I'd miss...' She stopped talking, she was going to say 'like she'd miss her own hand', then she remembered poor Catherine. 'Anyway, nothing I can say is going to bring him back.'

'No. I know. But talking about your memories will help keep him alive, and sharing your emotions might help you cope with losing him.'

She shrugged. She did not think anything would help. All she could do was grit her teeth and carry on.

'We don't need to talk about it, though.' His hands slid into his trouser pockets. 'You're cracking at darts, by the way. You should join the women's league.'

She might be good, but she and Naomi hadn't won. Naomi was not a natural, and as she hadn't played before she had no skill.

Maggie glanced at Ron, as her arms folded across her chest. She was cold. 'I had a misspent youth. I am cracking at all the pub games. Darts. Dominoes. Skittles.'

A bark of laughter choked out from his throat. 'I know you did not have a misspent youth, remember, I knew your dad.'

'When he and me were older. Not when I was young. When my aunt thought we girls were old enough to be left to our own devices, she married and left our house. The others were old enough to do what they wanted when Dad went to the pub, but I was too young. So, if none of them were at home Dad took me to the pub and I played games while he talked to his mates.'

'What a hell of a man,' Ron grinned. 'He taught you how to dance beautifully, throw a dart and smash skittles down. I bet you strike the lot down every time. Any other attributes I should be warned about? What else are you good at?'

'Dad used to love my steamed puddings.'

'Well, those I am going to have to try then.'

'I can bat and bowl in a game of cricket too. Dad taught all of us to play cricket in the park...'

Their conversation continued easily, refreshing flippant banter, the sort of conversation hardly anyone had at the moment. It was nice to have someone to talk about nothing in particular to. He even succeeded in dragging a note of humour from her throat a couple of times.

A ginger cat appeared, the cat that was always somewhere around the gates of the park. It regularly followed Maggie and her friends. Lily had named it Mr Tabs the other day. Mr Tabs decided he would accompany them along the last hundred or so yards of Faringdon Road.

Dusk had fully settled in; the sky and the world had become a deep hazy blue. Maggie no longer missed the electric lights that would have come on at this hour before the war, darkness was the normal thing at night, and she was used to navigating it, even when clouds made the night as black as tar.

Ron, along with Mr Tabs, walked alongside her right up to the wrought-iron gates of the GWR park.

The cat brushed against his trouser leg. 'Hello, little chap.' Ron bent for a moment and rubbed his ear.

'That's Mr Tabs, he follows us to and from work most days, on this side of the railway tracks anyway. I don't know who he belongs to.'

'Do you want me to walk you as far as the Lodge door?' Ron offered.

She smiled at the cat, watching it wrapping itself around Ron's legs, strolling in a figure of eight. 'No. I'll be fine.'

'I'll wait here then, until I know you're through the door and home safe and sound.'

She looked up, to say goodbye, but as she looked at him, she wasn't sure what to do. If he was a friend she would hug and kiss him on the cheek. An acquaintance, or work colleague, she would say, '*see you soon*' and raise a hand in parting as she turned away. Ron... She wasn't sure... She wasn't sure what this was. He was not really a friend, nor an acquaintance, and this had been a date. It was her first ever date too, so she had no idea what the normal thing to do was. Should she kiss him? She felt a desire to do so, and now she had stopped and said nothing at all it would seem odd if she just walked away, saying simply, thank you and goodbye.

His gaze held hers, as if he was deliberating the same questions.

Should she make the first move and lift onto the balls of her feet and press her lips against his?

In the end, he moved first, his hand lifted and rubbed the edge of her upper arm. It felt brotherly. 'Goodnight, Maggie. I've enjoyed tonight, I hope you have too.'

'Yes, I did.' Or the end part of it anyway, when they'd played darts and the walk home.

'Shall we do it again then?'

'I would like that. Thanks. Goodnight.' She stepped back. Glad that she'd not kissed him and made a fool of herself. Then without saying anything else, she turned and hurried away, the cat following her.

The latch on the iron gates grated as Ron closed the gates behind her.

The back door into the kitchen opened as she turned the handle, it was unlocked.

She glanced over her shoulder. She could see the park gates. Ron was still standing on the other side, watching, checking she got inside safely. She lifted a hand and waved. He waved back, then turned away.

'Shoo, you nosey thing,' she said to the cat, gesturing with her hand for it to go away before she went in.

She found Lily sitting alone at the kitchen table, in the very last of the daylight, scribbling away in the smallest writing she could manage to make the most of the piece of paper she was writing her letter on. She looked up. 'Did your date go well?'

'I think so.'

'Did ee kiss you?' A cheeky grin split Lily's lips.

'If he did or didn't it wouldn't be any of your business, Lily Franklin, but as it happens, he didn't, and I didn't want him to. But we are going to go out again.' Maggie walked across to the window and pulled the cord so the blackout lining dropped and covered the window. She pulled the curtains too, then reached out and flicked on the light switch, illuminating the room and making Lily blink. She pulled out the chair beside Lily and sat down. 'It just feels too weird. Dating, I mean, doing anything normal that might make me feel happy doesn't feel right. Not when Dad's not here. I don't even want to try to be happy, that would feel like I didn't care about him any more.'

Lily dropped the pen on the tabletop. 'What would your dad say to that? Ee'd tell you to stop talkin nonsense.'

'I know he would say I shouldn't stop my life, when he is perfectly happy in the afterlife with Mum.' Maggie smiled as she imagined him saying it. She could see him and hear his voice as though he were sitting at the table with them.

'Then that's your answer, don't let it feel odd. Your dad wants you to be as appy today as you were before ee died.' She picked up her pen and looked at the paper, poised to write again.

'What are you telling Lenny about?'

'I'm not writin to Lenny. I'm writin to Art. I saw is son today. Ee's gorgeous. Betsy brought im out for a walk an we met in the park an sat on a bench for a bit. She let me old im. Ee's a perfect little chap. I reckon ee'll grow up cheeky, just like Art.'

'I didn't think you liked babies…' Maggie said. Lily had protested quite a few times that she was never having children. But mind you, she had also said she'd never get married, and now she had an engagement ring on her finger.

'I like them. I love some of them, the ones that are related to me, that is. I just don't want one of them to rip my fanny in two or to av to wash the shit off their nappies an sheets.'

A peal of laughter bubbled up and out from Maggie's throat.

Lily laughed as well.

The sound brought Dot, Marjorie and Edith downstairs to investigate what was spurring the hilarity. Of course, what they really wanted to know, now that Maggie was home, is how her date with Ron had gone.

'Alright,' she answered with a shrug, and then refused to say more.

9

NAOMI ISAACS

Sunday 19 May

Naomi's heart beat more strongly as she walked through the long, narrow, low-ceilinged tunnel deep beneath the train tracks. She was returning from the GWR factory, after her shift, to walk home via the Railway Village. Asher would be waiting on the other side. They didn't try to find each other on the busy factory site, but whoever came through the tunnel first would wait at its mouth on the other side. He was always there first.

Her friends rarely worked Sundays, they attended the Railway Village's Anglican church. She and Asher worked because they celebrated the Jewish Sabbath over Friday and Saturday.

Sundays were Naomi's best days of her week. Most of the time, when she saw Asher, it was with her friends, or his, or at home with her parents and Dietrich there. On Sundays they were alone during their lunchtime breaks, and during their walks down and up the hill to the Old Town.

Asher lodged in Violet's house, sharing the room with his best friend, Ron, but even though he lived just beyond the factory wall, he always insisted on walking with her. He would climb the hill to collect her on a Sunday morning and walk back up it to accompany her all the way home after their shift, even though he had to then walk back down.

Excitement raced through her heart as she neared the end of the crowded passage and caught a glimpse of the top of Asher's head. He didn't see her, even though he was looking her way, there were too many people around her. He was taller than most, she was shorter, so it wasn't surprising he didn't see her.

When she reached the end of the tunnel, she saw his brown eyes looking everywhere, his gaze sifting through the people, obviously searching for her. Their gazes collided. His expression instantly lit up, his smile rising and his eyes gleaming with joy. That look, that pleasure he expressed in the first moment he caught sight of her, always brought a smile to her lips.

'Hello.' Her voice came out breathless. 'What time is it? Will they be at the station?'

He reached into the chest pocket of his waistcoat and withdrew his pocket watch. He had shown her the inscription on the reverse of the watch once.

Mature in the faith, my son.
  Abba.

'It is ten past three.' His eyes lifted from the watch to Naomi. 'What time did you say their train will be here?'

'It was just after three, we might still catch them at the station if we hurry. I would love to see their faces when they arrive.'

'Then we had better hurry.' He reached for Naomi's hand, took hold of it and pulled her into motion.

His legs were a couple of inches longer than hers, which meant his stride was longer too, but he held back his pace so they could run side by side. She was glad she had her overalls and boots on, and that she didn't have the encumbrance of the gas mask box. Hardly anyone bothered carrying their gas masks now. In the eight plus months of war, the only attack from the air had been one small event in the Scottish isles.

The RAF used to fly aeroplanes low over Swindon, but it was rare now. She frequently saw the aircraft, though, higher up, flying off to somewhere much further away than Swindon.

She freed her hand from Asher's, to make it easier to run.

Her feet struck the pavement lightly, and her arms pumped back and forth, like train pistons pulling her forward faster and faster as she fought to reach the train station in time. The tall wall of the embankment at her left side ran the full length of the pavement – from the Railway Village to Swindon Station.

Asher could have overtaken now they were not holding hands. He did not, he continued pacing his strides to hers. She pushed herself harder. Her breathing heavy. She'd missed Golda and Esther. Their chatter and laughter had been a blessing in an otherwise sad and quiet house. The house was even quieter now her brothers had gone, and poor tortured Dietrich could not be expected to be jolly or particularly conversational.

'Go steady!' a woman pushing a pram shouted and waved a hand as Naomi and Asher ran towards her, taking up the full width of the pavement. She shook a fist at them to express her annoyance as Naomi tried to run around her, only to nearly collide with the pram and Asher.

Asher caught her arm and stopped her from falling.

'Sorry,' she said to the woman, then ran on.

A pillar of smoke and steam drifted into the air in the distance, from a train coming from the direction of London. If that was the train the twins were aboard... if it had not arrived yet... she might even be able to reach the platform and meet them off the train.

She found another spurt of pace from somewhere, hurtling along the pavement for the last few yards and into the station. She had no time for a platform ticket, but when trains of refugees arrived, they often left the gates open, and she had her GWR badge pinned on her chest, to say she was working shifts. So, they would know she was staff.

The soles of her boots drummed up the wooden steps to the platform. The shush-shush-shing of the train's pistons as it slowed, the squeal of the brakes and the click-clack of the wheels on the rails told her the train was arriving before she reached the top of the stairs and could see. The smells of the oil, steam and coal smoke greeted her as she ran onto the platform.

Full carriages rolled past as Asher joined her. Steam and smoke drifting along the platform with the rolling stock.

Her chest heaved as her lungs recovered from the run.

Her mother stood much further along the platform. Naomi didn't shout or go to her, she looked at the carriage windows. The twins could be in any one of the carriages, it was better if she and her mother remained spread out. As the carriages rolled past at a slower and slower pace, Naomi peered through the glass, scanning the seats for the girls' faces.

One last carriage rolled past as the train slowed almost to a halt.

'There.' Asher pointed just before a carriage door passed them.

Naomi turned and walked quickly, following the door along the platform as the brakes growled and the train stopped. Her heart beat as hard as it had at the thought of meeting Asher outside the factory. In the few weeks the twins lived with them last year, she'd fallen in love with these girls, then she thought she'd said goodbye to them forever.

She walked along to the first window. The glass was grimy and hard to see through, she rubbed the side of her hand across it, looking at the faces of the children inside. They looked back at her wide-eyed, as if she was the troll from the story of the three billy goats gruff.

But then she saw the girls waving, eagerly, further along, gathering their belongings.

Her heart flopped around like a fish out of water in her chest, tail flicking. The joy that sparked inside her at the sight of them was a little ridiculous. But perhaps it was because of the war and the difficulties Jews faced that she'd felt close to them so quickly. The girls picked up the same rucksacks they'd arrived with in September last year, and their gas masks, and hurried towards the door.

Not many of the children were disembarking in Swindon, most were going further south, so there was no queue to get out the door.

As the girls spilled out, rushing towards her, she opened her arms, then wrapped them both up in a hug, as they wrapped themselves around her. Coats, rucksacks and gas mask boxes getting in the way; it was more like a pile of jumble than a hug, but the warmth of it spread from Naomi's toes to the crown of her head.

She kissed the top of Golda's head, then Esther's. 'You've grown,' she said as they stepped back. 'You're at least two inches taller.'

The girls grinned, looking as excited as Naomi felt. She had expected sad faces because they had to leave their home behind again. They were very homesick the first time. But their mother said in her letter she'd told the girls this was a holiday, to stay with their friends in Swindon. It must feel very different from the day they boarded a train with no idea where they would end up.

When they arrived last year, they were quiet and nervous. Like a couple of little mice silently scurrying around the house, whispering to one another. Not wishing to make a fuss or be a bother. It had only taken a few days for them to settle in, though, before they became their boisterous selves. They had only ever been a joy to have in the house.

Dietrich had lived with Naomi's family for nearly a year, and he was still not wholly able to be himself. But that was understandable – how could anyone settle and feel any level of contentment when their family was missing in a nation run by Hitler and his Nazis? Since he had been helped to escape in the Kindertransport, everyone he'd left in Berlin had vanished.

He was fifteen now, and nothing like a child. Hitler had stolen his childhood in Germany, and here he had dropped out of school to become an apprentice at the factory as soon as the war began – to fight in some regard until he was old enough to actually fight.

Golda and Esther were eleven now. But apart from being taller and a little slimmer, they looked and seemed the same. They still had their hair cut into neat matching brown bobs, to the length of their chins, and they wore matching red gingham dresses, with smocking across their chests and white lace collars.

'You two are a perfect pair,' Asher said.

Naomi glanced over her shoulder. He stood beside her. She looked back at the girls. 'Do you remember Asher?'

They nodded keenly, though their eyes looked beyond Asher.

'My lovely girls!' Naomi's mother called.

Naomi glanced over her other shoulder and saw her mother rushing towards them. The girls dropped their coats and gas masks on the platform and raced to hug her. They had obviously become as attached to Naomi's family as her family had to them.

Asher picked up the discarded items and they joined her mother and the girls.

An odd sensation, perhaps because Naomi was tired after her shift, crept across her, a weight, embracing her. But it was a nice feeling of being in the right place with the right people.

They walked up the steepest part of the hill to their house, with Naomi holding Golda's hand, Golda holding Esther's and Esther holding Naomi's mother's. Asher walked in front carrying the girls' coats and gas masks. The day was lovely, sunny, bright and warm, a lovely day in every way. Golda swung Naomi's hand as they walked, and both girls prattled on, telling tales of their journey and their parents.

'A girl in our carriage on the way here had a nosebleed,' Esther regaled. 'One of the older girls made her lie down with a key at the back of her neck, and then she pushed on her nose until the girl screamed.'

'And a little boy fainted at the station!' Esther declared in a high-pitched voice that seemed to attempt to outdo her sister's tale.

'Gosh,' Naomi's mother said. 'You have had an adventurous journey.'

Asher looked across his shoulder and Naomi caught his slight smile of amusement.

This was why she loved these girls. Because they always made her smile and filled her heart with happiness – even when they squabbled.

Naomi hurried up the front steps of the house that was perched on a sharp slope of the hill. The pavement sloped a good four foot in height even from the front door to the bottom of the cellar window. She turned the doorknob, the door opened. Dietrich and her father were at home.

'Hello!' she called into the house. 'We are home! The girls, Ima, me and Asher!'

A door opened and closed upstairs, and Dietrich appeared at the head of the stairs. The fringe of his dark hair flopped forward over his brow as he ran down the steps.

'Welcome, Golda, Esther,' he greeted them. The 'w' of welcome holding a tone more like a v with the German accent in his English. 'I made you some welcome back presents. They are in the kitchen.'

Naomi had seen them. He'd carved the girls a pair of amazing little wooden horses. The horses' legs, neck, head and tail all swung at their joints. He liked carving wood, it was a distraction for him. It kept his hands and his mind busy, and he was very clever.

She'd told him, *After the war you must become a sculptor.* He was working in the sawmills at the GWR factory now. She'd thought he was too talented to remain there. Though, after seeing the beautiful hand Joe Marsh made for Catherine, there might be a place for Dietrich's artistic skill in the factory after all.

He had smiled weakly at her suggestion. For good reason, Dietrich could not see as far as the end of the war. His mind looked back, not forward, hovering on the people he had left behind at the beginning of the war. How could he forget them?

Naomi's family had all been asked many times, *'Where do you think my family are?'* and *'Why did my countrymen turn against Jews? Some of them were my father's and mother's friends.'*

Her mother, father and Naomi had answered his second question numerous times. *'Your countrymen did not turn on you. The bad people who chose to follow the Nazi doctrine turned on Jews.'*

His first question none of them could answer. No one knew, and that broke her heart.

The twins' bright smiles made a sharp contrast to Dietrich's shallow, heart-sore expression, their smiles shone like the sun to Dietrich's moon as they unwrapped their little horses from the handkerchiefs Dietrich had used to hide the gifts.

While she watched them, Naomi felt the warmth of Asher's arm surround her, and his hand rest at the indent of her waist.

Her mother happened to look up and her gaze caught on Asher's hand.

Naomi stepped away from Asher's touch. 'We have some rhubarb cakes, would everyone like something to eat, and tea?'

'Yes, please, Naomi.' The girls spoke in unison.

Yes, and here they were, home – Naomi stopped herself short. They were not home. This was not their home. But their cheeriness did make this house feel more homely.

'Hello, young London ladies.' Naomi's father came into the room and he leaned to embrace the girls. His expression, though, as he looked across their shoulders, was grim.

'What is wrong?' Naomi asked quietly.

'What's happened?' Her mother had noticed his expression too.

He released the girls, leaving them to play with their horses. 'The BBC broadcast a statement that people must not send any letters to military men.'

'Pardon?'

'Why?'

'They did not say why,' he answered. 'But what other reason can there be? The Allies must be losing and retreating.'

Dietrich's eyebrows lifted, expressing silent emotions. The dark tone in skin around his chin and upper lip, where he had begun shaving, sometimes gave him a sinister appearance. 'Are you sure?' he asked.

'That is a very big assumption, Jacob, from the single truth that we can't send letters,' Naomi's mother challenged her father, in an overly calm voice, which Naomi assumed was for Dietrich's sake.

But Naomi knew he was right. Of course he was. Since the Germans had invaded France, most people had not heard a word. The Allies were losing. If they were moving forward, it would still be possible for the post to reach them, so they must be moving back and so quickly they could not be sure where the regiments would be.

The girls showed her father their horses. He pretended fascination, as though he had not seen them before. At least the children were unaware of the Nazis' threat, but it was better that way. Naomi looked at Asher. His forehead had creased into a deep frown of concern. He shook his head, discouraging her from asking him any questions. The muscles in his cheeks were taut, implying his teeth were clenched. He must be fighting thoughts, memories perhaps, and the anger they inspired.

There was nothing they could do, though, except live day by day – and make bombs! As many bombs as she possibly could!

'Shall we build a racecourse?' she said to the girls. Then looked at Asher and Dietrich. 'Will you help? Perhaps we can lay out some books…'

'Cutlery would make better fences,' Dietrich said. 'Not so thick.'

'I'll fetch a handful of forks,' Asher agreed.

Good. Building fences for the girls' horses to jump would help them forget the Nazis were heading towards England.

10

LILY FRANKLIN

Tuesday 21 May

Lily squatted down, the hem of her skirt brushing on the dusty pavement. 'Mr Tabs, don't you av an ome to go to?' The cat rubbed his cheek and ear against the hand Lily offered. The ginger tomcat followed them to and from work every day. No matter the hours of their shifts, he was always somewhere around the park gates and rushed to say hello.

Violet squatted down too and stroked a hand over the cat's striped ginger coat. 'You must be hot in that coat in this weather, Mr Tabs.'

'Baking like a little potato,' Maggie joked. 'His coat would make a good fur stole for you, Vi. That tabby colour would go well with your red hair.'

Violet looked up at Maggie. 'That's a horrible thing to say.'

Lily clasped the poor cat to her chest and pressed a hand over his ear. 'Don't talk about skinnin im! That's cruel.'

'I was only joking,' Maggie clarified, rolling her eyes. 'He's very sweet just as he is.'

'I know you were jokin, but you didn't av to say it when the cat is ere. Gosh, he's skinny,' Lily said. Every single rib protruded beneath his fur and the notches along his spine. When had he last eaten? He did not have a collar, nothing identified him as someone's pet, so maybe he was a stray.

She gave him some food once, a tiny piece of spam from her lunchtime sandwich. Perhaps he always came to say hello to her and followed her along the street in the hope of another morsel of food.

Pity punched her firmly in the chest. 'Don't you belong to anyone?' she said to the cat as she stroked her hand across his head, and he rubbed his skinny body against her thigh.

'Meow,' he answered. 'Meow.'

Violet's fingers stroked his side. 'Perhaps his owners stopped feeding him because they didn't have enough rations to share.'

'Maybe his owner died,' Maggie said.

Lily looked up at Maggie. 'I think we should take im ome. Ee follows us every day. Ee must be really ungry.'

'Mr Faraday might like him if he can catch rats and mice,' Maggie responded. 'Mr Faraday said he was going to get a crate of chicks and build a chicken coop, so there will be plenty of rats coming after the chicken feed, enough to fatten a cat.'

The Faradays were special people, more generous than anyone else she knew; they had given her, Maggie and her sisters a home; she was sure they would welcome a homeless cat.

'Come on, Mr Tabs.'

'He'll have fleas,' Maggie warned as Lily scooped him up and rose with the cat in her arms. 'And he might scratch you,' Maggie threatened.

'Ee won't, not when I'm the one that feeds im.'

'How will you feed him?' Maggie protested, walking beside Lily as they headed towards Park Lodge.

'I'll eat less,' Lily answered.

She knew Maggie was not really against the cat, just tired after her shift and fed up over everything – everyone was, and not everyone had lost their dad.

'I can spare some scraps too,' Violet volunteered, following them. She was coming to the Faradays to be social. The house had become very like a single women's hostel now Maggie and her sisters had moved in, and Violet was nearly always there too.

'Anyway.' Lily looked directly at Maggie, speaking with a smile and a joking lilt in her voice. 'Another man around the ouse will be good for us all.'

That succeeded in sparking a laugh from Maggie. 'Oh, go on then. Let's see what Mr and Mrs Faraday think of our new lodger.'

'Ee'll be my responsibility. I'll be is landlady; I'm subletting to im.'

Maggie's smile twitched, then she laughed. Her hand rested on Lily's shoulder for a couple of paces. 'I guess he does make you smile, and if he makes the rest of us smile too, it'll be worth it for a mouthful or two less.'

When Lily walked through the back door into the kitchen, she discovered Marjorie and Edith busy making dinner.

Marjorie was rolling out a potato pastry on the kitchen table. They had started mixing the mashed potato with the flour to make the flour go further.

'Meow. Meow,' Mr Tabs cried.

Marjorie looked up from her task.

'Good Lord, what on earth have you got there?'

'A cat, obviously,' Maggie answered.

'The cat that is always following us, we've called him Mr Tabs,' Violet told her. 'He's a stray, he needs fattening up.'

'Well, get it out of the kitchen. If it's a stray it'll be riddled with parasites,' Edith cried. She was mixing whatever they were going to put in the potato pastry pie, stirring it in a pan on the gas stove. All the girls had been doing as many of the household tasks as they could, cooking, washing and cleaning, to express their gratitude to Mr and Mrs Faraday for offering them a home.

'I'll take im into the yard, then run up to the shop for some flea powder,' Lily said.

'I'll pour him a saucer of milk,' Maggie offered.

'You stay with him, Lily, I'll go to the shop,' Violet volunteered. 'You're his favourite, he'll worry if you go and he might run off if he's left alone in the yard.'

Lily smiled, happy to hear them adopting her scrawny little orphan. 'I'll take im outside anyway. Ee can drink is milk out there while you fetch the flea powder.'

'And don't you bring any fleas back in here,' Edith shouted as Lily opened the back door.

Before Lily could leave, the door from the hall into the kitchen opened. Mr Faraday came in. 'Who do we have here?' His gaze immediately focused on the cat in her arms. Her dad would have shouted, snatched the cat and probably literally kicked it out the door – Lenny's dad gave the meowing cat a warm smile.

'Mr Tabs. Ee needs an ome. Can ee stay with us, please?'

Mr Faraday's eyes widened and his bushy salt and pepper eyebrows lifted. 'Well, we are becoming a lodging house, aren't we? I suppose one more small one will do no harm. Hello and welcome, little fellow.' He walked across and stroked Mr Tabs's head.

Mr Tabs purred, shamelessly trying to charm the man who would be paying for the roof over his head.

So, just like that, as quick as a snap of a thumb and finger, Mr Tabs became a member of the Park Lodge family. 'Thank you, Mr Faraday,' Lily acknowledged with a wide smile. 'I knew you'd welcome im. You're always kind. You'd never leave anyone or anythin to suffer.'

'I've just remembered,' Mr Faraday said, his gaze passing from Marjorie to Edith to Maggie. 'A letter arrived for you girls this morning. It is on the hall table.'

'Do you remember what the postmark is?' Edith asked. 'We aren't expecting any letters.'

'I didn't look,' he answered. 'Shall I fetch it?'

'No, I will.' Maggie dashed around him and ran into the hall. The cat's saucer of milk was forgotten, so Lily kept Mr Tabs in her arms. He seemed comfortable there anyway.

'The postmark is Ramsgate!' Maggie shouted from the hall. 'It's from Aunt Alice!'

As Maggie came back into the room, Mr Faraday left, leaving the women to it.

'Is that your father's sister?' Lily asked Maggie.

Maggie nodded, looking really glad to have the letter, as her thumb slipped under the lip of the envelope and tore it open. She pulled out the letter and unfolded the paper. 'My darling girls...' she read aloud and glanced up at Edith and Marjorie, smiling. They smiled too, stopping in their tasks to listen.

It was one of the looks that Lily envied; an acknowledgement of valued longstanding love. Mr and Mrs Faraday and Lenny shared looks like that all the time. Lily did not even share looks like that with her sisters or her brothers, not even Art. She hadn't had a childhood full of love like Maggie and Lenny. Her fingertips combed through Mr Tabs's fur and he purred again.

Dot came through the door from the hall and joined them in the kitchen. 'Mr Faraday knocked on my bedroom door and told me you had a letter from Aunt Alice.' She was carrying a little Bible, held tight in one hand that pressed against her bosom. Lily had not known how religious Dot was until they moved in, though she had seen her at the church talking to Father Arnold. Dot read her little Bible all the time and carried it around the house when she wasn't reading it, as though she needed to feel constantly connected to God's word.

Maggie lifted her hand, waving the letter in front of Dot. 'I was about to read it.'

'Sit down, Dot,' Edith said. 'I'll make us all a pot of tea once we get this pie into the oven.'

Dot did not sit, but walked across to the stove and leaned over to smell whatever Edith was stirring in the saucepan. 'It's smells nice, what is it?'

'Kidney and oxtail. It was all I could afford to have enough to go around all of us, and onions from the garden. Two onions to stretch it out and bay leaves from the bush to make it extra tasty.'

'I'm ready for the filling,' Marjorie declared, as she cut away the edges of the potato-fortified pastry from the pie dish. Edith picked up the saucepan. 'Pour it into the middle,' Marjorie said.

Dot put her Bible down on the table. 'I'll put the kettle on and make that tea.'

'Is anyone going to listen to this letter!' Maggie complained, shouting across them all.

Mr Tabs flinched, his claws sinking into Lily's forearm. 'It's okay.' She stroked his ear.

'I'll go and buy the flea powder and leave you to it,' Violet said, and exited via the back door.

Dot turned on the tap and held the kettle beneath the running water.

Maggie rolled her eyes comically, raising a smile on Lily's lips, as Maggie waited for the noise of the water to stop.

Lily tickled Mr Tabs under the chin, until he purred happily again, his claws receding.

'Oh, hello!' Violet's voice could be heard through the door.

Answering hellos followed.

The answering women's voices drew everyone's interest.

The door opened and Violet reappeared. 'Look who I found about to knock.' She stepped out of the way, to let Catherine and Naomi into the kitchen. 'I'm off to the shop. I won't be long.'

'Ello,' Lily welcomed them.

A fresh round of greetings from the others followed as Violet left for the second time.

Maggie nodded her hello to Naomi and Catherine, her frustration with all the interruptions obviously growing.

Naomi came across, her hand lifting to stroke Mr Tabs. 'Who have we here?'

'Our new lodger, Mr Tabs,' Lily answered.

'He's gorgeous.'

'Vi's gone to buy flea powder so we don't infest the place,' Maggie informed them. 'I was going to pour him a saucer of milk so we could put him outside. Then I got this letter from our aunt.' She waved it in the air. 'Which I am failing to have any chance to read.' Maggie's lips pursed at the end of her speech.

Maggie's sisters laughed at her expression. It became a brief look of hurt. The different expression was only there for a moment, a fleeting hint of Maggie's true feelings. Lily often saw moments when Maggie expressed something that appeared submerged. A look that spoke of feeling deeply unhappy. Maybe it was only that her sisters were being annoying. Lily had seen Maggie struggling to have a voice among them.

'I'll get that saucer of milk,' Catherine offered. 'I'm practising with my new hand whenever I can.' She slid her handbag off her forearm, rested it on the table and walked over to a cupboard for a saucer as she spoke. Because she'd lived here for a while, she knew where everything was.

'Lord in Heaven, is anyone going to listen to this letter!' Maggie declared.

Dot looked over her shoulder as she lit the gas for the kettle to boil. 'Don't take the Lord's name in vain.'

A loud huff of annoyance left Maggie's mouth.

Edith and Marjorie laughed again.

Lily bit her lip, stopping herself from laughing at Maggie too – she did sound funny when she was annoyed.

'My darling girls...' Maggie began again, ignoring all of them and reading it whether they were ready or not.

'Who is it from?' Naomi mouthed the words silently towards Lily.

'Their aunt who raised them,' Lily replied and received a side glance from Maggie that said, *please shut up.*

'I hope this letter is worth listening to after all this,' Marjorie joked.

'Marjorie! Please!' Maggie snapped.

Lily could see from Marjorie's grin that she'd interrupted in order to tease Maggie.

'My darling girls, how are you?' Maggie began for the third time, holding the letter high up in both hands. 'I have thought of you every day since we lost dear Pip.'

'Who is Pip?' Catherine interrupted.

'Dad,' Maggie answered. 'It broke my heart that I was too ill to travel to the funeral. I wish I could have been with you then, and now I am feeling a lot better I will see you very soon. We will come to Swindon. I love all your letters, and Maggie, dear, you do tell me some tall stories – the Germans using mice as spies, indeed.' Maggie's lips parted in a grin, before she read on, 'This new home of yours sounds perfect, girls. I hope the move has gone well.

'I am writing with a purpose, though, because things have become quite concerning here.' Maggie's grin fell, and a frown marred her brow instead, as she looked more intensely at the writing. 'For the last couple of days, we have heard bombs exploding. They sound like the heaviest thunder, booming through the air.' Maggie had read with a theatrical voice before, but now her voice became grave. 'The sounds come from the other side of the English Channel, from the French coast. Even though the explosions are that far away, they rattle the windows of our little cottage. It is quite frankly terrifying, to know the fighting is so close to us. At night we see the glow from the fires that remain after the explosions. The coast of France is lit up like a Guy Fawkes bonfire. Heaven knows what is happening over there, to our soldiers and the French...'

Lily hugged Mr Tabs tighter. Naomi and Catherine were pale. They had relatives and sweethearts among the soldiers Maggie's Aunt Alice feared for.

'The British aeroplanes pass over constantly, going and coming, to and from France,' Maggie read on, her voice becoming grimmer. 'We know they're fighting the Germans' aeroplanes, but the papers say nothing of it, of course, for fear Hitler might think we are afraid and he's beating us, or that he may learn something about our defences. We must be losing, though, because the soldiers are asking everyone in Margate to leave their homes and move inland...'

'Papa said they were moving children...' Catherine said, 'not everyone.' She looked as shocked as Lily felt.

Maggie swallowed awkwardly, obviously overwhelmed by the news herself, even though she had no personal link to anyone fighting.

Lily stared, open-mouthed. What she'd been afraid of and imagined… was real! The fatigue from the constant hours of work and lack of sleep punched her in a quick swift blow of exhaustion. Loving people involved in the fighting was hard.

Her vision blurred and she sniffed as the tears rolled. She lifted a hand away from Mr Tabs and wiped her eyes, smearing the tears across her cheeks. Catherine did the same, before bending down to put the saucer of milk on the floor. Lily leaned and set Mr Tabs on his feet, he eagerly lapped up the milk as Lily straightened, facing a truth she wasn't sure she could handle. 'Lenny and Art, your Charles, Cath, and your and Naomi's brothers are somewhere among those bombs and fires…' Her heart sank all the way to her heels like a heavy lead weight.

Naomi's palm pressed against her stomach, as though she felt ill too.

Catherine breathed deeply and sighed. Then, her lower lip wobbling, she wiped a tear away from her eye with a wooden fingertip. 'At least we know why no letters have come,' she said, as Mr Tabs noisily drank.

'I suppose so,' Naomi replied. 'And why we cannot send them.'

Lily reached for a chair, pulled it away from the table and sat down before she fell down. She did not just feel sick, she was going to be sick. Her left hand pressed over her mouth and she felt the hard edge of Lenny's engagement ring against her lip.

'You look green, Lily.' Edith had come to her side. 'Get a bowl, Dot!' she yelled as she realised why.

Dot reached for a Pyrex bowl and handed it to Lily.

Dot didn't look much better herself, she was pale too.

It was lucky Lily had not eaten for hours so there was not very much to be sick with.

Maggie handed Lily a cloth to wipe her mouth, and Catherine's left hand touched Lily's shoulder. 'Lenny and Art will be fine. But I will add them to my prayers.'

Lily nodded, saying, *thank you*, as Naomi passed her a handkerchief so she could blow her nose too. Dot took the bowl away to wash it out.

Lily looked up at Catherine. 'I'll pray for Charles an your brothers too.' She looked at Naomi. 'And yours.'

'Should I read the rest?' Maggie was looking at them. 'Or would you rather not know?'

'If Charles is living it, I will not hide from the knowledge of it.' Catherine sounded more horrified that Maggie might not read on.

Maggie's wide eyes and raised eyebrows asked Lily, *do you want to know?*

Lily nodded. 'Yes. I must know.' She would only imagine things that were not true, otherwise.

Maggie looked at the letter, her expression no longer showing any gladness.

'I have heard, from friends,' Maggie read on. 'Though no one official tells us anything, it's not only Margate where people have been asked to leave their homes, it's along the whole east coast of England.'

'They've been moving children away from the coast for at least a week,' Catherine interrupted, 'and...' she took a deep breath, then continued, '...I am not sure if I should share this, but I know none of you are spies and no one else can overhear... Papa told me this morning that telephone communications with France have been cut. There are staff managing the GWR trains that were shipped over to Europe to transport troops, and no one has heard anything from them, the lines are dead.'

A bitter taste filled Lily's mouth. She was so cold she was shivering as though she had a fever. Catherine's hand returned to her shoulder.

'Do you think we've lost the war?' Edith asked no one in particular.

'It doesn't sound as though they're winning any battles.' Dot's tone was gloomy.

'Aunt Alice says, some soldiers told us the Nazis will bomb the coastal towns soon,' Maggie read on. 'Then they'll come across the Channel from France in boats and land along our coast. That's why the army wants us civilians out of the way. Which comes to the whole point of my letter, really – as I said at the beginning, I will see you soon because we are coming back to Swindon. We will be with you in a couple of days. I hope not for long. I have no idea where we will stay. We will have to resolve that when we arrive.'

Maggie looked up, looking from Dot to Edith and Marjorie. 'What on earth will Mr and Mrs Faraday say?'

'They'll say, welcome,' Lily answered. 'We can fit them in, with a bit of jugglin of beds.'

'We can share,' Maggie looked at Dot.

Dot nodded.

'No. They must stay with my parents.' Catherine raised her wooden hand and silenced everyone. 'There are several rooms spare. I'll tell Papa and Mama this evening.' The tone of her voice refused to engage in any discussion. Though they all knew she'd left her parents' house, until her accident had meant she had to return, partly because her father and mother had not offered up rooms to refugees.

'When will they arrive?' Catherine asked.

Maggie looked at the envelope. 'The postmark is dated two days ago. They might even be here tomorrow.'

'I will have to ensure we're prepared for them, then.' Catherine smiled.

'Do you want to stay for dinner?' Edith offered, looking at Catherine and then Maggie. 'The pie will stretch.'

'No. Thank you for the offer, though,' Naomi said.

'I need to get home and tell my parents we'll be having guests,' Catherine answered. 'But I have some news too.'

'What news?' Lily asked.

'I'm starting work in the machine shop in a fortnight. The foreman is happy there's plenty of work for me to do.'

Edith's hands clapped together, which began a round of applause from all the girls.

Roses bloomed in Catherine's cheeks.

'Will you move back ere?' Lily asked.

Catherine's head shook. 'No. It's full already, and I can manage at home. Papa and I are using bicycles, rather than burn unnecessary diesel.'

'Good for you,' Maggie commented. 'I'll be glad to have you back in the workshop.'

'Me too,' Lily agreed. 'It's never the same when the five of us aren't on a shift.'

The back door opened. 'Flea powder,' Violet declared as she walked in, holding a small brown bottle. Her chest heaved with each breath. She must have run there and back.

A metallic clunk told Lily that Marjorie had put the pie in the oven and shut the door. Edith opened the larder and took out the freshly pulled carrots and cut kale from Mr Faraday's garden. There were always fresh vegetables to eat in this house. Living with the chief gardener was to everyone's benefit.

Lily's thoughts spun to Lenny – he loved gardening. He wanted to become a head gardener for a grand house. He'd thrown that plan aside to fight the Nazis.

Thinking about him reminded her of the danger. Her stomach rolled and left her feeling green again, but she refused to be sick. She rose from the table. 'I'll put the powder on Mr Tabs outside.' He'd finished his milk, but he was still licking the saucer. She held out a hand to take the bottle from Violet, and with her other hand scooped up the cat.

Marjorie opened the back door for her. 'Dinner will be in three quarters of an hour.'

'Thank you.' Lily nodded.

The door closed behind her. But a moment later it opened again. Catherine stepped out and shut the door.

'You looked like you could do with some company, so I thought I would join you,' Catherine said. 'Are you frightened for Lenny?'

'Yes.'

'Me too. I mean, for Charles, and Lenny and all the men. My stomach is tied in knots. I knew something was wrong when Papa said the Government were moving more children.'

'Can you elp me with this, Cath?' Lily held out the bottle, showing Catherine the instructions printed on the label. 'I can't talk about Lenny, or Art. I'll throw up again if I think about what they're facin.'

'Good idea. Worrying is not going to help. You're right, Lily, I just need to pray and believe in them.'

Yes. Lily should believe they would win too. She tried to. She imagined Lenny using a rifle like a sword, battling a Nazi and knocking him down on his arse in a muddy puddle. The image made her smile. She should think like that all the time.

It was not until she climbed the stairs, alone, to go to bed later that evening, that she let herself consider her emotions again.

She held Mr Tabs in her arms, her fingers stroking his silky ear. Calming herself.

Before brushing the flea powder into his coat, she and Catherine had washed him in the garden, scrubbing him with a bar of soap, rinsing him off with a shower from a watering can and rubbing him dry, much to his annoyance.

In her room, she put Mr Tabs on the foot of her bed. He watched her undress with a head quizzically tilted to one side.

She always tried to be positive, to think the best of things, but it was hard when she knew about the fighting on the coast of France, and she couldn't even expect a letter from Lenny.

Lenny had written in his last letter that he had to retreat. She hadn't told anyone in case he wasn't meant to have told her. No amount of thinking could make what was happening positive. They – Britain – were losing.

The letter she was writing to Lenny lay on the dressing table. If she climbed into bed, she wouldn't sleep, so she sat down at the table instead, to write. Just because she could not send the letter didn't mean she couldn't write to him. She would send it later. It might be as long as a novel by then, but he'd know she'd not stopped thinking about him for one minute. When she held the pen in her hand, though, she couldn't think of a single word to write beyond, *I love you.*

Mr Tabs jumped off the bed, strolled over and hopped up to squeeze himself onto her lap. Her fingertips stroked through his fur as he curled up.

She stared at the blank page, as the words 'I love you' circled her mind.

When she saw him, she would say it against his lips a hundred times. It had taken her too long to realise Lenny wasn't just a good friend. What if she never saw him again?

She sucked in a noisy breath that expressed her pain and put down the pen. She couldn't write after all.

Tears welled, rolled onto her cheeks and dripped from her chin. She sniffed, as she cried, and allowed herself selfish embarrassing sobs in the privacy of her room, sounding like one of her younger brothers and sisters.

Her mind's eye saw Lenny's body, lying face down in the mud of a French field, not the German on his arse.

She wanted this war to stop, she wanted Lenny and Art to come home.

Footsteps on the landing outside the room silenced her.

'Goodnight,' Maggie said.

'Sleep tight.' That was Edith.

'Sleep well.' That was Marjorie.

Marjorie's and Edith's footsteps creaked on the stairs to the attic rooms. The door of Lenny's room opened. But a moment later a slight tap knocked

Lily's bedroom door. 'Lily,' Maggie's voice whispered through the door. 'Can I come in?'

Lily didn't want to talk. She sat silently, her fingers combing through Mr Tabs's fur.

'I heard you crying. Let me in.'

Lily didn't move a muscle, sitting quiet and still.

'Lily, I know you're awake. If you don't answer me, I'll come in anyway because you're worrying me.'

Lily sniffed the tears from her nose and wiped a sleeve across her cheeks, then got up. She opened the door.

Maggie stood in darkness on the blacked-out landing.

Lily was illuminated by the twilight sky as her window was uncovered; she never used her electric light.

'Sometimes Dot brushes my hair when I'm sad. Would you like me to brush your hair?'

The only precious items Lily owned, beyond the engagement ring Lenny had given to her, were the silver-backed hairbrush and tortoiseshell combs that had belonged to her mother. But no one else had ever used them. No one else had ever brushed her hair.

'Oh, Lily.' Maggie's arms enveloped Lily in a firm hug. 'I'm sorry. This war is horrible.'

To have someone to hold – and hold her – was what she needed.

She wrapped her arms around Maggie and hugged her back just as hard, as Mr Tabs trailed a figure of eight around their legs.

After a moment, Maggie released her. 'Sit down, let me brush your hair for you, and you can tell me some lovely stories about you and Lenny, or about your brother Art. I know what it's like to miss someone.'

Of course she did, it was only a few weeks since her father's death, and here was Lily worrying over something that may or may not happen.

'I love your curls,' Maggie said as Lily sat down in front of the mirror. The sheets of her letter to Lenny in front of her.

'Is this your comb?' Maggie reached for Lily's precious heirloom.

'You av to comb the curls singularly, it takes ages,' she told Maggie. 'But otherwise, they get knotty.'

Maggie separated a single jet-black curl with her fingers. Lily had her mother's hair, she had always been proud of it. It was a comfort to know she was like the mother who had died when she was born. Her hair, like her colouring, came from her mother's black heritage. Her family came from St Kitts, in the West Indies, in the Caribbean Sea. At school, she had liked looking at the island on a map. Her mother had told Art her family owned land on St Kitts. Now Art's son had their mother's hair and colouring too, and he would hear all the stories her mother told Art and Art had told Lily.

As Maggie worked, Mr Tabs jumped back up onto Lily's lap. She stroked him, as the gentle tugs of the comb distracted her thoughts.

'How did you and Lenny become friends?' Maggie asked.

'On the first day of school...' Lily began telling her their whole story.

11

MAGGIE ABBOT

Wednesday 22 May

Maggie bent over and looked inside the empty shell of a 25-pounder bomb. She reached inside and stroked her fingers across the cold metal, checking it was smooth and clean and ready to be packed up and sent off on a train to wherever it was these bombs were loaded with explosives. Everyone in the weaponry supply chains only knew about their part. The less any single person knew, the harder it would be for Nazi spies to discover the whole truth.

Since yesterday, all Maggie could think about was that the Germans might be landing on the beaches and sailing up the river estuaries, like the Vikings did.

Maggie glanced over her shoulder. 'All clear!' she called out to Violet who was operating the loading crane.

The clang of a hand bell stopped Maggie before she looked at the next bomb on the conveyor. Susie Adams stood on the stairs to the foreman's office ringing the bell in swift up and down strokes, announcing the start of the lunch period.

It was a long time since the factory's hooters had sounded when it was the start and end of lunchtimes. They'd been silent since the war began, reserved to call out the warning of the air raids that had never come.

'Come on.' Violet caught hold of Maggie's upper arm and pulled her away from the production line.

Because it was a lovely sunny day, they were going to eat their lunch in the GWR park.

'Hurry up, Lily!' Violet shouted across the workshop floor, releasing Maggie's arm. 'Naomi! Come on, Cath and Dietrich will be waiting for us!'

Lily joined them as they reached the hooks where they hung their thin brass discs to show who was in and who was out.

Maggie walked to the sinks in the cloakroom and washed her hands.

'Hello.' Naomi joined her.

Maggie smiled her hello as she picked up her lunch tin. She walked out of the workshop and held the door open for Naomi, Violet and Lily to follow.

They linked arms, as they often did, and walked along the path to the tunnel.

'How was your morning?' Maggie asked Lily particularly.

They'd shared Lily's bed last night, in the way she and Dot slept together when one of them was sad. This morning, Lily had declared she was going to be more stalwart and stop blubbing like a baby. Maggie wouldn't say it was babyish to be concerned about people who were in places where bombs the size of the ones they were making were exploding – she didn't tell Lily that. Thinking about the bombs would probably scare her.

'It was alright, thanks,' Lily answered, and smiled slightly.

Maggie released her arm from Violet's as they neared the tunnel. Every day she walked through the tunnel there were fewer men in the crush of workers and more women. The men in the factory did not have to fight – they were in protected occupations – but they left because of their conscience or because they wanted to *'bash the bloody Nazis'* or just because they'd reached the conscription age.

Lily's Lenny was one of the latter. He turned nineteen one day and signed up the next. How on earth did he feel over there among the bullets and bombs? Maggie couldn't imagine it.

What she did know, was that the bombs she'd helped finish this morning would blow up Nazi tanks and equipment, and she hoped one bomb might stop a tank firing at her friends' relations.

Her heartbeat quickened as she walked into the low-ceilinged tunnel. It always did. She threaded an arm around Violet's again. It wasn't easy to walk in a four, but there was space to walk two by two, and Maggie hated this tunnel. She hated small, narrow, crowded spaces. The walls moved inwards and the ceiling downwards. She swallowed, fighting the sickly feeling that grasped the back of her throat, and she breathed in through her nose then out through her mouth.

'Relax, love,' her father's voice told her. 'Nothing bad will happen.'

She had been walking this route four times a day on workdays since last September. Nothing bad had happened. But this nonsensical fear continued to pump through her heart to the point she felt giddy on every occasion. Because she knew it was silly, she'd only told her father she felt like this.

Sixteen. Seventeen. Eighteen... Counting the steps from one end to the other helped her fight the fear. *Twenty-one. Twenty-two...* She continued counting in her head all the way to the point that she knew there were only a few more paces before she would be in the open.

As soon as they walked out the other end, she took the deepest breath, and her arm released Violet's.

They turned to walk along Bristol Street to the GWR park. Many of the men around them were greeted with swift embraces from women and children.

Her mind's eye pictured herself greeting Ron when he appeared from the mouth of the tunnel. She saw herself rushing into his arms to be received in a warm bear hug, caught up in the delicious scents of the wood saps that were carried in his clothes and cap.

Ron had asked her to go to a dance with him on Friday evening. This time it would just be the two of them. Asher and Naomi would be with Naomi's family because Friday was the day of a religious meal for them. Maggie had agreed to go, but she was unsure about being alone with him. She was not really in the mood to be dating anyone. But she didn't want to throw away her chance with Ron, she'd wanted to be his girlfriend for years.

'Joe!' Violet shouted, raising a hand and waving. He was walking a few yards ahead of them. Heading to what Maggie assumed was her old home. Violet ran ahead, as he'd stopped.

Maggie followed with Lily and Naomi.

'We're meeting Cath in the park for lunch,' Violet was saying, 'if you want to come? I am sure she'd love it if you joined us.'

Joe smiled, with a look Maggie would call polite. 'Thanks for the invitation but my housekeeper will have a meal on the table for me, and I can't let her down after she's put all that work in, nor waste my rations. But tell Cath I said hello, and I hope she's getting on well with that hand.'

'She is,' Naomi said.

'Really well,' Lily added.

'All of us are as grateful to you as she is,' Violet gushed.

Maggie couldn't speak. She was grateful to him too, for Cath's sake. But it had struck her heart when she thought about his dinner waiting on a table in a kitchen where her dad used to sit and eat his meals.

'That's kind of you, ladies, but I better get home.' He raised the brim of his bowler hat, lifting the hat off his head by an inch. The hat told everyone Joe was a foreman whether he was inside the factory or not. The working men, like Ron, wore flat caps, so the foreman's bowler hats stood out even in a crowd. 'Good day,' he said.

'Bye, Joe.'

Maggie raised a hand in a pathetic wave, as the others said their goodbyes, then they headed on towards the park.

The sound of several Hawker Hurricanes flying in formation shook all other thoughts from Maggie's mind. She looked up. The aircraft were flying high. They looked like tin toys from the ground, small impressions against the blue of the sky. The trails of smoke behind them left lines that would remind her later in the day how many aeroplanes had passed over.

The pilots must know what was happening in France. How on earth did it feel to be up there and see everything from a bird's-eye view? She should ask Edith to ask her pilot.

She kept watching the Hurricanes as they flew towards France, wondering if they were carrying bombs she'd helped make. 'Go on! Stop the Nazis!' the shout blurted out, and she threw a fist in the air, as though it would punch the Nazis all the way over the Channel in France.

'Yes! Get them!' Lily shouted, waving her arm back and forth.

'Good luck!' Naomi shouted more placidly, waving at the pilots calmly.

'Be safe! And successful!' Violet shouted as they disappeared above a cloud.

The girls burst into what Maggie felt was nervous laughter.

'I wonder if they saw us waving,' Maggie said as their excitement calmed down.

'If it was a train driver, they would have blown their whistle if they did,' Violet answered.

'I don't think they av whistles...' Lily's voice was so serious they all laughed again.

'Of course they don't,' Maggie said, staring upwards. 'There's no one up there to tell to get out of the way.'

'I do know why they don't av whistles. I was only jokin,' Lily answered, a little petulant.

'I know, I was joking too,' Maggie said. 'I didn't mean to tease you. But can you imagine if they did have whistles and pulled the cord to blow it?'

Lily giggled along with the others as they pictured it.

Maggie reached out, caught hold of Lily's hand and squeezed it tight for a moment. She would have let go then, but Lily clung on.

A group of young girls had drawn a hopscotch grid on the pavement with a piece of chalky stone. Maggie walked around the game, tucking herself behind Lily, careful not to step on the lines, as one of the girls with a fall of curly brown hair bent over to throw her stone onto a square. It landed on the square with six drawn in the middle of it. Her friends cheered, so it must have been the square she was aiming for. She hopped quickly from one foot to two, then back to one, then balanced on one foot to pick up her stone, before doing the pattern of one- and two-feet hops back.

Maggie glanced towards Violet. They used to play like that. It was nice, though, that these girls seemed oblivious to the daily headlines of horror in the newspapers and played as if nothing in the world had changed.

'I must ask the twins if they know that game,' Naomi said.

A flood of loss swept through Maggie's heart. For the days of her childhood, when her father was with her. To be back in the house Joe had probably reached by now.

Lily's hand let her go. 'Cath!' she shouted and waved.

Catherine stood near the park gate dressed in a smart pair of navy slacks, a pale pink blouse and a cream cardigan. Catherine's customary striking scarlet red, lipstick-painted lips parted in a smile, and she lifted her right arm, then changed it for her left to be able to wave her hand. After they'd all said how much they missed Catherine's presence at work, they had arranged to meet Catherine for lunch. Maggie had really missed her. It was bad enough that her world was haemorrhaging men, she didn't want to lose the company of her female friends too.

Lily's adopted ginger tomcat strolled around the corner of the end terrace house, with his swanky way of walking, acting as though he didn't have a care in the world. It was obvious he had heard Lily shouting to Cath. He'd appeared to greet the woman who would fill his little belly when he asked.

'Mr Tabs!' Lily cried out as excitedly as she had when she saw Catherine. She squatted down and lifted the cat into her arms.

A strange sense of having been here in this moment before caught at Maggie – with the noise of the girls playing hopscotch behind them, Catherine waiting for them not in work clothes but in her fine clothes and Mr Tabs in Lily's arms brushing his head into the crook of her neck. It was déjà vu. Not a real memory but an imagined one. Probably because she was so tired. But it was a new memory she would hold on to, a pleasant moment in her sad life.

When she told the others that, as they ate their lunches seated in a circle on the lawn in the Faringdon Road park, they focused on the word sad, not that she thought it a nice memory.

'I know why you feel sad, Maggie,' Lily declared. 'But your life is not sad. You av your sisters an all of us, I don't think it's a sad life.'

'And Ron's taking you out to a dance on Friday night,' Violet threw in. 'You'll be the lucky one, hardly anyone has a man to dance with, they're getting scarce. I wish I could go dancing with a man.' The last sentence held a note of envy.

'You could walk up to Old Town and go to the dance,' Naomi said. She'd heard the jealous tone in Violet's voice too. 'You don't need a man.'

'It's not the same dancing with friends,' Violet answered.

Maggie hoped Violet's jealousy was only over the dancing. A few months before, Violet had implied she fancied Ron too, and at one point Maggie thought Ron fancied Violet back. But it was Maggie he'd asked out.

'I haven't tried dancing with my new hand.' Catherine raised her wooden hand. 'I couldn't lead, but I could follow if you led, and I would come with you, Vi, if you want to go. Even if I am second best to a man.'

She had them all smiling again.

'I wasn't saying I wanted to go to the dance, or that you were all second best. I only meant it would be nice to have an evening out like we used to before the war...' Violet protested. 'And I think going dancing with a man would make my life happier if I was sad.'

Maggie smiled. She loved Violet, she loved them all, but Violet had been in her life for a long time, and they knew each other too well to hide emotions. She should talk to her about Ron again. If Violet really wanted to go out with Ron, she should.

'Then why don't we go to the cinema on Saturday afternoon?' Lily said. 'All of us. Naomi, can you come too if we go then? We've all got a shift-free day.'

'We could go to the swimming baths beforehand too,' Catherine suggested. 'The doctor keeps telling me using the baths would be good for my arm. We could swim and then go to the cinema.'

'That would be fun,' Violet agreed.

'It's a great idea,' Maggie said, forcing excitement into her voice.

'We'll have something to look forward to at least,' Catherine added, then she looked at Lily. 'Did you see the newspaper headlines this morning?' Catherine's voice became serious.

'No, Mr Faraday's adn't been delivered before I left for work, why?'

Maggie wasn't sure Lily should know, after the state she'd been in last night. She'd put the newspaper on top of a cupboard out of the way. But there was no hiding from this war, Lily would hear the news eventually.

'They describe what we suspected yesterday. The Allied forces have been forced back to the French coast. They're camping on the beaches and encircled by the German forces. There's nowhere else for the men to go. It's why your Aunt Alice can hear and see the bombing, Maggie, because the Germans are bombing the Allied troops' camps at the coastal positions.'

'They're sitting ducks then.' Violet expressed the horror they all felt.

Mr Tabs, who definitely preferred Lily, walked to her side and stroked his body against her arm, as Lily's eyes swam.

'He knows when you're upset,' Maggie said.

Lily swallowed, her throat shifting, she swallowed again. This morning, she had been determined not to cry any more. She wrapped a hand around Mr Tabs and pulled him onto her lap.

Catherine took a deep, long breath, her eyes glittery with tears too. 'Sorry to tell you when you all must go back to finish your shifts. My father told me the reports have come from German sources, from their radio broadcasts, and of course they will tell us they're winning. He said we should take the information with a pinch of salt, as it may not be true.'

'But it sounds true, from what Maggie's aunt wrote, and if it is...' Naomi said. 'What does that mean?'

'I can only think about what it means for Lenny an Art,' Lily answered.

'Bloody Germans,' Maggie said in such a droll voice she made her friends laugh again – she'd intended to make them laugh. Even Lily choked out a sad-sounding chuckle.

The sound of aeroplane engines silenced them, and they looked towards the sky in unison. Another squadron of five Hawker Hurricanes flew over them in a V formation. Like the rows of noisy geese that flew over Swindon on their migration from Scandinavia and Russia to spend their winters on the lakes in the parks.

'They're loaded,' Lily said. 'You can tell from the sound of the engines. They definitely aren't practisin.'

Maggie had heard the different tone of the engines too.

'Go get those bastards!' Violet yelled towards the sky, waving at the pilots.

Maggie and all her friends spluttered into more laughter because that was something Maggie might say, but not Violet. Violet didn't swear. Maggie caught Violet's eye and grinned, as Violet turned a vibrant red – having sworn.

A new sound drew Maggie's gaze to the park's gate.

'Right. Left. Right. Left. Right...' a man's voice called out. The rhythm of boots striking the tarmac of the road accompanied the calls.

'Now that's another bastard,' Lily said quietly.

Maggie looked where Lily was looking and her gaze struck John Finch, walking front and centre, literally, in the middle of the front row behind the lieutenant who was shouting out the rhythm.

'I can't believe they'd give that bully a gun. It's bad enough when ee's on the platform behind the air raid gun, an now ee can walk around town all day with that thing angin over is shoulder.'

'What I do not understand,' Naomi said, 'is that they arrest people all the time just because they come from a particular country and might be dangerous, when they have not vetted the factory volunteers before putting a gun in their hands. Who is to say they're not fascists?'

'Or just nasty,' Lily added.

John Finch's head turned, he must have sensed them looking. His gaze found Lily and lingered as he glared back. Maggie's shoulders shivered, in the way that people said was like someone walking over your grave. Ever since the incident between him and Lily at the dance the night that Maggie's father had died, she was wary of John Finch on Lily's behalf – he was a creepy man. She lifted her fingers and made a V sign towards him with her forefinger and middle finger, showing the back of her hand. Lily did the same in the same moment, and in the next moment, all of girls, including the prim and proper Catherine, were holding up the rude two-finger sign to tell John Finch what to do with his gun.

12

MAGGIE ABBOT

The workshop door opened unexpectedly. Maggie looked up, her concentration lifting away from the lathe she was working with. A young man came into the workshop. He was dressed in a three-piece black suit, not a dirty one, but the clean suit of a clerk.

Susie Adams, the checky, met him a few steps away from the door.

'Back to work!' Mr Baker's shout boomed across the room, clearly audible even over the sounds of the machines. He stood on his high perch, at the top of the steps, at the open door to his glass-walled foreman's office.

Nearly everyone had stopped work to look at the clerk invading their area. He was waving a piece of paper in Susie's face now.

'Maggie Abbot! Get back to work or I'll dock your wages!' Mr Baker targeted her with his complaints.

Maggie leaned down and focused back on the lathe, watching Susie lead the man across the shopfloor through the corner of her eye. Mr Baker walked down the office stairs.

The lathe ran, but Maggie wasn't working. She was too nosy for her own good half the time. She tried to hear what the man was saying to Susie and Mr Baker. It sounded like Mr Baker was complaining about the clerk being in the workshop.

Maggie decided to focus fully on her work – distraction meant accidents.

Catherine and Lily had learned that the hard way. She would end up with an injury if she didn't stop listening and concentrate.

'Miss Abbot!'

Maggie jumped half out of her skin, her hand flying out in a risky way. Susie caught her hand, lowered it to safety and pressed the off button on the lathe.

Mr Baker and the clerk stood beside her.

'I only stopped working for a minute, I—'

'That is not why we want to speak to you.'

'There's a telegram for you, Miss Abbot,' the clerk said. 'It was delivered to the factory.'

Why would anyone send her a telegram? Maggie wiped her sweaty forehead with the back of her glove, then bit the loose top on the forefinger and pulled the glove off with her teeth. She reached out then, with a naked hand, and took the envelope the clerk held out. People only sent telegrams in emergencies. Like when someone died... She broke the seal and tore the envelope open. There was only one line, one sentence on the piece of paper inside it. Maggie's heart hammered as she took the paper out.

```
MAGGIE DEAREST, WE WILL ARRIVE AT SWINDON TRAIN
STATION AT 3.20 P.M. TODAY.
    AUNT ALICE
```

Maggie's eyes lifted to look at the foreman, then even higher to look at the clock on the far wall. Its large black hands pointed at just after twelve and three. It was 3 p.m. She wasn't due to finish her shift until four thirty. She looked at Mr Baker. 'I need to go,' she said.

'What is it, Miss Abbot?' he asked.

News of dead and missing sweethearts, husbands, sons and fathers arrived in telegrams. His expression said he thought her message had brought news like that.

'It's family business,' was all she said, leaving him with the misconception. He was more likely to excuse her and not deduct anything from her wages if he thought it was that sort of message. 'Can I leave right now? I wouldn't ask unless I had to.'

'Yes, of course. You go on,' Mr Baker answered, nodding, his voice half the pitch of his normal volume and expressing concern, proving that he did have a heart in his chest after all.

As she hurried across the workshop, she untied the straps of the pinafore she was wearing over the blouse and skirt she'd put on this morning because her overalls were on the washing line. Her friends stopped their machines when she passed them and looked her way. She lifted a thumb to tell them nothing was wrong and headed to the checking board, where she hung her little round brass token to say she'd gone. It hung there in lonely isolation as she glanced up at the clock.

She had fifteen minutes to get to the station to meet the train. She hurried out of the room, sliding her arms free from the pinafore, hung that on her hook, picked up her handbag, opened the outer door and ran.

The pathways through the factory site were empty, with everyone working. It was odd, the walkways were always full of people when she walked to and from the workshop at the beginning and end of her shifts. There was a ghostly feel to this emptiness.

'Aye, slow down, Maggie Abbot! There are no wolves chasing after you, Little Red Riding Hood!'

The shout came from the man standing on the scaffold that held the air raid gun. She presumed he was referring to her red blouse. She ignored him, not even looking to see who was up there.

The chuffing sounds of the steam-powered pistons of a train coming from the direction of Bristol Temple Meads roared, and the iron tracks on the edge of the factory site jangled with the sound of its fast approach. That would be the train her aunt and uncle were on.

She rushed down the slope to reach the subway, careered around the corner and raced into the tunnel. She had never been alone inside it before. She hated the space when it was squashed full of people. She discovered she hated it even more when she was the only one inside it, as the walls came closer and the ceiling lower. She ran.

Her breaths, quickened by running, became even sharper from panic as she reached the middle of the tunnel. Even when she'd sat in the outdoor lavatory at their old home she'd left the door ajar because it felt too enclosed. She hated the Faradays' indoor lavatory because she couldn't leave the door ajar; her heart beat as hard as it did now when she used that small room. If she went into the walk-in larder, she would pin the door open with something so it couldn't close.

A logical part of her brain knew nothing bad was going to happen to her, as she raced towards the end of the tunnel, where a man sat in a little box at the Railway Village entrance, making sure no strangers came through. But the illogical part of her brain refused to believe what she knew.

When she reached the tunnel's end, her heart beat like the bang of a drum. 'Good day, Ben!' she called as she reached the man. He'd been a friend of her father's.

'Good day, Maggie, where are you off to in such a hurry?'

She didn't stop to answer him. 'I'll tell you later!'

The air on the other side of the tunnel carried both the scents of steam and smoke from the train from Bristol and the sounds of the engine's pistons chuff-chuffing as it ran along the track not far from her.

Maggie raced the train at full pelt, her arms pumping, her handbag swinging from the handles she held firmly in her hand, the breeze of the warm spring day catching the short hairs on her forearms.

The plume of smoke and steam was swept down from the embankment and into her path by a breeze as the train approached the station, the engine's brakes growling as she approached the station entrance.

Her lungs heaving, she ran to the machine to buy a platform ticket and pulled her purse from her handbag. She found out a penny, slid it into the slot, turned the handle, heard the penny fall inside, then a paper ticket popped out. She tore it free and rushed to climb the steps.

The carriages stood alongside the platform, and people disembarked via many open doors along the train. Looking left and right, and left again, Maggie searched for the faces she knew.

It was only then she remembered her sisters might want to be here. But Maggie was the one who'd known Aunt Alice as a mother the most, because she was the youngest when her aunt came to look after them. She was also the one who wrote the most letters, and that would have been why Aunt Alice sent the telegram to her. But she would expect Maggie to tell the others, would she expect them all to be here, even though they might be working?

Lifting onto the balls of her feet, raising the heels of her flat work shoes, Maggie looked over the heads of others as misty drifts of steam from the engine trailed along the platform. The engine hissed its desire to move on, more excess steam escaping.

Doors began slamming closed all along the train.

Where were they?

The only people still disembarking were those lifting luggage off. She immediately wondered if all these people were refugees from the Continent or from the English coast, like Aunt Alice. She could not imagine anyone travelling on a holiday today.

Right at the tail end of the row of carriages a man stood beside two suitcases and reached into the carriage to withdraw another case. His trilby hat rested at a slight angle, and he turned in a way that meant she couldn't see his face. But his movement was familiar, his stature.

She walked in his direction, unsure if she was right.

He wore a long overcoat, even though the day was warm and dry, presumably so he would not have to carry that as well as the cases.

He reached back into the carriage. This time, instead of lifting out another suitcase, a hand held his and a woman stepped down.

'Aunt Alice!' Maggie screamed, her hand waving high. 'Uncle Dan!' She hurried through the other passengers leaving the platform, twisting a path between them. She caught a smile from her aunt and waved her hand again as Uncle Dan slammed the carriage door shut and turned the lock.

The stationmaster blew his whistle, telling the train driver he could leave. Then the train's whistle blew, the sound made louder as it was captured beneath the platform's canopy. Chuff chuff, chuff chuff, chuff chuff, the pistons built up speed and the carriage wheels rolled forward as Maggie broke from the crush of people and raced towards her aunt.

Aunt Alice opened her arms. Maggie hung the handles of her handbag over her forearm as she rushed the last few paces before entering her aunt's embrace. They hugged one another as tightly as they had when Maggie was small.

Aunt Alice smelt of so many memories of childhood, of the violet sweets she ate all the time and her lily of the valley perfume.

'You look well, love. Rosy-cheeked and ripened by the sun,' Aunt Alice said when she released Maggie.

Maggie's handbag bumped her shoulder, as hers bumped Maggie's bottom.

'I don't see a lot of sun, I'm always in the factory. But maybe it has been ripened by the heat of the workshops, or the welding. Dad used to tell me colour was unbecoming in a woman's skin, anyway.'

'Nonsense, a bit of colour means you are a hardworking lass,' Uncle Dan said. 'Hello, love.'

Maggie turned, hugged him and kissed his cheek quickly. 'Was it a good journey?'

'Not bad,' he answered. 'But we didn't have time to pack properly, we left a lot behind. We're not sure how long we'll need to stay away. We saw a dogfight between the British and German aeroplanes in the sky over the sea yesterday. The sounds of their bullets and guns had everyone stopping to look up.'

'It was scary to watch,' her aunt added. 'My admiration for the young men involved in this war has gone up considerably.'

'Did anyone say what Churchill is going to do when they asked you to leave Margate?' Maggie picked up a case for them. 'If it's that bad, they can't leave the army over there. The newspapers said the Allied troops are trapped on the beaches.'

'I don't know how the Government can get so many men back...' Uncle Dan answered. 'There must be thousands of them. I mean, if it really is most of the army all pushed back to the French coast, how could they get them out while the Germans are dropping bombs from above and pushing their tanks and army through the towns?'

'Surely the Government can do something. They can't just leave them there.' She thought of Lenny and Charles, and Art...

Her uncle carried the other two cases as they left the station.

'Lord, it's hot in this coat,' he moaned as they descended the stairs. 'Where are we off to? Is it far?'

'Park Lodge is not too far, darling,' her aunt said. 'Do you think there might be room for us, Maggie, for one night at least, until we can find somewhere to live? I feel terrible for imposing but it will be hard to find somewhere for tonight.'

'You won't be imposing,' Maggie said as they left the station and she led the way along the path. 'I've found a lovely place for you to lodge. The family are happy to accommodate you. It is the home of one of my friend's parents.' She looked towards her uncle. 'Do you know Mr Pearce, Uncle Dan? Did you ever meet him?'

'Mr Pearce... There's several Pearces in Swindon, love,' he said.

'Not Milly's and Bobby's grandson?' her aunt asked. 'The lad who worked himself up to chief clerk after I left?'

'Yes, that's him. It's his house that you'll be staying in.'

Her uncle's steps halted instantly. 'Maggie, lass, are you serious? We can't stay with the likes of him.'

'Why not?' Aunt Alice answered. 'If his daughter is a friend of Maggie's and he's willing to take us in, I'll accept his kindness.'

Maggie met her uncle's gaze, smiled and lifted her eyebrows.

He slowly smiled in return, nodded and then walked on.

'We'll go to Park Lodge first. I only just got your telegram, so I didn't know you were arriving. But my friend Cath isn't at work. I'll call her. She said she would collect you in her father's car so you don't have to carry the luggage on the bus to Old Town.'

'That's kind.'

Maggie wasn't sure if her uncle was glad of the offer or not, his words resonated with grumbling sarcasm. 'She is one of the kindest people I know,' she said.

When they approached the park, Maggie saw Mr Faraday working on his knees pulling up some more of the early carrots, to be shared out among the Railway Village community. She waved. 'Hello, Mr Faraday, this is my uncle and aunt. Do you remember Dan Richardson, and my Aunt Alice?'

'I do indeed.' Mr Faraday rose to his feet, wiping his hands on the front of his corduroy trousers. He walked towards her uncle with one hand held out. 'Hello, Dan. It's good to see you.'

'Hello, Hector.' Her uncle put down the suitcases and shook the muddy hand that he'd been offered.

'Alice.' Mr Faraday reached towards her aunt, and they shook too. 'Come along in, Valerie will put the kettle on and make us all a cup of tea, though it'll be mint, we don't have any of the good stuff at the moment.'

He led the way to the front door, saw them through, then left them to walk around to the kitchen door in his muddy boots and work clothes.

'Leave the cases here,' Maggie told her uncle as she put down the one she'd carried, 'and go on through to the kitchen.' She pointed at the door. 'Mrs Faraday is probably in there. No one stands on ceremony in this house. They have a telephone, so I'll call Cath and then join you.'

Left in the hall on her own, Maggie picked up the handset of the phone.

Their railway cottage hadn't had a telephone, it was a novelty she wasn't used to. She turned the dial, calling the operator.

'Good afternoon, this is the Swindon Switchboard, how can I help?'

'Can you put me through to Mr Pearce in Bath Road?'

'Wait a moment... Putting you through now...'

There were a few seconds of silence, then. 'Hello, Catherine Pearce speaking.'

'Hello, Cath, it's Maggie. My aunt and uncle have arrived. We're at Park Lodge, could they come to stay with you tonight?'

'Of course. You said they might arrive at any time and it could be today. Mama and Papa are expecting them. Shall I come and collect them now?'

'No rush, they'll have a cup of tea and a chat, but you're welcome to join us.'

'I'll bring Mama with me, she will want to get to know them from the start.'

During the conversation over tea, Aunt Alice spoke about Catherine's grandparents, telling Mrs Pearce her memories of them. The connection helped them make friends.

When they had finished their tea, Maggie waved them off, as her aunt and uncle waved from the back windows of Mr Pearce's Austin 7. Catherine drove cautiously, using her wooden hand and good hand, Mrs Pearce sitting beside her in the front passenger seat.

13

LILY FRANKLIN

Saturday 25 May

It wasn't a long walk from Park Lodge to the GWR health hydro, scarcely five minutes, but Lily's steps were slow, her feet and heart heavy. She held her rolled-up towel containing the swimsuit she'd borrowed from Mrs Faraday in both arms. She'd never been to the baths. To her, the notion of sharing a pool while she was half undressed was odd. But the others were keen on it, and she was not going to be the one to throw a wet blanket over the day. Not when everyone needed a bit of fun. This whole week had been hard – with the news from abroad and being pushed to produce the bombs faster.

The King had spoken on the wireless yesterday evening; he said Hitler and his Nazis were motivated by pure evil. Those words, in his posh serious voice, had replayed in her mind and kept her awake last night.

'*...The struggle is now upon us... Let no one be mistaken, it is no mere territorial conquest, it is the complete and final overthrow of this empire and of everything for which it stands and after this, the conquest of the world. If they succeed, they'll bring hatred and evil designs...*'

He told everyone this Sunday, tomorrow, would be a day of national prayer. Everyone across the empire and the soldiers on foreign ground should join in the same prayers and '*humbly but confidently commit our cause to God...*'

The King was resorting to begging God to intervene because they were losing – that's what Lily thought. They were losing! Those were the words that throbbed through her thoughts with every heartbeat. *We're losing.*

So, what now? What would happen next? What about Lenny and Art, and the others?

She was utterly exhausted from making the equipment for them to fight with, how could they fight if they felt this tired, or worse?

She'd been praying all night, why wait until Sunday? And now they were going to the baths and the cinema as if nothing was happening on the other side of the English Channel.

A bitter feeling, a need to be sick, twisted through Lily's stomach. She couldn't stop thinking about the bombing and Lenny. She gritted her teeth. Lenny would not be proud of her if he knew she was blubbing every five minutes, and the Germans would take advantage of her weakness if they got here.

Catherine's rigid wooden hand slipped around Lily's waist. 'I don't know about you, but I am sick with worry. Did you sleep? I struggled.'

Catherine had cycled down from Old Town and left her bicycle at Park Lodge.

'Me too.' It felt so good to say it, and it felt better to know she was not alone in remembering their men as they walked along this street as if it were any other day.

In Park Lodge last night, as they listened to the King's speech, huddled around the large wood-encased speaker, no one had shown their emotions. Or perhaps they had, perhaps they were showing their shock in their silence, as the King made it clear how dire the situation in France was.

'I wanna scream an cry my eyes out,' she said quietly to Catherine.

Lily had gone to bed after the speech. She'd needed to be alone to express her anger. She'd thumped her pillow and screamed into that, so Maggie wouldn't hear her.

'I wailed last night,' Catherine whispered. 'While everyone was downstairs, I hid in an attic room so they wouldn't hear and screamed.'

Perilous, is the ordeal we are facing... had been the King's words, or something similar, but she remembered the word perilous. Even the King feared Britain would lose; its Allies had lost.

'The King said the Nazis will take away all that makes life worth livin...' Lily whispered.

'Which is why we must carry on and live life today. It is going to be hard to keep a smile on our faces. But I'm doing it to spite Hitler. The King also said we must keep a smile on our lips and our heads held high, and tomorrow we'll turn our fear to God. The men won't fail, Lily.'

'Are you talking about the King's speech?' Naomi asked. She'd been walking a couple of paces ahead. She stopped and waited for them to catch up. 'My stomach's been churning all night. What will my brothers do if they're captured? Dietrich told me the Nazis put Jews in ghettos and make them work like slaves.'

'Don't say that. I can't think about it.' Lily shook the thought out of her head as a shiver ran up her spine despite the warmth of the sun on her back.

They turned the corner into Faringdon Road.

By the sounds of it, everyone was thinking like Lily, but most of them were shutting their emotions inside. That was the curse of the British stiff upper lip.

'I wish we had a shift today,' Violet said. 'At least then I'd be helping the men over there. I'm glad we're spending the day together, though, I need to be busy. I'm all jittery. Nervous, I suppose.' Violet had obviously been listening to Lily and Catherine too.

'The King made it sound as though the outcome of the war is balancing like a charabanc hanging over a precipice, rocking towards a fall.' Maggie joined the conversation. 'It feels so odd, when we've seen and heard so little of war here until a few days ago, that we could be in a win or lose situation. Even though I know we've been at war, it's shocking.'

Lily now wished they would all shut up... She didn't want to think about losing... it brought the anxiety back, the image of Lenny dead in the mud. The fear swelled, clawing at her throat. She reached out blindly and found Catherine's wooden hand as the fear tried to strangle her. Her chest heaved and her heart pulsed much quicker than normal.

'Lily!' Catherine turned and held Lily's other arm with her good hand.

'I... need... to sit...' she said, and collapsed on the pavement, her towel rolling onto the floor, Mrs Faraday's costume spilling out. She couldn't breathe.

Catherine knelt on one side of her, and Naomi on the other. Naomi rubbed Lily's hands between hers. 'We'll get through this, Lily. We will.'

'That's what Lenny would want you to do,' Catherine added. 'He'll want you to keep your chin up and carry on. He's fighting so you can. Shall I count to help you breathe?'

Lily nodded.

'Breathe out slowly. One... See if you can make your outbreath last to five. Two...'

Lily ran out of breath before three.

'It's alright, breathe in,' Catherine reassured.

Maggie squatted down on her haunches in front of Lily. Everyone else in the street must wonder what on earth was going on. They were beside the doctor's house and the hospital was on the other side of the street, in the same building as the swimming pool. The nurses would be rushing out in a minute, and then Lily would feel like a real twit.

She knew Catherine was right; Lenny would expect more of her. If he didn't make it back and the Nazis came over here, he would expect her to be strong and to try her hardest to stay alive. He was risking his life so she could survive. He wouldn't want her to give in to fear like this.

'Now breathe out again.' Catherine was still trying to make her slow down her panicked breaths. 'One... two...' Catherine counted slower.

Lily followed her directions. The more times she did, the easier it became and the slower her heart pulsed. Her hands shook as Naomi carried on rubbing them between hers, as if Lily were cold.

'Do you feel any better?' Violet asked. She was still standing, but probably only because there was no room left in the circle of concerned faces around Lily.

'Yes. Thank you.'

'We are all here, no matter what happens,' Maggie reassured. 'Like the King said, the whole country will be praying for the fighting men, and for the people who love them at home. I know it's hard.'

'Hard' did not describe it at all. There were no words to explain what Lily imagined and feared, or the sickening feeling it stirred in her stomach. But then she remembered Catherine felt the same, and Naomi... She shut her eyes, closing off the tears that brimmed there. Hundreds of thousands of women felt like she did. She was a selfish cow, making such a fuss. Lenny would be embarrassed.

She swallowed and swallowed again. Trying to sort her stupid head out. She was British. She could do this. The King had said, keep your hearts proud and your resolve unshaken, and here she was, sat on the pavement in the street a few hours later.

'Even if the Nazis come here, Lily,' Naomi said quietly, 'we'll stay together. If we have to, we can hide. Asher said thousands of Jews are in hiding in Holland. We will keep each other safe.'

Lily pulled her hands free from Naomi's. 'Thank you. I'm sorry for bein such a wuss an lettin you all down.' She pressed a hand on the pavement and got up as they all got to their feet.

'You didn't let us down, you couldn't,' Maggie answered. 'That's the point of friends, you can tell us all your worries.' Maggie's words stopped with a blunt note. The look in her eyes and the blush in her skin said Maggie had worries she hadn't told them.

Maggie bent down and picked up Mrs Faraday's costume.

Violet moved around Maggie and picked up the towel, in a way that appeared as though she was avoiding looking at anyone. She took the costume from Maggie and rolled it back up in the towel. A scarlet blush in her cheeks. Maggie's words had struck a chord for Violet too.

Lily felt guilty again, for making a fuss when everyone had problems. And there were whole countries with more problems than her fear for Lenny and Art. The King had mentioned Poland, Norway, Belgium and Holland, let alone France, and all the other countries on their borders would be feeling like Britain did.

Tomorrow, she hoped all those countries would pray too.

'Let's hurry up and get in that pool. I feel like a good swim, I need to distract my mind,' Naomi encouraged.

'I'll tell you what else will distract my mind,' Violet said, 'is if Maggie tells us about her date with Ron. He came back home last night grinning from ear to ear.' She handed Lily the rolled towel and raised one pencil-drawn eyebrow (Violet didn't like her natural auburn eyebrows so she plucked out all the hairs and drew them in brown). 'Did you kiss him?' Violet asked Maggie and presented a teasing smile.

Maggie shook her head. 'I wouldn't let him get away with it. It was only our second date.'

They walked up to the kerb, to cross the road. There were hardly any vehicles on the roads because of the lack of petrol so the road was clear. They crossed in a row.

'How many dates does it take before you let a man kiss you then?' Violet asked.

'At least a dozen,' Maggie answered.

Laughter rang around Lily's friends.

'Lenny an I didn't av a single date before we kissed,' she said. 'But we ad a lifetime of friendship.'

'I think that counts, as making him wait the right length of time,' Maggie answered.

'What was Lenny like as a child?' Catherine asked.

'Annoying,' Maggie said, and chuckled. 'I remember him throwing a load of rose petals all over me when I was in the park one day.'

'I used to do that with im,' Lily said, remembering the stupid game. 'We would shout "confetti!" an throw it over a wall at people.' The memory brought a smile to her lips.

'He was a sweet child,' Violet answered. 'I was struggling to lift a crate of cabbages out to the front of the greengrocer's where I worked, and he came over and helped. I thought then what a nice kid he was.'

'Ee was always kind,' Lily answered. 'An fun.'

'He does have a good sense of humour,' Naomi responded. 'Dietrich used to tell me some of Lenny's antics at work. He was always trying to make Dietrich smile, and you know how hard it is to bring a smile to that boy's lips.'

When they arrived at the door to the women's baths, Violet pushed it and held it open for them all to enter.

Lily's gaze spun everywhere, the décor, the iron and glass work, was magnificent. But everything that the GWR men built was magnificent, like the Mechanics Institute. So, of course, even the place they built to see a doctor, surgeon or dentist, and to exercise or rest in a Turkish Bath and steam room, was grand.

In the women's changing room, her eyes soaked up the pretty tiles and the row of high windows as she unlaced her boots. When she stripped, even though her friends were undressing on either side of her, she pulled her clothes off, stepped into the costume and pulled it up quickly, embarrassed by her own nudity.

'Sorry, Lily, but what's that on your back?' Maggie asked quietly. 'It looks like a cross.'

'The scar?'

'Yes.'

Lily felt her whole body flush red, it turned her brown skin bronze. 'It aint some sort of miracle,' she answered. 'Dad did it with the fire poker when I was young.'

'Lord, your father's mad.'

'That's one phrase for it,' Lily answered. 'Or just mean.'

Maggie looked around, checking no one else was listening. 'Does he hurt the others?' she asked.

Lily shook her head. That scar had been made so long ago she rarely remembered it was there, and she was out of her father's reach now. 'No. If ee did, I couldn't av left without takin them all with me. Can you imagine us all turnin up at Park Lodge? It was just me an Art ee picked on.'

'I can imagine it, and Mr and Mrs Faraday are so kind, I can see them taking you all in too.'

Lily smiled. That was true, she thought they would too. They were like guardian angels.

Mrs Faraday's costume was an inch or two too long in the body, and loose around the waist, but it covered what it needed to cover.

Violet led the way out from the changing room, through a shallow pool where they washed their feet, into the swimming pool space – and that room was like a cathedral made from iron arches and panes of glass.

'The shallow end is this end,' Maggie told Lily, pointing. 'You'll be able to touch the bottom so you can stand up.'

'I'm not sure if I'll be able to swim without my right hand. So I'll stay in the shallows with you,' Catherine said.

'I'm going to dive in at the deep end,' Maggie told them. 'Come on, Vi, jump in with me, we can hold hands.'

Lily watched them run along the side of the pool, take hold of each other's hands and with their free hands holding their noses, they jumped into the water and disappeared beneath the surface with a huge splash. They reappeared a second later, brushed the wet hair away from their eyes and smiled at one another as they trod water.

'Do you want to hold my hand as we walk down the steps?' Catherine asked Lily, as she held out her stubby forearm. The scarred stump at the end was a vivid red, it looked sore.

Naomi was already walking down.

Lily held Catherine's scarred forearm, thinking it would probably give Catherine more confidence about having her arm on show too.

With every step, the water rose higher up Lily's legs. As it reached her waist, she let go of Catherine, rested her hands on the surface and swept them around, making ripples.

As she stepped off the last step and the water came up to her chest, she pictured Lenny wading into the sea on a beach in France, the waves crashing into him the deeper he got, while he tried to escape the German tanks and soldiers.

If she stopped imagining things like that, she would feel better. But if she didn't think about what he might be facing, it felt like she would be deserting him.

Then she would carry him across the sea in her thoughts and prayers, she would carry him through the water all the way across the Channel to her, so he was safe.

'Take my hand, Lily, and float. On the water. Let your body rise up behind you,' Catherine encouraged.

She took Catherine's left hand and held her right forearm, trusting Catherine, and the water, to take her weight. Praying Lenny could trust the sea in France, and that someone would help him and bring him home.

'Kick your legs,' Catherine said.

'Like this, with straight legs.' Naomi showed her the movement with her arms. 'Bend your knees a little.'

'You're good, you're a quick learner,' Catherine said. 'Shall I let go of you?'

'Move your arms like this.' Naomi showed Lily the motion. 'One at a time. Keep your fingers together. Use your hands like paddles.'

Lily let go of Catherine and swam on her own, for the very first time. She swam for Lenny, trying to send her strength to him, so he could get home.

After their swim, when they walked from the Health Hydro to the Savoy Cinema in Regent Street, Lily stopped at the newsstand, where a man was yelling, 'Getyour*EveningAdvertiser*!' in a way that merged all the words into one sound.

She had her purse in her skirt pocket. She took out the money to pay for it.

'Thanks, love,' he said as he swapped her coins for a newspaper.

She unfolded it so she could see the front page and caught up with her friends. The newspaper headlines talked about the King's speech and described the fires on the other side of the English Channel as tremendous – great flames shooting up into the sky for miles. There were more stories about the police arresting and locking up people they thought might be enemies, and there was a German spy found in Dublin who'd been reporting on the structure of the British ports.

She scanned it all.

Then her heart sank. One headline, not printed in a large typeset, and in a smaller paragraph than the news about the King's speech, said that the Germans claimed to have taken Calais. Calais was the closest French port to England... She breathed slowly, refusing to panic, folded the paper back up and tucked it under her arm. Yes. She would carry on. She would damn well fight with all of her heart, and hope and pray that Lenny could get home to keep fighting alongside her. And Art too.

Was it really only last week his child had been born, and that she'd first heard the Germans were on the French border? How had the Germans moved so quickly through France? Like Maggie said, they'd been at war for ages, but this was the first time she'd felt really scared, and it was shocking.

Despite her determination to not be afraid, a shiver raced up her spine and goosebumps rose on her forearms.

14

LILY FRANKLIN

Sunday 26 May

'Have you seen this?' Edith's shout reached from the bottom of the stairs and passed clearly through Lily's bedroom door.

'Seen what?' Marjorie shouted.

'This!' Edith called back.

Marjorie's feet hammered down the attic stairs to see whatever it was Edith was shouting about.

Lily came out of her room. She was dressed, ready to go to church, apart from her boots. She ran down the hall stairs barefoot, her toes pressing into the carpet that flowed down the centre of the stairs like a waterfall.

Behind Lily, Maggie's and Dot's bedroom doors opened, and Marjorie raced down the stairs so quickly she passed Lily.

'Come and look at all these people!' Edith beckoned from the front parlour doorway.

'What is all this fuss?' Mr Faraday came through the kitchen door into the hall as Lily jumped from the bottom stair.

'The people...' Edith answered, wide-eyed and smiling.

Mrs Faraday came through the kitchen door too and they all went into the parlour.

'Look!' Edith pointed to the window.

It was not hard to notice what was different. The street on the other side of the park was full of people and they were all walking towards St Mark's church.

'They have all come to pray.' Mrs Faraday pressed a hand to her chest as her eyes swam with emotion. 'How wonderful!'

'We'd better be on our way ourselves,' Mr Faraday said. 'Or there won't be a seat left.'

'There won't be any standing room either at this rate,' Edith answered.

The others dispersed, rushing to finish getting ready.

Lily lingered, her arms wrapping about herself, crossing over and holding onto her elbows.

All these people walking past the railings on the other side of the park proved that nearly everyone felt as scared as she was.

Surely God would listen to this many people praying.

'Lily! Come on! Hurry up!' Maggie shouted from upstairs. 'I want to get into the church!'

15

CATHERINE PEARCE

All dressed up in her Sunday finery, Catherine walked along the pavement in between her mother and father, behind Mr and Mrs Richardson, towards Christ Church. Her steps followed the rhythm of the church bells, as they called out one after the other for Christians to come to prayer.

She'd put on a wide-brimmed hat because she expected to cry when she prayed, and she could tilt her head forward and hide her face. But as she walked along the street, the handles of her handbag resting over her wooden fingers, and both hands held in front of her waist, she was not inclined to hide herself. Instead, pride surged in her chest, to be one of many who were prepared to display their emotions as she walked among about a hundred or so people spread along the paths on either side of the Bath Road. Everyone walked in the same direction, towards Christ Church.

She glanced at her father, smiling, wondering over the number of people.

'The King called for a National Day of Prayer, Catherine,' he answered her glance factually, to explain all the people.

'I know.' She had not expected this many people to respond.

A woman stepped out from a door ahead of them, then encouraged a row of children to follow her out. The back of their necks were a vivid red, as though they had just been scrubbed hard to make sure they were clean for church. Three women, walking together, with arms linked, in the way Catherine walked with her friends, joined the street from Prospect Place. Two elderly men joined the silent lines of people at the corner of Wood Street. Then many people who had walked up Devizes Road joined, and so the numbers of people gradually swelled into a large crowd.

When Catherine turned the corner from the Goddard Arms Hotel and saw the churchyard, her lips parted in an O of surprise. A queue ran the whole hundred yards of the path to the church door.

'Perhaps we shan't have a seat,' her mother said.

'I shan't bother about that,' Mrs Richardson answered. 'I'm only too glad to see all these people. If you'd seen all the fire and smoke the day before we travelled… We need God to intervene.'

Catherine slid the handkerchief out from the cuff of her right sleeve and dabbed it beneath her eyes. She'd encouraged Lily to be confident yesterday. Today, she didn't feel confident of anything, and this crowd of people was an expression of fear.

'Indeed,' her father agreed with Mrs Richardson. 'Thank the Lord, so many are here. It is a blessing to have such a visible display showing how we back our boys to win.'

Catherine's mother also withdrew a handkerchief and dabbed her eyes.

Of course, her mother was scared for her sons.

Catherine glanced around as they joined the queue to enter the church, wondering how many people knew men abroad.

The queue moved slowly, a pace or two at a time. Catherine and her party reached the church door at the same moment the minute bell began chiming, the single bell tolling out its warning that the service was about to begin, normally urging any straggling worshippers to hurry. She glanced over her shoulder. The queue behind her reached to the churchyard gate and followed the railing all the way to the corner of the Goddard Arms Hotel, and it must have reached beyond that too.

'Good morning,' the churchwarden greeted them. 'I'm sorry, Mr and Mrs Pearce, there are no seats left, but there is space to stand if you follow the wall around to the eastern nave.'

'Thank you.' Her father took her mother's hand and led the way.

Catherine stepped aside to let Mr and Mrs Richardson follow, then trailed behind, and others followed her. They were packed in, squashed as flat as kippers. She didn't care, she was only glad to have so many people praying.

The single bell chimed its last ring. It must be eleven o'clock.

'Good morning, everyone!' The vicar had climbed up the steps of the pulpit and shouted from there, looking one way then another across the sea of hundreds of people packed into his church. 'There are still people outside, and I want to include everyone we can, so we will wait a little longer to welcome as many as we can into the church. For those we can't fit inside, I have agreed with the churchwarden that he will stand at the door and repeat my words.'

Catherine had come prepared to spend the service on her knees, instead she followed the prayers led by the vicar on her feet, with her left hand encircling her wooden hand, surrounded by a crowd repeating the same prayers, for their fighting men, for the those here who feared for them, for the men, women and children abroad who faced and endured the Nazis' evil even now.

She thought of Charles and her brothers, of Lenny, and Naomi's brothers and of Dietrich's family too – sending her prayers up particularly for them.

'Lord, in the name of Jesus Christ, hear our prayer...' The same words spoken by hundreds of voices echoed through the church at the end of every prayer.

The vicar's sermon was short and to the point, encouraging everyone to do as the King had advised, to 'remain confident in Christ's love... To strive for peace in all that you do... We must acknowledge the truth, yes, and we must fight against this threat of evil, but we will do so with a clear conscience because we fight for peace, and it is life or death for us all. Yet our greatest gift, as Christians, is that we are not afraid of death. We may fight with no fear of death because if we die the Lord will receive us with open arms. So, hold your heads high, have confidence in Christ, and live with courage and resolution. We shall endure and accept the need for self-sacrifice with a unity of purpose, and within we will have peace always.'

The women around Catherine sniffed back tears and dabbed their cheeks with handkerchiefs and some men heartily blew their noses.

'As we must do things a little differently today,' the vicar called from the pulpit. 'It will not be practical to serve Communion as normal. However, we shall do our best for those who want to take Communion to provide the opportunity at the end of the service if you come to the altar.'

A desire to take the bread and wine lurched through Catherine's heart, a need for the spiritual connection she felt with Christ when she accepted the offerings.

She queued for almost half an hour, then finally had her opportunity to kneel beside her father at the altar rail. She saw his hands shake slightly as he held them out, cupped one beneath the other, to receive a tiny piece of bread and the blessing over it.

In all the years Catherine had knelt beside him at the altar, she'd never seen his hands shake. In general, he was not a nervous or emotional man.

As she held out her hands, her living hand beneath her wooden one, a tear rolled onto her cheek. One more prayer whispered through her thoughts. *Please protect Charles. I would rather lose my life than he lose his.*

Self-sacrifice, she remembered the word the King used in his speech. The military men were risking themselves to save everyone. She had risked her hand to save others. She would never shy away from the risks of stopping the Nazis.

'Amen,' she said aloud before she raised the small crumb of bread to her mouth.

A moment later she was offered the wine, from the silver cup that was shared by the whole congregation. 'Amen.' She swallowed a sip, then crossed herself, rose to her feet, bowed her head towards the gold cross at the centre of the altar and walked away, leaving space for someone else to kneel.

Surely God must have heard them today, when there were so many people praying for peace.

Yesterday, she had fought to keep smiling, pretending, just as her friends had done, that inside she was not broken-hearted. Today, everyone was solemn as they walked away from the church, quiet. Not one person smiled, and she didn't hear anyone talk in the street. At home, they ate their lunch mostly in silence too, and with their guests also at the table it was even stranger. Yet for the life of her she could think of nothing appropriate to say, so she presumed everyone felt the same.

Her father looked only at his plate as he ate, or his glass as he reached to sip from the wine Catherine had fetched from the cellar. His thoughts were obviously preoccupied. Probably drifting off to some GWR factory task, or perhaps drifting all the way to France, as hers were, and as she imagined everyone else's thoughts were around the table. To the French beaches and the fire and smoke Mr and Mrs Richardson described.

They ate a slow-cooked shoulder of mutton, with diced carrots fresh from the garden, and potatoes from last year's crop, the onion had come from last year's crop too. There was also a large helping of newly cut spinach, but her mother had oversalted that.

Her father's knife and fork chimed on the edge of the empty plate as he placed them together. He patted his lips with his napkin then rested the napkin beside his plate and smiled in her mother's direction.

'Thank you, darling,' he said. 'Very satisfying, especially enjoyable as our rations drop again next week. We will need to become cleverer with our food, won't we?'

'More imaginative,' Mrs Richardson said.

'Yes. That's the word.' He nodded towards Maggie's aunt.

'I think Mama has already become a wizard in the kitchen.' Catherine smiled at her mother.

'Thank you, darling, I am trying hard.'

'And succeeding by all accounts,' Maggie's uncle confirmed.

'But anyway,' Catherine's father looked at her mother. 'I am sorry, my dear, I have to get to work.'

'Today!' she exclaimed. 'It is Sunday, Roger.'

'Do you think the Nazis will stop because it is a Sunday?' he answered as he rose to his feet. He nodded towards Mr and Mrs Richardson. 'I do apologise, but we have a war to fight after all. Will you excuse me?'

'Of course.' They both spoke the words, in the same moment, sounding a little in awe of her father's responsibilities in the factory.

'I will use my bicycle,' her father said to her mother.

'How long will you be?'

He shrugged and raised a hand that expressed his inability to manage things within a certain timescale.

Catherine left her cutlery in disorder on her plate, pointing at odd angles and crossing over. Partly because she hurried and partly because she had not mastered the use of a knife with her wooden hand yet. She stood with a desperate need to be doing something to help fight the war today. 'If I came with you, Papa, may I help?'

'No, Catherine.' He shook his head. 'I don't think so.'

But the note of his voice held a hesitation, implying he'd considered the idea before rejecting it.

'Let me come, even if I only help you by sorting some papers while you work. At least then you will have company, and someone to...' She hesitated because she had been about to say type, then remembered she could not type any more. 'To help if you did need me,' she said instead.

He stood as still as stone for a moment, looking into her eyes, the thoughts behind his gaze weighing up and balancing her offer. 'Oh, very well.' He puffed up his chest as he breathed in, then… 'Come with me.' He raised a hand that beckoned, saying, *come now* in a furtive way.

She nodded towards Mr and Mrs Richardson, and her mother, then hurried after her father.

'What is it?' she asked him in the hall. He reached past her and closed the kitchen door, shutting them off from everyone else.

'Come up to the attic, I will tell you there. I dare not risk us being overheard. I would trust your mother but I do not know your friend's family.'

She ran upstairs ahead of her father, turned to the attic stairs, climbed those quickly too and stepped over the threshold into the first attic room. He glanced over his shoulder checking the Richardsons had not followed, then pulled the door to the stairs closed, shutting them in.

'What is it?' she asked. 'What is happening?'

'The Government are withdrawing the troops.'

'Withdrawing?'

'Retreating, Catherine. They are sending the Navy and every other merchant vessel they can commandeer to the beaches where our men are isolated, and sending word to any regiments in land to get out.'

Catherine pressed her hand to her chest, covering her beating heart.

'The Allied army is cut off. The only way to save them is by sea. It is not solely out of concern for the men that they are going to try and get them back. It would be foolish to send others to risk being killed when there is only a small chance of getting our men out. But we need soldiers to stop Hitler taking Britain. They can't leave them there to die or be captured.' His eyes expressed the importance and the dangers of this mission. This was why his hands had shaken this morning.

'*It would be foolish to send others to risk being killed when there is only a small chance of getting our men out…*' The way he spoke made her think the Government must have considered not trying to get the men home. Her right arm lifted, she replaced it with her left and her hand covered her mouth – '*small chance…*' he'd said. Which meant the greatest likelihood was that Charles would die on one of the beaches.

'When we get the men back...' her father continued. Her heart leapt at his use of the word 'when' not 'if'. He believed this plan would succeed even if the Government weren't sure. '...the ministry need trains to move the wounded and weary away from the coast as fast as possible, to safer locations. If the men remain on the coast when they reach England, they'll be sitting ducks for the Luftwaffe who can easily fly to this side of the English Channel and continue their bombardment. If you want to help today, what I need are people to plan the transport routes and coordinate the rolling stock to move these men quickly. We are working with the other train companies to run as many trains as possible away from Dover. But you can't tell anyone. The clerks are working shifts and sleeping beside their desks. I have no idea how long this will take, Catherine, but if you come, you can't come home. I will not take the risk of the information leaving the factory, and now there are strangers in our home who will know—'

'They are not strangers, they knew your grandparents.'

'But you and I have no idea who they know now, and who they might write to. If you come with me, you cannot come home until the job is complete. I will not risk information about the transport routes slipping out in the house. So, you may be gone for days, not hours, and you cannot tell your mother why we are absent either. This exercise must be secret.'

'Of course I will help, Papa. You know how much I want to. Should I pack a bag?'

'No. No one in this house or the houses around us can think you will be gone for some time. Anything that may give away what this country intends may kill our men.' The emotion in his voice implied he was thinking about the whole army, but particularly her brothers, his sons, who were among the stranded soldiers. 'We will take our bicycles and ride off as if it were any other day.'

'I'll fetch a hat and cardigan. People in the street may think we are just cycling for pleasure.'

'Say a quick goodbye to your mother, but in a way that she will expect you back in a couple of hours. You can send a note to say you will sleep over with your friends later.'

She nodded quickly, confirming she understood.

'I will bring the bicycles out via the alley at the back of the house.'

She pressed a quick kiss on his cheek, opened the door and hurried out to race back downstairs.

Despite the awful news of retreat, she felt happier knowing she could do something to help. Just as she envisioned the power and impact of the bombs she'd helped make, her mind was now eagerly taking responsibility for getting every single man who made it safely back to Dover somewhere comfortable and safe further inland.

16

LILY FRANKLIN

Monday 27 May

The back door handle turned, the door opened in a rush and Marjorie ran through.

Lily had worked the night shift on Sunday, and snatched a few hours' sleep this morning. She'd not long woken, but she hadn't stayed in bed as with such a noisy house there was no chance of getting back to sleep.

'The Government are bringing our men back!' The excited words burst out of Marjorie. 'They're sending ships and boats, big and small, to take them off the beaches and bring them back over the Channel. Don't ask me where I heard it, I can't tell you, but it's true. They've set up evacuation points along the French coast. They're picking men up at Dunkirk, Boulogne and Dieppe. The army are retreating as fast as they can to get to the evacuation points, and the Navy ships and every boat they can commission are going back and forth over the Channel, to get the men out of France.'

'How many ships?' Dot asked. Her head had lifted sharply when Marjorie mentioned the Navy. She was sitting at the table beside Lily, with Mr Tabs on her lap, making friends with their new lodger.

'Every single one they can use, that's what I was told. There are hundreds of thousands of men over there.'

One of those men was Lenny. Lily's heart pulsed quicker. He was coming home. They were all coming home. Art and Lenny and Catherine's Charles, and Catherine's and Naomi's brothers. They'd prayed for peace yesterday, this was not peace, but it was an answer to her prayers. She'd asked God to keep them safe and bring them home.

She stood up and hugged Marjorie, and they jumped up and down together.

'Thank you, God!' Maggie shouted, looking up.

'Yes, thank you, God,' Dot agreed more calmly.

Marjorie bounced up and down a few more times with Lily, then broke the embrace and stepped back, grinning as broadly as Lily was.

'The friend Aunt Alice spoke to on the phone said… Oh darn, I told you. Oh, anyway, she said they have evacuated lots of towns now – Great Yarmouth, Lowestoft, Felixstowe, Harwich…' She used her fingers, counting on them as she recited this list of towns. 'Clacton, Frinton, Walton, Southend, Margate, Ramsgate, Broadstairs, Sandwich, Dover, Deal and Folkestone.' After reeling off that list, Marjorie took a deep breath, and smiled, as though she was proud she'd remembered them all. 'So, if the Nazis bring the fight our way, we'll have our men back and we'll bloody well be ready.'

'How on earth does Aunt Alice's friend know all of this?' Dot said scathingly.

Marjorie's palms rested on the table as she leaned down, looking Dot in the face. Dot was still stroking the cat.

'Because her friend is a WREN who works in a naval administration centre.'

'Then her friend has a loose tongue that she needs to mind,' Dot answered.

'The Germans must know it anyway, they aren't blind. If Aunt Alice's friend can see the ships in the Channel, so can the Germans.'

'I would have told Aunt Alice to keep her mouth shut,' Dot answered. 'Not run around passing it on. Who else have you told?'

'Just you two. I couldn't keep it to myself.'

'That's why they say don't tell anyone anythin,' Lily said. 'You shouldn't av told me, but I'm glad you did.' She smiled. She clapped her hands, the emotions inside her reeling. 'Do you think they'll let the men come back to their omes? At least for a bit?'

'Who knows?' Marjorie shrugged.

Lily wanted to know. She wanted to know everything. Knowing a little was worse than knowing nothing. It was five hours before her next shift, she had time to walk up to Old Town, under the pretence of visiting Catherine, and use her visit to quiz Maggie's loose-lipped aunt.

When she reached Catherine's parents' house, her plan backfired, exploding in her face.

'Catherine isn't here, Lily, dear,' Mrs Pearce said before Lily had even made it past the front door. 'She told us she stayed at Park Lodge last night, and she has not come home since.'

Lily didn't deny it. She said instead, 'I'm sorry, I must av made a mistake. I thought she said meet ere. But I was workin last night, an I didn't see er this mornin. Sorry I disturbed you.'

'Would you like to come in for a cup of tea?'

If she did, she could talk to Maggie's aunt, but if she started asking lots of questions out of the blue it might seem odd and give it away that Marjorie had told her things. It would have been alright to bury them in a conversation with Catherine.

'No, thank you, but thanks for the offer. Goodbye.' She nodded, then turned away.

'Goodbye,' Mrs Pearce replied, sounding confused.

Lily walked all the way back down the steep hill to the Railway Village, wondering if Charles had come home already. That was the only reason she could think of to explain why Catherine had lied about where she'd spent her night.

Marjorie, Dot and Maggie were at Park Lodge. Edith had gone to meet her RAF pilot – though Lily thought he could not be much of a pilot if he had time to meet Edith in the middle of this big battle.

Lily didn't tell anyone about Catherine's lie. And Marjorie didn't tell anyone else what her aunt had said. So, Lily ate her meal feeling as though everything might be different in a day or two... or three... But kept her lips firmly shut on her desperate hope that she would see Lenny and Art soon.

She and Maggie left for work at the same time as Dot and Marjorie. Dot and Marjorie were working the same shift, in a different workshop. The sky was light, the sun low, and the moon already visible on the other side of the sky, one half more visible than the other.

At least the sailing vessels had good light and weather to work. But would that make it more dangerous if the German pilots could see easily too?

Dear God, keep them all safe and help the sailors do their work. Bring cloud if they need it. She prayed as she walked. She recalled how it felt to swim yesterday, and willed Lenny to swim for his life if he needed to.

Violet waved when she saw them approaching, much more excitedly than usual, and she walked so quickly, it was a sort of run, as she crossed the road to join them. 'You won't believe this,' she began even before she reached them. 'They're bringing the men back.'

'Are they?' It was only Maggie who was surprised.

'Mum's been asked to find volunteers,' Violet continued as they walked on towards the mouth of the subway. 'GWR are sending all the trains and carriages to the coast to meet the ships and move the men further inland as soon as they arrive, they expect to be running the trains day and night for a week or so. Mum needs people to clean the carriages in between runs.'

'But we're all working,' Maggie said.

'There are plenty of married women, GWR wives and ex-employees, who can clean the trains and get them ready to send them back. It is hardly skilled work,' Violet answered.

'That is brave of the company to take on married volunteers,' Maggie joked.

'It's not funny,' Dot snapped at her. 'We need everyone to help get the men back home. Think about it, if no one is holding the German frontline back, there must be hundreds of thousands of men trapped along the Flanders and French coasts. It'll take a miracle to get them all out before the Germans are on top of them.'

'Don't say that,' Lily bit back. 'They av to get them back.'

Violet wrapped an arm around Lily's shoulders. 'They will. Lenny will be home soon.'

'I ope so.'

'Come on, let's hurry up, we need to make more bombs to scatter those Nazis with.' Violet's fingers pressed on Lily's shoulder, then released her as they were swallowed by the tunnel.

The evacuation must be happening, though, just as Marjorie had said, if GWR were running trains to the coast.

It was difficult to concentrate on work, and they were operating the pressing machine, the one that had caught and crushed Catherine's hand, so Lily knew how important it was that she did concentrate. She'd refused to put the metal into the machine. She wouldn't do that job again, and she wore her engagement ring on a bootlace around her neck now, not on her finger, while she was working. Today she was removing the pressed rings and loading them into the crate to be taken away to the next stage of the 25-pounder bomb casing production.

She was hot and sweaty, she wiped her sleeve across her forehead. It was nice being warm in here in the winter, but as the days got hotter, as the year headed into summer, it was like working in an oven sometimes. The furnaces in the iron workshop next door heated the bricks between the buildings as well as the sun shining down on the black-painted glass roof.

'Lily?' a voice shouted. 'Lily Franklin?'

Lily turned and faced Susie Adams and another woman. 'Yes? Am I doin somethin wrong?'

'No. But I need to talk to you privately. Eve will take over from you.' Her hand lifted and beckoned the other woman forward. 'Thank you, Eve.'

Eve smiled at Lily, Lily smiled back then glanced at her friends. *What if she was going to be told something had happened to Lenny, or Art?*

Maggie's smile became a grimace, implying she feared the same thing.

'This way,' Susie said, touching Lily's arm and leading her towards the workshop's door, not the foreman's office.

'What is it?' Lily asked.

'I can't say,' Susie whispered so that no one else would hear her over the noise of the machines. 'I don't know, to be honest. Cath Pearce is outside and she has permission to take you off production.'

Lily didn't understand. To take her off production... Catherine...?

'There.' Susie pushed the door of the cloakroom open and there stood Catherine.

As the door shut again and Susie left them alone, Catherine embraced Lily briefly.

'Where were you last night?' Lily asked as Catherine released her. 'Your mum said you stayed at Park Lodge.'

'I was here working on Operation Dynamo. They're bringing back the men.'

'I know. Everyone knows.'

'It's like a huge jigsaw puzzle working out what trains can go where and when so we avoid collisions.'

Lily nodded, unsure why Catherine had pulled her off the production line to tell her this.

'One of the places they're going to take the men to is not far from Swindon. There will be nurses to help the wounded, but they need volunteers to feed the men and give them blankets and things like that. Will you volunteer with me? I thought of you immediately when I was asked if I knew people who I would trust. I know it will be like trying to spot a needle in a haystack but you never know, we might see Charles or Lenny, or our brothers. That is what I'm hoping. Will you come?'

'Of course,' Lily said immediately, snatching at the opportunity, pulling off one greasy leather glove then the other. 'Can I fetch some clean clothes to take?'

'No, we must go now. There's a train leaving in twenty minutes. It will be the last one we can take. All the trains will be solely for the use of troops after that. The first of the men have already been evacuated from Flanders and northern France. They are on their way back over already!' Catherine's left hand shook Lily's arm with excitement. 'Come on.'

Lily left her gloves behind, lifted her coat off the hook and slid her arms into the sleeves.

'A few people are going,' Catherine said as they walked across the factory site, her hands, even her wooden one, sliding into her coat pockets. 'Men as well as women. We're meeting the others at the station.'

Lily answered with a quick nod, her heart was doing an Irish jig in her chest.

Catherine's left hand lifted out of her pocket and reached for Lily's. Lily held it.

'I know it's a long shot,' Catherine said. 'I mean, that we might see Charles or Lenny, but I have always been a bit of a gambler, and I would take any chance at any odds.'

'Me too. Thank you for puttin my name forward.'

Their footsteps echoed about the buildings along the dark path. The clear evening had become a cloudy night, making the shadows they walked through pitch-black, and the pavement dark beneath their boots.

'Come on, let's run,' Catherine said and tugged on Lily's hand. 'We don't have to, but I am too excited to just walk.' She smiled, her eyes glinting like a child's.

Lily felt childlike too, at the thought of seeing Lenny again. Lily was the one who broke into a run first and pulled Catherine into motion.

When they reached the tunnel, it was too dark to run through in the middle of the night, instead they walked blindly, putting one foot in front of the other. Lily stretched out her free hand, searching the blackness as though there might be something in their way, but of course it was clear. She felt the bricks in the wall with the fingertips and used that as their guide as she walked on.

At the far end, the nightwatchmen nodded and lifted a hand as they passed his box.

Lily looked up at the clock on the Mechanics Institute's tower. Ten minutes left to reach the train station. But when she looked ahead of her, she stopped dead instead of running on, pulling Catherine to a halt too.

'What are you doin runnin around with your posh friend at this our, Lily?'

Her father stood in front of her in his black Air Raid Precaution warden's uniform. She'd never seen him doing the job he was meant to before, he usually spent his night smoking cigarettes in the back room of the bakery. It was typical that tonight was the one night he was actually checking the area.

'We're goin to the station, Dad, we're goin to elp the soldiers that are comin back. We volunteered. They'll be waitin for us.'

'I aven't eard about any volunteers that need to be runnin about in the middle of the night.'

Catherine's fingers closed tighter around Lily's, expressing without words that she was standing there, right beside Lily. Her father didn't know Catherine was Mr Pearce's daughter.

'That's because you don't know everythin that's goin on, Dad,' Lily snapped at him. 'If you don't let us go then we'll miss our train an you'll be obstructin the war effort. Let us get past.' Whenever she'd spoken to him like that, he'd hit her. But she was a different Lily now. It was months since she'd left home. She wasn't afraid of him.

'Come on, Cath,' she said, tugging Catherine's hand. 'You can't tell me what to do any more, Dad,' she told him, then broke into a run and raced past him, alongside Catherine.

'You got a brass neck on you now, girl!' he called after them.

'You should have let me tell him who my father is,' Catherine said as they ran on.

'Ee'd av shit is pants if you told him that.'

Catherine laughed at Lily's coarse joke.

But Lily was proud of herself for not needing any help. Lenny would be proud of her too.

'Do we need a ticket for the train?' she asked Catherine as they slowed to a walk.

'No. The guard knows we're coming.' She released Lily's hand.

The stationmaster stood in front of the metal, telescopic gate. As they approached, he pushed it back, sliding it open a couple of feet to let them through. 'Good evening, ladies. Go straight up the stairs.' He closed the gate behind them and locked it.

All the signs had been taken down at the station, all the names and maps. Anything, everything, that might help the Germans find their way about the country if they came to Britain. The British were not going to make it easy if the Germans invaded.

The train arrived a few minutes later, its brakes growling and the steam hissing as it drew to a standstill.

'Good luck to you, ladies and gents,' the stationmaster said as they boarded.

Lily wondered if he knew where they were going. She thought he didn't, but he would know it was something to do with the war.

Catherine pulled the carriage door shut behind them. The carriage was dark.

The stationmaster's whistle blew, but there was no train whistle. Chuff. Chuff. Chuff. Chuff. The engine pulled and the carriage moved.

'Where we are going is not far,' Catherine said. 'Just along a branch line.'

17

VIOLET TURNER

Tuesday 28 May

Violet turned the handle and opened the front door, sleep threatening to weigh down her eyelids before she reached the bed. But she should eat something for breakfast before she slept. Bread, if there was any, with a scrape of honey because they had used their butter ration between the four of them this week. When the honey soaked into the bread, even if the bread was stale, it made it edible.

'Morning, Vi.' Ron's voice greeted her, calling through from the kitchen. 'How was your night shift?'

'Long,' she called back, as she stripped off her coat and hung it from a hook on the hall wall.

'Good morning, Vi,' Asher said as she joined the men in the kitchen.

'Good morning,' she said in return. 'Where's Mum?' The chair her mother used was empty.

'She's been out all night, preparing the carriages to send off to the coast. Including the hospital carriages.'

The men were eating scrambled eggs. 'Are there any eggs left? I'm starving.'

'Look in the pan, I cooked enough for you. I begged a dozen off a friend at the factory,' Ron told her.

'Oh, you're a star.' She turned to the stove. There was a good portion left, and two slices of fresh bread had been cut and put on a plate for her.

'Do you know anything more about the evacuation?' she asked as she spooned the scrambled egg onto the plate.

Ron raised a newspaper that had been beside his elbow as she returned to the table.

'The Ministry of Food announced the country is being divided into regions, so our food supplies are to be separated.'

She shook her head, too tired to understand any importance in that. 'Why?'

'I presume because if we are invaded, with food divided, we can defend different areas of the country and still have supplies. The Germans have raced through France like a wildfire, our Government must have learned something from that.'

'And more important news,' Asher interrupted, 'is that the Belgian king has surrendered to Hitler, without even consulting his parliament. The Belgians were protecting our men as they leave. Now they'll expose the British and leave them open to attack. Some damn ally they were.'

'Yes, but the newspaper said most of the Belgian army are ignoring their king and still fighting,' Ron answered.

Violet walked to the sink, turned on the tap and washed her hands before she sat down to eat. While the women wept and worried, the men were becoming war strategists from the comfort of their armchairs.

'We're going to help them,' Ron said as she sat down. 'We're filling our stomachs then we're off.'

'Who are you helping?' she asked before slipping a forkful of scrambled eggs into her mouth.

'The troops,' Asher answered.

'The country doesn't need carpenters right now,' Ron said. 'We're making things to keep the country running, not to help the men fighting. So Joe Marsh closed the carpentry shop. For now, anyway. He told every one of us to volunteer to help get the men who make it over here away from the coast. Asher and I will be firemen, shovelling coal into the firebox on the steam engines.'

'To shovel coal…' She didn't understand.

'It's all hands, Vi. If they are going to be running trains day and night for days, they need men to work in shifts to keep the fires burning in the steam engines. No man can keep shovelling for more than a few hours straight. So, we'll be in the engines, and I'll be glad I'm doing my bit to get our lads home safe.'

'Me too,' Asher said. 'Dietrich is joining us. He'll be on the same train as me.'

She nodded as she chewed a mouthful of bread. She was proud of them. It was inspiring, to see everyone rallying, and playing a part to bring the soldiers back.

Except her... Guilt punched her in the chest. Her plan had been to go to bed, while everyone else was helping. She swallowed the mouthful. 'What can I do to help?'

'Your mum said they need more women to clean the carriages,' Asher told her.

'Alright. I'll eat, then fetch Maggie and her sisters. They will all help, I'm sure. Lily disappeared during our shift last night so I don't know what she's up to, but the rest of us can do something.' She didn't feel tired any more. She was wide awake now and ready to do her bit. She wanted to feel proud of herself too. She'd feel ashamed when this was all over if she did nothing today.

18

MAGGIE ABBOT

Maggie sat on the rug in the Faradays' front parlour, Dot seated in the chair behind her and Marjorie on the floor next to her. Mrs Faraday sat on the sofa and Mr Faraday in the armchair that was just for his use. Edith was working a shift in the factory, and Lily had gone AWOL last night. Disappearing without a word. None of them knew where she was or who she was with, but she had been called away by the checky so Maggie presumed it was something to do with war work and the evacuation.

Maggie and Violet had been cleaning carriages all day. Maggie had come home for a brief rest before her shift in the factory. The others had been sitting by the wireless, so she'd stopped to listen too, before heading up to bed, hopefully to squeeze in an hour's sleep.

'This war has now entered upon its first most critical stage...' the minister of information, Mr Duff Cooper, said, his voice crackling from the wireless speaker, '...it will be necessary to do our utmost to withdraw our army from the positions it now occupies.' The radio reception was awful, his deep, precisely spoken voice continually broke up. 'It will not be a defeated army that we shall withdraw. It will be an army whose courage is still high and whose confidence is still unshaken.

'The magnificent work the British troops have done since the invasion of Holland, France and Belgium will rank among the finest feats ever performed by the British army...'

Maggie shuffled forward on her bottom, to get closer to the wireless's speaker, as if where she sat would stop the crackle and make his voice clearer.

'The result of the few days' or the few weeks' fighting that now lie before us may determine the history of the whole world and the future of civilisation. Germany has committed the last or at least the latest of her hideous crimes in the brutal and cowardly assault upon two neutral nations who have never given her any cause for complaint...'

Maggie's heart beat hard as she listened to his firm, concerned and even angry voice.

'Now the whole people of Britain are united in one supreme effort, united behind a government which represents all parties in the state, united with one purpose only in their mind, and that is victory and the destruction of the cruellest, most cowardly, most treacherous enemy that we have ever had to fight in our long history...'

Maggie sensed Dot looking at her. She looked across her shoulder and saw her emotions reflected in Dot's glistening eyes, it was not fear, but anger and determination.

'In peace and in war it has always been the policy of Germany to divide Great Britain from France. She has now succeeded in driving a wedge between the armies of the north and the armies of the south.

'Do not, I beseech you, help her to repeat that success by hammering in a wedge of prejudice between our two great peoples...'

Mrs Faraday coughed, as she dabbed the lacy hanky she clasped in her hand against her eyes, catching tears. Of course, Lenny was her son, she would be fearful.

'However great the enemy's success in this great battle may be, however great the blow, we can recall how many defeats, how many blows this country has withstood and rallied from.

'The enemy have succeeded in forcing their way through the lines of the Allies and they have reached the sea. But the armies of the Allies have not been defeated and whenever we have met the enemy, whether on land on the sea or in the air, we have proved our superiority...'

Yet the men were fleeing. How was that superiority? Maggie sighed. All she wanted to hear was the truth. No – all she wanted to hear was that the men were safe and this was over.

'The defeat of the barbarians will be no easy matter, we must expect to suffer, we must be prepared to make great sacrifices. Barbarians love war as much as we hate it, and they have prepared for it during many years when we never suspected that they were thinking of anything but peace. The fruit of those long preparations is seen today. It is seen in the perfection of their organisation. In the long-laid plans, which are now being put into operation. It is seen in the enormous accumulation of armaments that they have been storing up through these many years.'

'So that's why Hitler's been successful in France,' Mr Faraday commented. 'The devil's been planning this for years, building weapons and tanks and aircraft and probably working it all out. I suppose he's been biding his time through the winter, trying to deplete our resources by targeting our supply ships and now he has the spring weather on his side, he attacks.'

'...civilised man is not going to be destroyed by the forces of darkness and of barbarism...' Mr Duff Cooper continued. 'The united forces of the British Commonwealth of nations and those of the great French Republic, bound together in...' Maggie could not hear the next few words, the reception crackling. '...will not lightly be defeated. They have as their Allies the men of all those nations who are already groaning under German tyranny. The men of Austria, of Czechoslovakia, of Poland, of Norway, of Denmark, of Belgium and of Holland. Great nations, each of whom has contributed to the building up of our modern civilisation. So many forces are bound in the end to obtain victory and they will go on fighting until that victory is complete and until their enemy has been so utterly destroyed that never again will he be allowed to disturb the peace of Europe and threaten the survival of civilisation.'

The BBC broadcast went on to provide more day-to-day information about the changes to rationing and the need to collect new ration books.

Mr Faraday reached forward and turned the wireless switch to off. 'We are on the run indeed,' he said.

'But we are not defeated,' Mrs Faraday answered.

'And we will not give in,' Marjorie added.

'We will keep working and keep fighting,' Dot agreed.

'I'll pick up a gun to fight if needs be, if they come here,' Maggie said. She would too. She would defend her country with her life if she had to and shoot the Nazis.

Mr Duff Cooper had begun speaking of Germany as 'her', but at the end of his speech used 'he'. Because it was not Germany they were fighting, not really. It was one man, Hitler, who wanted war. *He* led his nasty-minded Nazis. They were barbarians, but without Hitler, she thought the war would end.

19

CATHERINE PEARCE

The matron reached forward and switched off the radio the workers and volunteers had crowded around in the communications tent, silencing the voice that provided further information following Mr Duff Cooper's speech. There were a few nurses here to help any wounded men who made it this far, but anyone arriving at this camp would be the walking wounded. The men had to walk five miles from the train station to reach the camp. The seriously injured were being taken elsewhere. Mostly, it was volunteers like Catherine and Lily helping here, and some women from the Auxiliary Territorial Service, the ATS, along with a couple of male officers who were giving orders to everyone.

Mr Duff Cooper said Hitler had been preparing to fight for years; Catherine thought of GWR's hurried adaptions last summer. The ships and trains that were stripped and re-equipped to be used as travelling hospitals, to treat and move the wounded. Those ships and trains would be full of seriously injured men for the next few days, doing their job.

If GWR had prepared those in a couple of months, though, how much had Germany prepared in years...? Were the Allies trying to fight mountains with molehills? Was that why they were losing?

Catherine sighed and looked at Lily. 'I should have asked Naomi to join us.'

'She wasn't workin. She was at ome, sick.'

Catherine's left hand held her right and found wood. Sometimes it still shocked her that her right hand was not flesh. She was going to circle her thumbs in an old nervous habit she had, but a wooden thumb definitely could not achieve that. It would cure the fidgety habit, though. Rolling her thumbs around each other annoyed Charles. He would think it was an improvement that she could not do it. Of course, he had not seen her wooden hand yet. She didn't know if he'd even received her letter telling him about it.

'How much longer before the men make it this far?' she asked Jenny, the female ATS officer who was managing the radio transmissions.

They knew men had landed in Dover, but none had been sent to them in Wiltshire yet. 'It's a slow start,' Jenny had told Catherine earlier. 'They are getting things organised in France, so the men can board.'

The receiver crackled then, and a woman's voice called out a code name for a position by the coast. 'Over,' she said, after repeating the code three times.

Jenny slipped on the headset without replying, and spoke what Catherine presumed was a password into the receiver, to confirm it was the correct depot responding.

There seemed to be a codeword for everything, obviously to confuse the Germans if they intercepted any transmissions.

Catherine couldn't hear what was being said through the headset. But then she probably wasn't meant to hear. She stepped back a couple of paces.

She and Lily had spent their day setting up wooden and tarpaulin camp beds in rows across the aircraft hangar, beds where the soldiers could at least get some sleep. Other people had erected marquees outside, where they were going to serve food to the men, a watery beef stew that was more like soup, and there were pans of water and a few hundred tin cups to serve the water and stew in.

In another marquee the men could be assessed for medical care and issued blankets and spare clothing.

'They're coming!' Jenny shouted as she slipped off her headset and stood up, calling out to everyone inside the aircraft hangar. 'We have a trainload of men on the way to us! Roughly five hundred!' She looked towards the commanding officer. 'Lieutenant Colonel Dowling, they are due to arrive at the station at twelve minutes past midnight. After their march we should anticipate their arrival here at forty-five minutes past the hour.'

'Wonderful,' the lieutenant colonel declared. 'I will send some volunteers down to the station to show them the way.

'Last chance for a nap, ladies,' he continued, smiling towards Catherine, Lily and the other female volunteers, his gaze ignoring the men, as though only the women needed sleep.

Catherine and Lily had already lain down on the camp beds, but they'd also been awake for many hours now and Catherine would need to be fully awake to help the men, so she would take this chance to sleep.

'Do you know which regiments are comin?' Lily asked Jenny.

She shook her head, her eyes watching the lieutenant colonel stride away, as if she was waiting for him to be out of earshot. When he was, she said, 'I am probably not meant to say, but it sounds like chaos at the coast. Some regiments are returning as a group, but other men are being plucked off the beaches or pulled out of the water just as quickly as they can get them aboard and they are not stopping to sort them all into any regimental order. Several of the ships have been hit and sunk, so many that the water is full of men, so even if the regiments boarded in an order, they have become muddled up when men are rescued from the sea.'

Catherine's stomach dropped at the thought of Charles being in the sea. But she could not fret, there was no time. Whoever was saved and came to this camp needed her help – and if none of them was Charles, then she hoped and prayed another woman would be offering him the same comfort and support in another camp with as much care and determination as she would give the men here.

She looked at Lily, the tan colour had been washed out of Lily's skin by her fear. 'Stay strong,' Catherine whispered. 'Stay hopeful.'

Lily's right hand lifted to her forehead, then lowered to her chest, before touching her left and then her right shoulder, forming the shape of a cross, implying she said a prayer in her mind.

Catherine did the same with her wooden hand, as with her left hand she held the locket that hung from the necklace about her throat. When she'd formed the cross, she raised the gold locket that contained a picture of Charles, and kissed it.

Lily's left hand curled into a fist, embracing her engagement ring.

'They'll come back,' Catherine reassured her, even though she feared it might not be true.

'I know,' Lily answered, as though they really could be sure. 'We should eat somethin ourselves, I suppose, an sleep for as long as we can, if we are goin to stay on our feet for the night.'

'Yes. Of course.'

After eating, Catherine lay down, but she could not sleep. Now she knew the men were on their way, these last hours of waiting were the worst. Her heart pounded too quickly, with swift beats of anticipation, and her mind spun with thoughts of what the men might be like. They had come from an unimaginable place. She pictured men limping through the miles to reach the camp.

When Catherine gave up any hope of sleep, she found Lily had given up before her and was standing outside with other women.

Catherine accepted a cigarette off one of the women, solely to have a task for her shaking left hand.

Lily refused the offer. 'They taste foul,' she said. 'An they make the back of your throat burn.'

They did taste foul and burn your throat the first few times, but Catherine had smoked a few of Charles's cigarettes, and like many things, they were an acquired taste – once you were used to them, they were enjoyable. Like sprouts and walnuts – she laughed at the likenesses her thoughts chose. She had hated sprouts when she was a child, but she enjoyed them now.

The cigarette did not last long before she stubbed the butt out beneath the sole of her shoe, and then she began walking in a figure of eight.

Lily sat cross-legged on the floor, smiling at Catherine's wandering.

It was dark when she heard the men, their feet, nothing else, the rhythmic strike of their boots on the tarmac road, marching at exactly the same pace – unlike the sometimes-shambolic sound that the GWR volunteers made in the Railway Village. No one called out any orders to align the steps of the approaching men, no words were spoken at all as they marched. It was only the sound of their boots that heralded their arrival.

Lily got to her feet, and all the women stared at the gateway.

The sound became stronger. Hundreds of footsteps, moving in time.

The anticipation of the unknown threatened. What state would these men be in, having fought so hard? Catherine's heartbeat struck heavily, jumping in her chest and ringing in her ears.

She shared a glance with Lily as the sounds of the boots grew louder and louder. Lily's hand reached for Catherine's and she squeezed it quickly, then let go. *Good luck*, the gesture said, as the first row of men appeared at the gate, an officer walking ahead of them.

In the moonlight their uniforms were grey not khaki, but she could see they were filthy. Many of the men marching through the gate had broad dark patches on their uniforms, and dark stains smeared across their faces and wiped on sleeves. Blood, she realised. Her stomach somersaulted, and even though it was not her role to do so, she rushed forward to help them.

'Halt!' the officer yelled to the men. 'Dismissed!'

'This way! This way!' Catherine shouted, calling them towards the marquee. 'There's food and drink here, and beds inside!'

'Form lines at the first tents, please!' one of the women from the ATS shouted. 'We will get you registered and give you what you need.'

'Sleep, love, that's all I need,' one of the men said. 'I ain't slept for four days, and only the Lord knows how I'm on my feet.'

'I'm starving.'

'I could do with some water, my throat is as dry as a desert.'

Catherine had never been so happy to hear men's voices, they sounded so... The only word that came to mind was – alive. A barrage of male voices had been normal in her life, and there were so many of them here now. They sounded like the factory used to after the GWR hooters announced the end of a shift. They smelt as sweaty as the GWR workers too.

As each line came through the gate, the men broke from the marching formation and reformed in queues at the marquees, talking to each other, their voices a low, dense, glorious sound.

Catherine hurried to her position behind a trestle table in one of the marquees. Her designated task was to hand out the bread rolls, after each man had received a ladle of the stew from Phyllis, a volunteer from a local village.

A baker from the village had brought the rolls an hour ago. He'd gone to make more. He'd told them he would use all the flour he had 'for our boys', but he suggested the women rip the rolls into quarters so every man could have a piece.

'*I doubt anyone local will have bread for a week or so, but I guess they won't mind for this cause,*' Phyllis had said.

Catherine would happily miss out on bread for the sake of the exhausted men queueing up in front of them.

As Phyllis tipped a ladleful of stew into the first billycan that was held out,

Catherine picked up the first bread roll. The bread smelt so fresh it made her mouth water. The stew may be thin but that smelt beefy and hearty too; the whole marquee smelt wonderful. She tore off a piece from the roll and placed it on top of the stew in the billycan that was held towards her.

'Thank you, ma'am,' the man said.

It did not take long for the pleasant smells of the food to be overwhelmed by the acrid smells coming from the men; stale sweat, mud, the smoke from the fires that must have permeated through the cloth of their uniforms, and... gunpowder... a firework-like smell – and dried blood.

She had grown up with four brothers and lived in a home with enough bumps and bangs to know what blood smelt like.

The tents ran like a production process at the factory. The men moving just like the bomb shells, from one station, one tent, to another. First, they were registered, so the army would know exactly who was here. Then they moved to another marquee to be checked over by the nurses for injuries. Then the line arrived in the marquee where Catherine and others served the food from a row of trestle tables. The men were given tin mugs full of water that most of them drank thirstily before they reached the food. Next, they were told to present their billycans or given a new one and received a ladle of stew and a piece of the bread.

Catherine used her wooden hand to hold the rolls and her left to tear a piece off and lay it on top of the stew. She could do it quite quickly, she was keeping pace with Phyllis's ladling.

Lily was at the end of the marquee, handing out blankets. She lay a blanket over each man's shoulder or arm as they passed. The ATS women stood at the exit, telling the men they could sit, sleep or rest wherever they liked but there were beds in the aircraft hangar. They were told they could return for more water, but the stew must be rationed. When they had more food supplies, they would hand them out.

In an upwards glance, Catherine whispered, 'Thank you, Lord.' God had not answered their prayers for peace, for Hitler to stop, but he had brought all these men safely back from the brink of death.

'Yur an angel, luv,' one man said as he held out a billycan for the stew Phyllis ladled into it. Catherine tore him off a piece of bread and rested it on the stew. 'Thank you,' he said to her.

'I need this, thanks, darling.'

'Thank you.'

'Cheers.'

'Oh. Yaki da. Some proper food. I can't tell you how long it's been since I had a warm meal.'

'That's bonnie, lass.'

'Thanks a million.'

'Oh, that's just the ticket, pet.'

'Hey, duck, that smells like heaven.'

She could not believe how polite, appreciative and kind the men were after all they must have been through. They looked and smelt like they had come from hell. It was unimaginable, and again, she felt the joy of being here with them. It did not matter if Charles was not a needle that turned up in this haystack, she would always remember being able to help these men.

Men who'd been delayed in the nursing tent and were freshly bandaged arrived to collect their food, with slashes and rips in their uniforms.

She noticed more about all the men then. Every one of them had bloodshot eyes, and their voices held the sound of fatigue. Few had enough energy to even raise a smile. Some men, too many of them, had blood on their clothing that could not be theirs because there were no corresponding wounds. On any other day, it would have sickened her, but today there was no time for horror. She focused on the need to tear the bread as the men kept coming.

By the time they had served the first five hundred, the boots of another trainload of marching men thundered along the lane towards the camp.

Within a couple of hours, men lay everywhere, not only on the beds inside the aircraft hangar, but on the ground outside. Once they had eaten, they had literally lain down wherever they sat and fallen asleep. Their exhaustion now absolutely obvious as they lay out cold, seemingly unconscious.

Phyllis nudged Catherine's arm, drawing her attention back from staring through the opening of the marquee looking at one group of men sprawled on the grass, side by side, not far away. 'Serve,' Phyllis whispered as a new line of men formed.

'Don't spill it, love,' a man said as Phyllis swung the ladle. 'That's too good to waste.'

'Can you manage the ladle for a bit?' Phyllis asked. 'My arm's killing me.'

'Alright.' Catherine just hoped she did not spill the stew and waste it, as her left hand was more awkward.

She thought about Lily handing out blankets. They hadn't had a moment to speak since the men started arriving. Perhaps she should swap with Lily, Lily would be better at ladling.

'Ta, angel,' the next man said as she handed him a chunk of the bread. Then Phyllis handed her the ladle and they swapped places.

Catherine filled the next man's billycan. 'Cheers, duck.' She was slower but able.

'*Merci*,' the next man said. She looked up from the ladle of stew at the sound of a French voice. A broad white smile shone from a face dirty with dust.

'*Bonjour. Merci.*' The next man was French too; there were several French soldiers.

'*Merci.*'

'*Merci beaucoup.*'

'Catherine!'

Her gaze flew to the man further back, who'd shouted her name.

'Catherine!'

He stood ten men back, with his hand lifted and waving.

Her brother! 'Alfred! Hello!' she shouted back, her heart leaping with relief and joy to know one of her brothers had made it home.

'Keep serving, Cath,' Phyllis grumbled. 'We have too many of them to get through.'

Catherine focused on her task again, grinning stupidly, knowing that Alfred would reach her in a bit.

'Grand, thanks, darlin.'

'Ta, duck.'

'You're a sweetheart.'

'Thank you.'

'Catherine, my God, I can't believe it is you,' Alfred said, as she served the man two in front of him. She wanted to hug him, but there was a table and a huge pot of hot stew between them, and a task to do.

'It's so good to see you,' *alive*. She did not say the last word.

She filled the next man's billycan.

'You are injured,' she said, as Alfred stepped in front of her and held out his billycan. His chest was covered with a large bloodstain.

'It's not my blood,' he said in a low voice. 'I dragged an injured man to a boat.'

'One of your regiment's men?'

'No, a stranger. I will probably never know if he survived. But it was like it was fate, the hospital ship was one of ours, I mean a Great Western Railway ship, they had painted her white with a clear red cross on her funnel. But the German bastards were still bombing her. I think she got out of the harbour, but we had to navigate a lot of wrecks. They have sunk so many bloody boats.'

'Cath,' Phyllis nudged again.

'He's my brother,' Catherine snapped. She had to be allowed to dally for a moment.

Alfred's eyes held the bone-deep weariness she'd been looking at for hours.

'Hurry up, mate. I want to get my head down.'

'*Dépêchez-vous, s'il vous plait.*'

The men in the queue behind Alfred moaned.

'I didn't realise we were saving the French,' she whispered to Alfred.

'It's madness, Catherine. Initially we were moving forward to the boats in regiments, but then a shout just went out to form a line and board. To keep up the fight if the Germans follow us home, we need as many soldiers to get back here as possible. So the Navy are bringing back any living soldier on those beaches.'

The man behind Alfred pushed him aside, nudging him on. 'I know you want to speak to your sister but do it later.'

'I will find you later, or tomorrow morning,' Catherine said to Alfred as Phyllis gave him a piece of bread, hoping she would find him again among all these men. The bread rolls would run out soon, the baker could not keep up with the men's arrival. The camp had been prepared to offer a temporary refuge to a thousand men, but there were more than that and more on the way.

'It is good to see you, Catherine. A great surprise. I am glad you are here.' He sent her a last weary smile before turning away, looking at the much-needed food.

Catherine returned her attention to serving the queue of men, her smile holding on her lips and her heart swollen with joy that Alfred was alive and well. Seeing Alfred encouraged her hope for Charles and her other brothers.

20

LILY FRANKLIN

Wednesday 29 May

A line of light drew across the horizon to the east as dawn broke behind the men Lily was passing blankets to. She had no idea how the Ministry of Supply had acquired so many blankets, but somehow, they had, and they left her hands by the second. The once orderly lines were often a melee of men by the time they reached her and they grasped a blanket from a pile in her arms.

Though some men didn't bother to join the queue and were lying on any spare area of ground, fast asleep with exhaustion and uncovered.

As her eyes constantly searched the men for Lenny, every darker-skinned face she spotted made her heart leap, as she thought of Art. But every time, when she looked harder, it wasn't him. It was hard to tell their skin tone, though, when so many of them were dirty and bloodstained.

The light increased, and the world became colourful again, as birds sung in the trees and hedgerows around the camp. At one point the dawn chorus became so loud it drowned out the voices of the men.

Was Lenny in a queue, taking a blanket from someone's arms somewhere else right now? she wondered for the thousandth time. She'd prayed at least hourly that he was on one of the ships coming home, or here in England somewhere.

'*Merci.*' A man took the last blanket off her arms.

She turned to pick up another pile of a dozen or so. This wave of men was waning. They'd been arriving in waves all night, by the trainload.

As the sun rose higher, she could see the dried blood marks on their uniforms more clearly, plus black soot, and the greys and reds of what looked like building dust – as well as the grime of mud and grass stains where they must have crawled on the ground.

'What was it like in France before you left?' she asked the next man.

'Don't ask, lass, you don't wanna know.'

21

MAGGIE ABBOT

Maggie was shaken awake by a hand on her shoulder. She opened her eyes. Dot leaned over her.

'Get up! They are coming through on the trains! The men! Hundreds of them! The trains are packed! Come on, everyone's on the platform, cheering the trains as they pass!'

Maggie hadn't heard this eager pitch in Dot's voice for months. She rubbed her eyes, then threw back the covers. 'What time is it?'

'Six thirty. I've been to the train station to see for myself.'

'But what about work?'

'Sod work for one day, no one's gone in. Hurry up!'

Maggie reached for her underwear and dressed quickly.

She and Dot ran to the rail station. There were others in the street doing the same, coming from all directions.

Some GWR station staff were on the street, organising a crowd. 'Form an orderly queue, please. No pushing.'

'Do we need a platform ticket?' Maggie asked Dot, as they queued to climb the stairs.

'No, not today.'

When Maggie reached the platform, she was squashed in a crowd. To move away from the top of the stairs, she had to nudge people aside with her elbows.

Dot caught hold of her hand so they would not be parted and led the way, forcing a path along the back of the platform where there was less of a crush.

'Sorry, no more people!' someone official shouted behind them. 'The platform is full, go home, please.'

They'd been lucky to get up here.

Near the end of the platform, Dot squeezed a path through the crowd and they managed to work their way to a spot on the platform's edge.

The stationmaster's whistle blew from somewhere at the opposite end. 'Ladies and gentlemen, please stand back from the edge! A train is coming through that is not stopping!'

Maggie shuffled back a step, forcing people behind her to step back too. Dot grinned as she looked along the trainline. She was the old Dot, the Dot she had known before the abortion and before their dad died. Her eyes as bright as her smile. Dot leaned forward a little, looking for the train. A grin formed on Maggie's lips too, Dot's emotion was infectious. She leaned forward, her gaze on the empty track. The iron rails began to tremble, making a ringing sound, then they heard the chuff chuff of the pistons running, and there she was, racing towards the station, shining as the sunlight reflected off the engine's glossy black paint.

The stationmaster's whistle blew again. 'Ladies and gentlemen, stand back!' He sounded angry this time.

As it headed towards the platform, and came alongside, Maggie saw the driver's hand lift, then the train's whistle toot-tooted. She thought the hooter was to say hello to them, but a moment later she understood it was a communication to the passengers. Men leaned from the windows in the doors, three or four squeezing through the space, and heads and hands appeared from the carriage windows all along the train.

Maggie waved with all her might, shouting, 'Hurray! Hurray!' Tears rolling onto her cheeks, as all around her people waved and shouted, and on the train the men waved, grinning out their joy to be back and safe.

'Well done!'

'God bless you!'

'Cracking job, boys!'

'Welcome back!'

Maggie smiled her hardest as the men flew past on the train, the steam and smoke drifting across them in a cloud.

'See?' Dot said to her as the last carriage passed. 'You had to be here.'

Maggie wiped her cheeks, smearing the tears and nodded. 'Do they stop here? The trains?'

'Only if the signal says the line's busy further along. Then they stop for a few minutes, but none of the men have disembarked here.'

Maggie remembered that Ron was shovelling coal into one of the engines along the lines. She'd loved him for years, and she loved him more for helping to bring the soldiers back.

The night of the dance, they'd walked home slowly, along Regent Street, looking into the dark shop windows, talking about nothing in particular. Then before he said goodnight, he'd held her hand, leaned forward, kissed her cheek and said, *You're a sweet girl really, Maggie.* Afterwards he'd let go of her hand and walked off. She hadn't known what to make of it.

The stationmaster blew his whistle hard, attempting to silence the excited crowd.

'Ladies and gentlemen, please!' he yelled, his voice sounding hoarse from shouting. 'I have a message from the GWR factory! Anyone involved in production, you need to get to work! We still have a war to fight!'

Maggie shared a look with Dot. She did not want to leave. She would happily lose a day's wage to stay. But it was true. The men were back but the war was not won; their aeroplanes needed bombs. 'I'd better go,' she said to Dot.

'Me too.'

She had no idea what Dot worked on, just as Dot had no idea what work Maggie was doing, but now they knew they were both working on armaments.

As Maggie left the station, forcing her way past those waiting to get in, she realised if there was a German spy in this crowd, they would be watching who left, to find out who to ply for information. She glanced around, but she didn't see anyone staring at them.

Dot linked her arm through Maggie's as they walked along the street. She was so like the Dot of old days that more tears brimmed in Maggie's eyes.

'It's a miracle, isn't it?' Dot said. 'I mean, that they have got men out of France. The Navy are doing a great job.'

'Yes,' Maggie agreed, with a smile pinned on her face, as she wondered if the father of Dot's baby was a soldier. That would explain why Dot was so excited about them coming back. Perhaps she'd been in the same situation as Betsy.

But then again, everyone was excited, it could be nothing to do with the father.

They walked to the factory among others, with their arms linked and Maggie had a skip in her heart. The British had lost this fight, that could not be denied. This was not a victory, but to see the men cheering and waving, it felt as if they had won solely by saving every single man who got away from the Germans.

Susie, the checky, was ready with her pen and ledger when Maggie entered the workshop. 'You're nearly an hour late, Maggie,' she accused.

'I was at the station. Welcoming the soldiers home.'

'What the soldiers need is bombs not cheers. You're on a lathe today. We left the lathes to the women who came late.'

'Miserable cow,' Maggie mumbled under her breath as she walked towards the machine, tying the apron she'd lifted off her hook to cover her clothes. She hadn't dressed for machine work this morning.

When she passed Naomi's workstation, she asked, 'Do you feel better?'

Naomi nodded, glancing in Susie's direction, then looked back down at her work.

Maggie leaned closer to her. 'I've seen some soldiers on a train at the station. We cheered them as they passed.' She gave Naomi a swift grin.

Naomi's lips parted as if she would ask a question.

'Get to work, Maggie Abbot!' Susie shouted before Naomi could speak.

Maggie walked on, but she could not resist shouting, 'Is no one else excited?' Her voice travelled above the sound of the machines. 'The Navy are getting our men out of France! They're coming home!'

'We do know, love,' one of the working men called back.

'Then, let's have a cheer!' she yelled. 'Hip hip!'

'Hurray!' a lone woman's voice called.

Maggie looked over her shoulder and saw that it was Violet who had responded.

'Hip hip!' she shouted again.

'Hurray!' more people responded.

'Hip hip!' Maggie yelled louder as she reached her lathe.

'Hurray!' over half the room yelled back, the energy of joy travelling through the women in the room. The men were not so exuberant. But Maggie knew then she was not the only one who wanted this shift over as quickly as possible. When it was over she would run back to the station.

Within a second of Susie ringing the bell to announce the lunch break, Maggie rushed over to Naomi. 'Are you coming to the station? I'm not hungry at all, I'm too excited.'

'Nor me. Yes, I'll come.'

'Are you going to the station?' Violet joined them.

'Yes, come on, let's hurry,' Maggie urged.

Maggie stripped off her apron quickly, then, alongside Violet and Naomi, ran all the way to the station. She even pushed her way through the crush of people in the subway tunnel without a thought for the narrow space.

On the platform, the number of people had thinned, and everyone there was armed with gifts to give to the soldiers who passed through Swindon. Maggie and her friends were told that every train was stopping now, so that the men could be handed food and drink, and anything else people wanted to pass over.

'I wish we'd brought something—'

'You wouldn't be able to,' a woman standing beside Maggie said. 'All the shops are empty, sold out, or given it away.' She grinned, her eyebrows lifting. 'There won't be anything left for anyone else for weeks, but we'll manage. These men deserve everything.'

It must be true. People along the platform were giving out delicious-smelling pasties and sausage rolls that must have been freshly made by the butchers. Maggie hadn't seen a sausage roll for months.

The newsagent, Mr Bradley, stood on the platform. He'd filled small paper bags with sweets from the large jars on the shop's shelves, and spun the bags by what her dad used to call the ears to close them up. The little bags would be easy to put into a man's hand.

'May I buy some of your sweets?' Maggie asked.

'You don't need to pay me, Maggie. People were coming in to buy whatever they could to give to the soldiers, I wasn't going to charge them. In the end, I thought I may as well bring the stock up myself. They deserve a treat or two. So, you take as many bags as you like and find the men who need something sweet.' He winked.

The stationmaster's whistle blew, and the exuberant joy Maggie had known earlier returned as people eagerly looked along the tracks.

'Please, everyone! Keep back! We don't want any injuries!'

'Is it stopping?' someone called out from further along the platform.

'Yes. But don't push forward. Give each other and the men some space!'

'Will they disembark?' Naomi asked Maggie. Naomi's hands held freshly baked currant buns that smelt delicious. One of the bakeries must have sent them to the station.

'No, none of the soldiers are disembarking. My mum is helping on the trains now, and she said none of the men are coming here,' Violet answered, '... and where they are going is secret. Did you see the newspaper this morning? People have already seen German planes overhead, watching what we are doing on this side of the Channel.'

'Then they'll see we're not beaten, just regrouping,' Maggie said. 'Let's see if we can get closer to the train, there's some space in the crowd further along. Come on.' Her hands full of packets of sweets, Maggie elbowed her way through, with Violet then Naomi in her wake.

She found a spot where the crowd was not as dense and moved forward. The woman at the front held out an arm. 'I've been ere all day, lookin for my fella on the trains, I ain't givin up my place for you, Maggie Abbot, just so you can be nosy.'

'I'm not being nosy, I want to hand them sweets.'

'You can stretch your arm then, can't you, an so can they.'

'That told you,' Violet whispered near Maggie's ear.

Maggie laughed. She could not be angry today, not with anyone, or for anything.

'I'm going to look for my brothers—' Naomi's words were drowned out by the approaching train's whistle. The steam and smoke rose in a tall tower above the moving train.

Maggie's heart beat in the same rhythm as the train's pistons.

Violet raised the sausage roll she held to her nose. 'This smells delicious. My stomach's growling. I think I'll dream about eating it. The man I give this to is going to be lucky.'

Maggie laughed, the tone of it carefree, the sound something she hadn't heard from her throat for a long time. As the train approached, she watched the men leaning from every door and window all the way along the carriages, and the hundreds of hands that reached from the tops of the viewing windows.

The people around Maggie screamed, waved and cheered long before the steam engine reached the station. Toot. Toot. The driver pulled the whistle. Even more heads appeared from the windows as the engine came alongside the platform and slowed. The first carriages passed too quickly for Maggie to see anyone's face, and the steam swept across the platform, creating a cloud. She tried to look for Lenny, but she couldn't possibly recognise anyone inside the packed carriages. The men waved and shouted, their voices travelling past Maggie. The women around her screamed their excitement and shouted out names.

'Hello!' Maggie shouted.

'Hello!' Violet called too.

The line of carriages slowed to a crawl and stopped.

The stationmaster blew his whistle. 'Passengers, stay on—' Whatever he said next was drowned out by all the people shouting.

'Here! Here!'

'A gift for you!'

'Take it, take it. It's a sausage roll.' Violet reached through a gap between the women in front and put her sausage roll into an open hand that stretched through a top window of a carriage compartment.

The men were packed into the carriage as tightly as the shelves GWR transported young chicks in, with hardly a spare inch. Maggie wouldn't have survived it.

The stationmaster's whistle blew again.

It sparked Maggie into life. She reached past the woman in front of her. 'I have sweets!' she called out. 'A bag of sweets! To say thank you!' She held out the first small paper bag, trying to connect to a hand.

A dark hand found hers and clasped the paper bag. She let go as the couplings clunked, a jolt, and then the carriage rolled forward as the chuff of the pistons sent steam along the platform.

'Thanks, lass!' a deep voice shouted.

'God bless you!' she called back as the hand disappeared out of view.

Her empty hand raised higher and waved hard as the last of the carriages passed.

She stared at the train as it shrank into the distance, her heart thumping. Giving a man a bag of sweets was such a small thing to do, but it felt so good.

She looked at Violet, then Naomi, and saw the same light of excitement in their eyes. They hugged each other, in a three. A triangular cuddle – and cried.

'It's wonderful,' Maggie said.

'Wonderful?' a man behind her repeated. 'That's what you call it, is it? Wonderful that these poor bastards have had to run for their lives? Don't you read the papers? Maybe they only have hours to get the rest of the men out of the way of the Germans, and those Nazi bastards don't give a damn who they kill – I heard they were mowing down refugees on the roads, including children.'

Anger rose in Maggie's throat, and rude words burned on the tip of her tongue, but she bit them back. She wasn't going to let this man ruin her joy. 'Then I am even happier, and I think it's even more wonderful that the men on these trains have got away,' she snarled back at him.

22

LILY FRANKLIN

Thursday 30 May

In a moment of quiet, Lily walked around the groups of men sleeping on the ground outside the aircraft hangar. She'd begun walking around the men yesterday, whenever there was a break in arrivals, looking at all the men sprawled on the ground or lying on the beds inside the hangar. Looking for Lenny or Art, in case she hadn't seen them arrive.

Some of the men had been asleep for eighteen hours or more. Others only arrived an hour ago and had already found somewhere to collapse. The blankets had run out long ago. There was still food and water to hand out, though.

'Fuck! Fuck!' a man further away shouted, thrusting out a fist.

He was lying on the ground alone, with his coat rolled up to form a pillow.

She walked quickly, to reach him. To help him if she could.

'Rupert! Rupert!' he shouted, still in the midst of his nightmare. 'No!' he yelled and then he screamed in a way Lily had never heard a man scream. She ran the last few paces to reach him. His eyes opened and he sat upright, his fingers curling into the long grass his body had flattened.

The setting sun caught on the grease in his lank blond hair, lightening it and creating a sort of halo. It looked as if his hair had been left unwashed for weeks, and there were a couple of days of stubble growing on his chin and upper lip. She squatted, then knelt on the ground beside him, and rested a hand over one of his as it clutched at the grass.

His eyes held terror.

'Are you alright?' It was a stupid question, because he obviously wasn't. 'Was it a bad dream about France? What appened…?' She dared the last question tentatively, not sure she would want to hear the answer, or he would want to say, but if he wanted to speak, she'd force herself to have the courage to listen.

'Yes, it was about France,' he answered.

She said nothing in response, leaving him to talk or not. She lifted her hand away from his and sat back on her bottom. The grass was a bit damp. She wasn't sure how the men were managing to use it as a bed so easily – but perhaps they were used to it.

'My brother died,' he said in the end. 'Rupert. An explosion caught him and threw me out of the way. We signed up together, to be in the same regiment, so we could protect one another. We had done, until then. But how could I have stopped a bloody bomb…? I let him die.'

'No, the Nazis killed im, you didn't let anythin appen. An wherever ee is, ee will be glad you survived. Would it elp if I sit with you for a while?'

His blue eyes looked into hers. 'Yes. Thank you. I would appreciate the company.'

'I'll stay until you can fall asleep again. What's your name?'

'Lionel.'

'Mine's Lily.'

The King had talked about holding pride in her heart, and she felt it, even though she'd heard the cracks of this man's broken heart. She was proud of all these exhausted men, and proud to be here helping them.

On the wireless today, they'd said the French army were holding open one last evacuation point, at Dunkirk, and the British forces left in France were fighting a route through the Germans to reach it. More of these men would come.

She asked him about his brother, about what his brother was like before the war, to lighten his thoughts, while her mind dwelt on the situation in France; internally she prayed for every man left in France and for God to help them protect Britain.

Some words in the announcement on the wireless replayed in Lily's mind. *'We conquered them once and we shall conquer them again...'*

She prayed for Lenny as she talked to this man, *Please, God. Let him be among men in a camp like this right now, already safe, with women to help him.*

23

MAGGIE ABBOT

Friday 31 May

Maggie sat at the Faradays' kitchen table, with Mr Faraday's daily newspaper spread wide open in front of her. Maggie and her sisters were alone in the kitchen. Mrs Faraday was at an urgent Defence Committee meeting, and Mr Faraday was already out in the park, cultivating and sowing vegetables.

Dot was leaning over her shoulder scanning the published names of the dead. Three destroyers had been sunk in the Channel between England and France, and several small auxiliary ships. They had been sunk either in the harbours or en route to or from the beaches.

The article described thousands of battle-weary men arriving on the south coast and stumbling into train after train. Another article warned of the risk of Hitler bombing England and encouraged the ARP wardens and schools to be ready.

Maggie read an article that talked about the empty shelves in shops all over England, because everyone had been doing the same as they'd done in Swindon, giving everything they had to the returning soldiers who came past in the trains.

Maggie, Violet and Naomi had swapped their shifts today, to work the night shift, so they could spend the whole day at the train station, cheering the men through. Maggie was knocking for Violet after breakfast. She'd finished eating but she wanted to know what the paper said was happening before she left. The newspaper articles and the Ministry of Information's speeches on the wireless were the only source of true information.

Dot straightened and turned away from the newspaper, and the table.

Maggie would guess Dot had been looking for a particular name, but she didn't say so, and Maggie didn't ask. She wasn't sure if Edith and Marjorie had noticed the way Dot seemed to be thinking about a particular man when they talked about the evacuation, but Maggie was sure of it. Of course, they didn't know about the baby and abortion either.

Dot turned to the sink to finish washing the pan and bowls they'd used for dinner. They were following the guidance to use only one pan for everything they ate, and heating less water, so they didn't waste gas. They kept a jug of vegetable water in the fridge, even though the fridge wasn't on, as well as a bowl of dripping. The two items were used to add flavour and vitamins and minerals to other meals. Nothing could be wasted, not if the Germans were likely to try to take everything.

Mr Tabs circled around Maggie's legs, meowing an unhappy sound. She reached down and picked him up by a hand looped under his belly and lifted him onto her lap. 'I told you, Mr Tabs,' she said as she stroked him. 'I don't know where Lily is or when she'll be home.' Her fingers tickled behind his ears. 'You know as much as we do, which is what we were told in the message from Aunt Alice. Lily is safe and well, and with Catherine. I'm sorry I can't conjure her up. I know she's your favourite, but for now, you have to put up with us.'

Mr Tabs turned his head, made a sort of yowling sound and jumped off Maggie's lap, expressing his opinion of having to put up with her versus Lily. Well, the feeling was mutual.

Edith laughed, then bit another mouthful from her slice of toast, with plum jam thickly spread on it, but no butter. There was no butter in the house today, last week's ration had gone and there was none in the shops. All the butter had been used to bake things for the soldiers. Mrs Faraday had also asked Edith to use less jam, as there wouldn't be sugar for preserves this autumn, but Mrs Faraday wasn't here and Edith had said, *Just one last thickly spread slice,*' as she'd spread the jam on her toast a quarter of an inch thick. *'Then I'll be good.'*

Maggie closed the paper and left it on the table for Mr Faraday. 'I'm going back to the station,' she told her sisters as she rose from the chair.

Dot looked over her shoulder. 'I wish I could come. I couldn't change my shift.'

'Nor me,' Edith said. 'I tried.'

'Me too,' Marjorie added. 'But I will come at lunchtime.'

'Do you think there will be as many trains today?' Edith asked them all.

'More,' Maggie answered. 'The newspaper said they're running dozens of trains an hour from Dover.'

'I heard the trains running on the line all night,' Marjorie told them. 'The drivers were blowing the whistles, so people must have been on the platform even then.'

'I heard them too.' Dot put the last of the dishes on the drainer, and picked up the tea towel. 'I spent half the night thinking about the men aboard the carriages, wondering who was on them. In the end I got up and went to the station.'

Maggie had been about to open the back door, but Dot's words stopped her leaving. 'You should have woken me. I would have gone with you.'

'You'd worked all day, Maggie, and you're working tonight, you needed your sleep.'

'You had worked all day, and you have to work today,' Maggie answered.

'I only stayed an hour. It was not like the daytime, most of the men were asleep. We gave a few of them something to eat, but it was cold and the carriages were too dark to see who was in them, so I came home in the end.'

Maggie was sure Dot was looking for a particular man.

Had she taken her little Bible with her and clutched it to her chest? Maggie had not seen her carrying it for the last twenty-four hours. Maybe, if this man came home, she would give up the idea of becoming a nun.

Instinct – no, love – took Maggie to Dot. She hugged her with all her might and kissed her cheek. 'I love you,' she said, then released her.

Edith and Marjorie laughed at her.

'Why does she get a cuddle and I don't?' Edith teased.

'Because she's my favourite sister,' Maggie answered, winking, before making a run for the door. 'I'll see you all later.' Violet would be waiting for her.

She folded her arms over her chest as she walked along the street. The sun hadn't managed to warm up the spring day yet and she had only put a thin cardigan on over her blouse. She passed two young boys sitting on the kerb playing jacks but with a marble and pebbles. One of the boys looked up at her. It was one of Lily's brothers.

'Hello, Jimmy Franklin, shouldn't you be getting ready for school?'

'My mum doesn't make me go to school.'

'Your Lily would. I will tell her if you are skiving.'

He stuck his tongue out at her.

Maggie smiled and wagged her forefinger at him. 'Mark my words, I will tell her,' she warned.

When she reached Mrs Turner's terraced cottage, she tapped her knuckles on the door.

Violet opened it almost immediately. 'Good morning.' She looked over her shoulder. 'We are going, Mum.'

'We' turned out to mean Violet and Naomi – Naomi followed Violet through the door and closed it behind her.

'I thought you were meeting us at the station,' Maggie said to Naomi.

'I came here in case Asher had come back. Dietrich has not been home at all since he volunteered to stoke the engines.'

'Nor Ron and Asher. I don't think anyone moving the soldiers has any time to do anything else,' Violet said. 'Mum came home last night. She said they are cleaning and turning carriages around in half an hour now, but she felt faint so she had to sleep. She's going back later.'

Their strides were as energetic as the day before, but when they reached the rail station there were fewer people on the platform. There were still crates of bread, pies, sausage rolls and sweets to be handed out, though.

Maggie walked over to ask for some bags of sweets.

'There are milk churns along the platform, with ladles and mugs, ladies,' the stationmaster told them.

A woman beside him smiled proudly. 'We pulled the churns off a train heading for Paddington Station this morning, like Robin Hood and his merry men, we were. The Londoners can do without their milk for a day, that's what I say.'

'Too right,' Violet agreed. 'I'll hand out mugs of milk.'

'Me too,' Naomi offered.

'Just remember to get the mugs back off of them, otherwise we shan't have any.'

'We will,' Violet agreed, then, being the tallest, rose onto her toes, looking over people's heads. 'There's more room at the front of the platform, and it looks like there's a churn that no one has opened.'

Maggie followed her friends to a place where the first carriage would stop.

'Good morning, Maggie. Violet.' The stationmaster stood near them.

'Good morning, Mr McGregor.'

'Hello, Mr McGregor.'

'And I don't know this pretty young lady. You don't live in the Railway Village, do you?'

'No, sir, but I work in the factory.' Naomi held out a hand, offering to shake his. 'I'm Naomi Isaacs.'

'I do know that name.' He accepted Naomi's hand and shook it heartily. 'You were the family in the *Evening Advertiser* last year, there was an article last summer about you taking in a Jewish refugee, a German boy. That was a good job. Nice to meet you.' He let go of her hand. 'But I had best check to see when the next train is coming in. Good day, ladies. They ran near two hundred trains from Dover yesterday, did you know that?' He raised his eyebrows at the same time he lifted his cap slightly then turned to his office.

He reappeared scarcely five minutes later.

'Is a train coming?' Maggie asked.

'Yes, indeed.'

'Will it stop here?' Naomi added.

'They are all stopping now, to fill the engine up with water but also to give the men a chance to collect the women's gifts.' He smiled before lifting his whistle to his lips and blowing a shrill call as he walked further along the platform. 'Ladies and gentlemen, stand back, please!'

Maggie's heart pulsed with excitement as the train came into view.

'I wish you could all help me look out for my brothers,' Naomi said, lifting the lid off the churn. 'But you haven't seen them, so you won't recognise them.'

Violet picked up the ladle, stirred the milk, then carefully scooped some out in the way that caught a little of the cream from the top. She poured it into a cup Naomi held out and filled a cup of her own as the engine chuffed towards them, spewing out steam and smoke.

Men leaned from every orifice of the train. It was madness. Bedlam. But… her mind still turned to the word 'wonderful'. It was wonderful to see them whooping, cheering and hollering as much as their welcome party on the platform.

'Milk.' Violet lifted a mug. 'Does anyone want a cup of milk? You'll have to share the cup, though. Give it back to me quick and I'll refill it.'

About ten of the men accepted the offer and the cup was drained again and again.

'Who wants a bag of sweets?' Maggie offered, looking along the row of faces.

A man leaning from a window near the door stretched out his hand. 'Give them ere, darlin, thank you, I'll share them.' She pressed the bag into his hand, and he took it. Maggie held out a second bag.

The window in the door was pushed as far down as it would go and one man leaned across it almost bent double, as two other men reached around him, one accepting a cup of milk from Naomi.

'Bring us some beer next time, love,' someone behind him shouted. 'Lord, I could do with a tankard.'

'I could do with a whisky.'

'I'm so glad to be home I could kiss you girls,' the man leaning right out of the window said.

'Why don't you then?'

Maggie looked over her shoulder.

Rose Lloyd was the one who'd said that. Betsy's sister. She stood behind Maggie.

Rose had a reputation for kissing lads. Maggie didn't kiss lads, but she was the one closest to the door as the man reached down to the outside handle and turned it. As the door swung open, he stepped one foot down onto the platform, leaving the other foot on the train so the train could not go without him.

His hand reached out and hooked about the back of Maggie's neck, and with no by your leave, pulled her close and pressed his lips hard against hers, his unshaven chin scratching on her skin and his lips salty with sweat. He smelt as horrible as he tasted, of sweat and dirt. Her stomach jerked with a desire to be sick, but she didn't want to push him away, it was only a kiss…

Then his tongue forced its way into her mouth, and the toast and milk she'd had for her breakfast threatened to come back up. She hadn't known a kiss could be as unpleasant as this.

The stationmaster's piercing whistle rang out and the man released her. She wiped the back of her hand across her lips before he'd even stepped back onto the train. He struggled to get the door shut with the other men pressing forward behind him. The train whistle blew and Maggie shoved the door with both palms as he turned the handle. The lock clicked home as the train's pistons moved. Chuff chuff, chuff chuff… the engine blew steam and smoke Maggie's way.

She did not want to dislike any of these men, but she hated that man. That had been her first kiss. She had wanted her first kiss to be something to remember, with Ron, not something that would make her feel sick for the rest of her life.

'Are you alright?' Naomi asked. 'You look pale.'

Maggie nodded, unable to speak. She did not want to admit that had been her first kiss when she was twenty-two now, not in front of Rose Lloyd anyway. She wouldn't hear the end of it. 'You can stand by the door if you want kisses, Rose,' she told the other woman.

Maggie moved back to stand closer to Violet as the train pulled away, men waving and hollering at the women on the platform who waved them off.

Violet hadn't waved, and her left hand was curled into a fist. 'Maggie,' she said in a quiet voice. 'Look.' She uncurled her fist and showed Maggie a scrappy little bit of paper.

'What is it?'

'A man pressed it into my palm. He was begging me to tell his mother he was alive and safe.'

Maggie picked up the small piece of paper and flattened it out. The words were written on a cigarette paper. She read aloud. 'Doris Etherton, Bude.'

Violet looked from the paper to Maggie. 'That's where my mum and dad come from. Dad's grave is there.'

Violet had never told Maggie that before. But then why should she mention where her mother came from unless it was relevant to a conversation?

'It's a bit of a mystery, isn't it?' Maggie said excitedly. 'You have to find her.'

'You could send a telegram,' Naomi, who had overheard, said. 'From the post office here, to the post office in Bude. I bet they'd find Doris Etherton.'

It was much better to have a message to pass on than an unwanted kiss. Maggie should have poured the milk, she could still taste that man in her mouth.

24

CATHERINE PEARCE

Saturday 1 June

When he saw her approach, Alfred's lips quirked at one side, a brief expression that reminded Catherine of her childhood, when he'd tickled or teased her. 'Hello,' he said quietly, trying not to disturb anyone who was asleep.

'Hello.' She smiled too.

As the youngest of five children, with four brothers, the youngest of whom was six years her senior, her childhood was full of boys' games and brotherly torment. Alfred was third in line. The middle child of the five. He was eight years older than her.

Because the boys had gone to boarding schools, and because she was a lot younger, she'd not been close to any of her brothers as a child. But as adults, before they went off and joined the army, they'd become closer. They'd all liked to protect and coddle their little sister as men.

Her legs folded and she sat cross-legged on the floor, sitting on the ground facing him, and tucking her skirt around her with her wooden hand. He'd had a camp bed when he first arrived, but like most of the men who arrived the first day, he'd left the bed for someone else to use and moved to the ground outside. Thank God, the weather had been kind and rain kept away.

'How are you?' she asked. 'How do you feel?'

He sat with his long legs stretched out, and his hands on the ground behind him. He'd shaven and washed in a stream the men were using at the far end of the field, but the jacket and trousers of his uniform still held the blood of the man he had tried to save. She could not wrap her mind around what he and the others here had endured to get home. How could he cope with never knowing if the man he had helped survived?

'Still in shock, I would say, Catherine. I am not sure I really lived through that. It doesn't feel real now I'm here on the green grass of home. But how are you?' He sat forward suddenly, reached out and picked up her wooden hand. 'I can't believe you did this to yourself. But this is beautiful.' He turned the hand over, which meant she had to turn her forearm, as he looked at all sides of the carved hand. 'It's very clever. The GWR men are going to have to start carving spares for soldiers.'

'I think they might, they are renowned for their artificial limbs all over Europe...' The mention of the Continent stopped her words. She swallowed and gave him a shallow smile. 'This was made especially for me by a friend.'

Alfred looked up, studying her face and her eyes, in an exaggerated way.

'What is it?' she asked.

His eyebrows lifted. 'I think Charles needs to marry you quick sharp, before this friend grasps your interest.'

'Charles wants to wait until after the war. He wants a big wedding.'

'Sod that, God knows when this is going to end, don't let Hitler plan your life. Anyway, I'd lay good odds it's his mother who wants the big wedding. How's Bonny?' he asked as he released her hand. 'Have you seen her recently?'

His wife lived in a village a short distance from Swindon.

'No. We haven't been using the car. The last time we saw her was Christmas.'

'Well, she has her mum locally. She's not alone.'

'I'll write and tell her you're safe when I get home.'

'I'll tell her myself, the army are giving us all forty-eight hours' leave from tomorrow. Then we'll have to report back to a duty station somewhere as the army generals rally and decide what to do next. Have you heard any news? Do you know what's been happening in France? I haven't seen a newspaper or got anywhere near a wireless for days.'

'There are still thousands of soldiers arriving on boats at the coast. The Navy have requisitioned every single boat that can make it over the Channel, from fishing trawlers to leisure boats. The French army are fighting to hold a route to the coast open so men who were nearer Belgium can get through to Dunkirk.'

'Bloody hell. Sorry to swear.'

'Believe me, I have heard a lot of swearing here, and now I work in the factory, you won't shock me.'

A deep chuckle came from low in his throat. Then he sobered. 'The man I gave my bed to told me he had walked fifty-five miles in thirty-six hours to get to the extraction point, and then he had to walk another five to get from the station to here. He stripped off his boots and socks and God knows how he had walked on those feet.' He breathed in deeply, leaned back on his hands again and looked up at a white cloud gliding across the sky. 'It has been seventeen days...'

'What has?' Confusion pinched her eyebrows together in a frown.

'This. This mess. This bloody shambles. The Germans walked into France seventeen days ago and drove straight through, like a bulldozer. In seventeen days they have completely defeated us and won Europe. Just like that.' He snapped his fingers. 'If I stop and think about it...' The tendons in his throat tightened as he swallowed back the emotions she heard in his voice. 'We have to stop those bastards somehow, Catherine. It is awful over there. You have never seen... Well, you don't want to see it. And I don't want you too, either. I don't want to think about it, but it won't go away.'

'Ello...'

Alfred's gaze lifted, looking beyond Catherine in response to the tentative-sounding greeting.

Catherine turned slightly, looking over her shoulder. 'Hello,' she said to Lily. 'Do you want to sit with us?' She looked back at Alfred. 'Alfred, this is my friend, Lily. We met in the factory and lived together for a while before my accident.'

'Ello,' Lily said again, this time speaking to Alfred.

'It is a pleasure to meet you, Lily.'

'If you don't mind, I'll join you? I av nothin to do until the next trainload arrives. I've been walkin around andin out water, but my legs need a break. If I don't sit down, I'll fall down.'

'Pull up a seat,' Alfred joked, nodding towards the grass.

She folded her legs and sat cross-legged beside both of them.

'So, have you bumped into anyone you know, Lily?' he asked her.

'No.'

'We were hoping to see Charles, and Lily's fiancé, Lenny,' Catherine explained. 'But we did know it would be hoping to find needles in haystacks.'

'You found me, though.'

'I did, and I'm happy I did.' Catherine looked at Lily. 'Alfred just said the men are being given forty-eight hours' leave, so Lenny and Charles should be heading home.'

'If they've made it out—' Alfred started and then stopped. Catherine presumed he stopped in response to Lily's horrified expression. 'I am sure they will be coming home to you both.'

Lily gritted her teeth and exhaled through her nose, as if she was strengthening herself to hear the worst news. 'If a man wasn't comin back... I mean, if ee died, or was captured, ow long does it take them to tell people?'

Alfred shook his head. 'I don't know. I have never seen so many men involved in a fight. This is unprecedented. It's impossible to say how long it will take for the army to unpick all the registers and work out who did or did not make it home, and whether they're dead or a prisoner of war.'

Remembering Lily's moments of panic, Catherine waited for Lily to start struggling to breathe. Instead, Lily inhaled deeply and slowly. Then nodded, as if to say, *I understand, and I will face this.*

She looked at Catherine. 'Do you think the camp can manage without me tomorrow? I wanna go ome. I wanna be at ome if Lenny comes back. Especially if ee only has two days.'

'I would like to get back for Charles too. We had better go and ask. Excuse us, Alfred?'

'Of course. Say goodbye to me, though, before you disappear?' he said.

'I will.' She kissed his cheek before she left him.

25

VIOLET TURNER

Sunday 2 June

Violet walked around the small, square kitchen table, putting a bowl down in front of Asher and Ron, one at her place and one at her mother's. There had been no meat in the butcher's shop, because everything had been cooked up into something for the soldiers. And no fish in the fishmonger's because the trains travelling up from the coast were too full of men to carry any fish. It meant their dinner was a vegetable curry, but at least she had found the curry powder in the pantry to add flavour and some dripping from the mutton they'd had a few days ago to fry the potatoes, onions, carrots and greens in before she had added the spice and vegetable water. It had been tasty when she tried it, and the rice from the store cupboard would make it filling.

She knew Asher and Ron were exhausted and very hungry. They'd arrived home less than two hours ago, both of them as black as the ace of spades with soot. Her mother had boiled a pan of hot water on the stove. They'd put up some sheets on the washing line in the yard. Ron and Asher had washed in the tin bath out there, while Violet had put their clothes in a bucket of salt water to soak. She doubted she would get all the stains out when she washed them, though.

The men had raced through the kitchen wrapped in towels, leaving wet footprints on the stone flags. Their feet had been heavy on the stairs as they had raced up to dry and dress.

Violet served the rice as her mother carried the pan of curried vegetables over to the table.

'It smells good, Rose – and Vi,' Ron said, remembering Violet had done the cooking.

'Vi has done us proud with what little we had,' Violet's mother answered.

'Believe me,' Asher said, looking at Violet, 'I would eat anything today, I am so hungry.' He lifted his bowl up for Violet's mother to spoon the curry into.

'Ah. Oh.' Her mother set the pan down on the table in a way that looked as if she had been about to drop it.

'Rose?' Ron stood, as if he might need to catch her.

'Mum?' Violet stepped closer, putting the empty pan they'd used for the rice on the stove.

'Don't fuss,' Violet's mother told them both, raising her left hand to keep them away, while her right pressed against her chest above her left breast. 'I'm fine.' She did not look fine, she was pale and beads of sweat shone on her brow.

'Forgive me,' Ron said, 'but you don't look well.'

'Honestly, I am fine, I am just tired after all these extra hours' working, and I had a stitch.'

Stitch pain was usually in the side of your ribs, not your chest. Violet knew better than to make a fuss, though. Her mother didn't mollycoddle and she didn't welcome it either. Violet was raised to be tough. *There's nothing wrong with you, girl...*' had been her mother's favourite phrase if Violet fell or bumped herself as a child. *Jump up.*'

Ron took over serving the curry as Violet and her mother sat down.

'Thank you,' her mother said as he served her.

'Thanks,' Violet said, when he filled her bowl.

When Ron sat down, he raised his glass of water. 'Let's toast to a successful retreat. The Navy saved hundreds of thousands more men than they thought possible.'

Asher raised his glass. 'To the men who have come home.'

'To the men who came home, and those who did not,' Violet said with a more sober voice.

'Yes.' Asher raised his glass again, his voice sobering too.

'To all our fighting men.' Ron lifted his glass higher before he drank the water.

Her mother didn't contribute to the toast, she still had a hand pressed to her chest and was breathing slowly, trying to stop the pain she was obviously experiencing.

'The last trains we ran were loaded with Belgians as well as the French,' Ron said between mouthfuls. 'Some of the Belgian army refused to accept the order to surrender, so the small boats took them off the beaches too. Any man who is willing to keep fighting, the army were glad of.'

'How many trains did you shovel coal for?' Violet asked.

Her mother picked up her spoon and started to eat, so her pain must have eased.

'I lost count after ten,' Ron said, 'and it was a lot more than that.'

'I lost count too,' Asher agreed.

'Have you seen Naomi?' she asked Asher.

His eyes lifted from his food, but he glanced first at Ron, then afterwards looked at Violet. 'I will speak to her tomorrow. I am too tired to walk up the hill now. I need my bed.'

'How is Dietrich?' she said. 'I imagine this is harder for him than for most of us, and it is hard enough for me.'

'He felt much better to be actively helping, when he could see the difference he was making. When the men boarded, we could see how severe the fighting had been,' Asher answered.

'Did you work on the hospital trains?'

'For some of the runs.'

'When we were giving out food at the rail station, one of the men on the train handed me a note,' Violet said. 'He asked me to tell his mother he was safe. I only had her name and the town she was from. He wrote it on a cigarette paper, with no room for the address. I sent her a telegram today, so she would know he was safe.'

Ron smiled around his mouthful.

'That was good of you, darling,' her mother remarked.

'Where did he come from?' Asher asked.

'Bude.' Violet's eyebrows lifted as she shared the coincidence. 'Where Mum comes from and where my father is—'

'You did not send it with your name?' her mother's sharpest of voices interrupted.

Violet's eyebrows dropped to a frown. 'Yes…' Her belligerent tone of voice said *'why wouldn't I?'* She was proud of herself.

'Child.' The note in that word said Violet had done something wrong. Her mother didn't say any more, though, and nor did Violet, she didn't like being told off in front of Ron and Asher. Violet frowned as she ate, feeling the telltale heat of a blush in her skin.

The men continued eating, pretending to be unaware of the change in the mood around the table.

As soon as Asher and Ron had emptied their bowls, they washed them up and excused themselves.

Violet's mother was strong-willed. Because she'd raised Violet alone, she had a good reason to be. But she was never normally angry or annoyed.

As soon as the kitchen door closed on the men, her mother stood, picking up her bowl and turning away to wash it up.

Violet stood too and met her at the sink with her own bowl in her hand. 'What did I do wrong?'

'Did you not think it might be a bad idea to communicate with anyone in Bude?'

'Why? I was excited, because my family came from his town, and it seemed to be fate that he'd given me the note.'

'He didn't choose you, did he? It just happened to be you—'

'Exactly, Mum. That's fate.'

Her mother looked at the closed door, then lowered her voice, expressing her fear of the men overhearing. 'Will it be fate if someone arrives here, and knows me, and knows I was never married to your father…?'

Violet sighed. She hadn't considered that, she'd just wanted to tell the man's mother he was safely home. 'I don't think people will remember a woman who left over twenty-two years ago, Mum, not at the current time.' She had never argued with her mother, never talked back to her like this. But today was not about her mother's secret. It was about the mother of the man who had fought and would have to fight again.

26

LILY FRANKLIN

Monday 3 June

Lily rolled to her other side. She had spent the whole night tossing and turning in the bed. She had been looking forward to returning to her comfortable mattress for a good sleep, but now she knew Lenny might be on his way here there was no chance of sleeping.

She'd hoped he would be here when she pushed open the back door at just after ten o'clock last night. She couldn't tell from the outside of the house if anyone was awake because of the blackout, so she had not knocked, she had used the key that was under the mat. The house was dark when she walked in, everyone had been in bed. They would have been awake if Lenny was home.

Even so, she had checked the parlour to see if Lenny was sleeping on the sofa because Maggie was using his room. Then, just in case Maggie had moved into a room with one of her sisters, Lily had crept upstairs and opened his bedroom door slowly and silently, peeking in. The room was dark, Maggie had drawn the curtains. Lily knew it wasn't Lenny in the bed because she'd learned the sound of his breathing when he slept with her before he joined the army.

She knew then, he was not home. *Yet...* 'Yet' was a word she was becoming used to relying on. She had fought to believe in the word 'yet' all night as she waited for the sound of a door opening.

How many other women were lying in their beds tonight wondering if their man, son or brother was one of those who was saved? Or one of the bodies left on the beaches? Or a prisoner of war? It was a gruesome lottery.

Her stomach growled. She had barely eaten in all the time she had spent at the camp, and she had lost weight because of working harder. But it was not just her stomach that felt empty, her whole body felt empty, and she was not even hungry really. She felt sick, not hungry. Heartsick.

She sighed, turned to her other side, lifted up, thumped the pillow to try to aerate the feathers, rearranged it to a more comfortable plumpness and lay back down. Her thoughts whizzed around in circles like a fairground Waltzer.

The men she had seen in the camp appeared in her mind's eye; the blood on their skin and uniforms. She knew from what they had said, and from the look in their eyes, that though they had survived, many men had been killed on the beaches and in the water. The thoughts broke her heart open like a cracked egg.

She lay still, unable to stop thinking about those men, and wondering whether Lenny and Art had been left behind among them.

The next time she found herself turning over, the light had changed in the room, no longer tones of black but shades of a very deep, dark blue. Dawn. Birds began to sing, though the number of songs was nothing like the symphony around the fields where the camp was. She reached for the alarm clock and checked the time, it was twenty minutes past four. A long time before the next shift at the factory would start.

As the foreman didn't know she was back from the camp, she would not be expected there today, and she did not want to work. She wanted to wait here.

She threw the covers back, got up, searched out some clothes to wear and dressed. There was no point staying in bed when she could not sleep, she might as well go for a walk.

She crept downstairs with her boots held in her hand, stepping cautiously to avoid the creaky floorboards. In the kitchen she stopped and poured herself a glass of water from the tap and drank that down. Then she put on her boots, pulled the laces tight and tied bows on each. She lifted her coat off the hook, it wouldn't be warm outside yet, it still took the sun a bit of time to warm up the days.

She unlocked the back door with a light heart, and stepped out, a feeling of calm descending. So many of the happiest days of her life had been spent in this park with Lenny. The park was a place that would always bring her happiness. Whatever came next she would always feel like she was with Lenny here.

She walked along the twisting paths of the parterre garden. The soil beds that had been filled with roses were now full of vegetable plants. But vegetables could be pretty to look at too, and the herbs planted at the edges of the beds smelt beautiful: the mint, rosemary, sage and thyme.

She walked to the metal gate that separated the beds from the general park, to take the path around the perimeter.

There was a figure on a park bench. On the bench beneath the oak tree. Where she and Lenny had often sat. A man. A man in a khaki uniform. Her feet moved more quickly, taking her towards the figure. He was looking up, not towards her but at the horizon, his attention absorbed by thoughts. With every step she walked, the sunrise progressed and the world seemed lighter.

It was him!

It was Lenny!

Her legs ran without any thought, her arms pumping like the pistons on the trains. The hand-me-down coat that had been her stepmother's, with the patch on the elbow, had been loose a year ago and was now like a sack as it swayed around her while she ran.

'Lenny! Lenny!'

His head lowered, his eyes looking towards her. He stood, and then ran towards her too, his arms opening. 'Lily!'

She wrapped her arms around his neck as his arms wrapped about her middle. He picked her up and spun her around and around in a circle. He spun her so many times the park was still circling when he set her back on her feet.

'You're a sight for sore eyes,' he told her as his palms pressed either side of her face and he kissed her. She kissed him back, hungrily, desperately. She hadn't been sure she would ever be able to kiss him again, and she let him know how much she loved him in that kiss.

He broke it and rested his forehead against hers for a moment, catching his breath. 'I wasn't sure I'd make it home.'

'I've seen some of the men, I was terrified you adn't.'

'But I have.'

'Why are you out ere? Why didn't you come inside?'

'I got back half an hour ago and I didn't want to wake you. I thought I'd sit out here until it was a more sensible hour of the morning. What are you doing out here?'

'I couldn't sleep, I was worried about you. I came out to walk around the park, but perhaps I knew deep down you were ere.'

His lips pressed against hers again, his hands slipping to her waist, hers remaining around his neck.

The next time he broke the kiss, he immediately let go of her and stepped back, slipping free from her arms. She didn't ever want to let go of him. He descended to one knee on the gravel path. She thought he was picking something up, but he reached for her hand.

'Lily Franklin, will you marry me? I mean now. Let's not wait another day. I've saved up for a special licence, they won't have to read the banns.'

She was already engaged to him. She had already said yes. 'Yes,' she answered breathlessly... 'But you'll need Dad's consent an ee won't give it. Ee'll say no, even if it's just to spite me.'

He rose to his feet. 'I'll sort things with your dad. He'll agree. Like your sister said, he'll be keen to be a relative of my father's. I'll ask Mum and Dad to help me. We'll charm him into accepting.'

'Do you really think ee'll agree?'

'Yes. I won't take no for an answer. Shall we stay outside on the bench for an hour or so? I'd rather spend some time alone with you before we tell everyone else I'm here.'

'I'd like that.'

They eventually walked into the house at five thirty, because they knew the whole of the Railway Village would be waking up and their moment of peace and quiet would be broken anyway.

Mrs Faraday was in the kitchen, in her nightdress, dressing gown and slippers, making a pot of tea.

'Oh!' She pressed her palms against her cheeks as her lips formed an O of shock, and her eyebrows lifted so high they disappeared beneath the curls of her fringe. 'Leonard!' Her eyes swam as she rushed to hug him. 'Oh, darling. You're safe. I couldn't sleep. I have not slept for days worrying over you.' She held him tightly for minutes, then looked at Lily. 'And you are home too. Where did you meet?'

'In the park,' Lily said. 'I got up an ee was out there. I snuck into the ouse late yesterday, you were all in bed.'

Mrs Faraday hugged Lenny again, in a way that implied she was relishing the solidity of him just as much as Lily had. 'What a joy it is to have you here.'

'May we wake Dad?' Lenny asked. 'I want to ask Lily's father to agree to her marrying me today or tomorrow. I have forty-eight hours' leave, so I need her father to give his agreement before he goes to work, and I need Dad's help to persuade him. I want to marry Lily because...' He sucked in a long breath. 'At least then she will have my army pension if I die.'

'Oh, Lenny!' his mother declared at that awful thought.

'No, Lenny.' Lily rejected any thought of his death in the same moment his mother did. She reached for his hand and held it tight. 'Do not talk like that, not now, please...' *Not when so many others have died.* She did not say the last sentence because he had seen them die, and it was obvious it was why he had thought about his own death.

He gave her a smile that lacked his normal energy and humour.

'Your father's awake,' his mother said. 'He couldn't sleep either. I will ask him to get dressed. He will be down in a moment.'

* * *

When Lily had imagined Lenny's homecoming last night, she had pictured sitting beside him at the kitchen table, talking with the others, laughing together as they used to. She had not imagined knocking on her family's front door at six fifteen in the morning, with Lenny holding her hand so tightly it hurt.

Mr Faraday stood behind her, with his hands in his pockets, having made a promise to Lenny that he would not thump Lily's father if he said anything rude.

Polly opened the door. Her eyes instantly opened wider, with surprise and joy. 'Lily! Ello. What are you doin ere?'

'Hello, Polly. I brought her,' Lenny answered. 'We want to speak to your dad. Is he here?'

Polly nodded, no longer looking happy but nervous.

'It's alright,' Lily said. 'We just wanna talk to im. This is Lenny's father, Mr Faraday, but you've met im before, aven't you?'

Polly nodded and pressed back against the wall so they could all walk through the hall. 'Dad's in the kitchen,' she told them.

'Good morning, lass,' Mr Faraday acknowledged her as he passed her.

Lily breathed in and held the breath for a moment, bracing herself as Lenny turned the handle and opened the kitchen door.

He'd never stepped inside her house, he didn't know how she had lived before moving into his parents' home. How she had grown up, how her brothers and sisters were so squashed around the table it was hard to lift a spoon to your mouth without someone knocking it from your hand. That there were always shirts, underwear and nappies on a line hung across the kitchen, in case things didn't dry on the line outside. How the house usually stank of piss or puke because at least one of the little ones had had an accident or an illness of some sort.

Spoons chimed as they struck the bowls on the table as the children abandoned their watery-looking porridge.

'Lily!'

'Lily!'

'Lily!'

'Lily!'

Her siblings rose from their chairs and surrounded her in a swarm.

Her dad was sitting in his normal chair, the one armchair at the table. His knife and fork clattered down on the plate. He was eating bacon, not porridge. His gaze narrowed on Lily, his eyes accusing her of the worst crimes. 'Sit down, you lot,' he ordered her brothers and sisters, and they did not disobey her dad, so all the children returned to their seats.

'May we talk to you privately, Mr Franklin?' Lenny asked.

'Why?' Lily's father answered.

'We apologise for interrupting your breakfast, Mr Franklin, but it's quite important. Could we speak to you? If you don't mind?' Mr Faraday dived in. 'Perhaps we could speak in your parlour.'

Her father nodded quite calmly and stood.

Polly had said weeks ago that Lily should ask Lenny's dad to influence their father, because he would be impressed by having the chief gardener as a relative. It looked like she was right.

Lily's stepmother stood, as though she was going to come with them.

'Stay ere,' Lily's dad told her.

Lily glanced at her stepmother.

She made a stewed prune face at Lily that expressed her annoyance at being excluded from the conversation.

Her dad walked through the middle of Lily and Lenny, past Mr Faraday and led the way.

He opened the parlour door, stepped in and held it for Mr Faraday to follow, then let it fall for Lenny to catch. As the last in, Lily shut the door, she didn't want her brothers barging in, and they would.

'Would you like a seat?' her father offered.

'No, thank you,' Mr Faraday replied in a jovial voice. 'We don't intend to keep you for long, I know you have work to get to.'

Lily looked at Lenny as he took a deep breath… 'Mr Franklin, I have forty-eight hours' leave, and I would like your consent for me to marry Lily today or tomorrow, whenever Father Arnold can fit us in. I have the money for a special licence, we won't need to wait for the banns to be read. If we marry, I can provide for her whether I'm alive or dead, as she'll be entitled to my pension. So I'd rather marry now.'

'If you agree, we shall become relatives, Mr Franklin,' his father added in an amused tone. 'So of course you will be welcome to any vegetables from my own garden, as well as the park. I also have a crate of chickens on order, which means there'll be eggs too.' It was pure bribery, very nicely said.

Lily bit the inside of her lip to stop herself from smiling.

Her father looked from Mr Faraday to Lenny to Lily and back around them all again.

A very young baby wailed upstairs. Lily looked up at the ceiling as if she could see through it. It must be her nephew. It must be Betsy up there with the baby.

She looked back at her father, who was looking up. 'As Art come ome?' she asked. 'All the men av forty-eight ours' leave.'

His gaze lowered and he shook his head. She thought she could see what he was thinking – that if he didn't let her marry Lenny and she got herself knocked up, then she might be thrown out of the Faradays' house and he would have two unmarried mothers on his hands.

He nodded towards Mr Faraday, then nodded more strongly towards Lenny. 'Yes. You av my permission to marry er.'

'If Father Arnold can marry us during the lunch hour, I'll send a message and you can meet us at the church to sign the certificate,' Lenny told him.

Her father nodded again.

'Thank you...' Mr Faraday reached out, offering to shake her father's hand. They did shake.

'Thank you,' Lenny said. 'We'll get out of your way now.'

Lily returned to the kitchen, opened her arms and quickly circulated around her brothers and sisters, hugging them all. She wanted to ask Polly to be her bridesmaid but she knew their father wouldn't allow it. She hugged Polly the tightest.

'Why did you come?' Polly whispered in her ear.

'We used your plan. We're gettin married,' Lily whispered back.

Polly was grinning from ear to ear when they let go of each other.

'Av a good day, the lot of you,' Lily said, lifting a hand and waving.

'Goodbye,' Lenny called from the hallway.

Their fathers were still in the parlour. Lily let herself out, Lenny followed and a few seconds later, Mr Faraday came out and closed the door behind him. He moved in between Lenny and Lily as they walked along the street and rested a light hand on Lily's right shoulder and Lenny's left. 'Well, children, I think that went very well. Much better than expected.'

27

CATHERINE PEARCE

Tuesday 4 June

Catherine hadn't travelled back with Lily, she'd waited until Alfred was able to leave and travelled with him. They returned to their parents' house yesterday, just as Mrs Fletcher, the housekeeper, was serving lunch. They'd eaten the warm bread she had not long taken out of the oven, with cheese from a farm near Wroughton and honey from a neighbour who kept beehives.

'This is like dining in heaven,' her brother had said around a mouthful of bread and cheese.

Mrs Fletcher had blushed at the comment.

Their mother had shaken her head. 'I am glad to see you, Alfred, but do not speak with your mouth full.'

He had grinned.

A smile lifted Maggie's uncle's lips too.

That afternoon, Alfred returned to the station and caught a train to Purton to see his wife and children. Catherine's father had been at work, and had not known Alfred was safe and well until Alfred had already left.

There was no news about her other brothers, or Charles, yet. She had walked to his parents' house as soon as Alfred left to see if Charles was there, or if his mother had heard anything. If there had been a telegram it would have been sent there.

'*No. I haven't heard a word,*' she had told Catherine and welcomed her in for a cup of tea. She'd poured the tea from a bone-china pot with shaking hands. '*It's very nerve-wracking waiting. I feel quite sick.*' So had Catherine, and she still did.

She'd been finding tasks to distract her mind all morning.

A part of her wished she was working in the factory, but then the scarring on her right arm, having worked so many hours at the camp, was too sore to wear her wooden hand today, and when Charles did come, she wanted to be here. She was currently, clumsily, dusting her father's books, left-handed. She had rolled up her right sleeve, leaving the scar open to the air to let the blisters dry and heal. Before the war, her mother would have suggested rubbing butter on the blisters, but butter was too scarce now to waste on wounds.

A quick rap of the door-knocker sounded.

Catherine climbed down the short steps she was balanced on.

A second quick knock.

The undemanding sound spoke of someone who knew the inhabitants and knew the knock would be answered sooner or later so did not insistently knock again.

Charles! Her heart leapt with hope. She didn't bother wasting time looking through the window, she ran straight from her father's study to the front door, forgetting to even put down the dusting rag.

She pulled the door wide. 'Charles!' She screamed his name and threw herself into his arms.

He did not say her name, he did not hold her with his usual firm bear hug, but his arms did surround her and his face pressed into her hair and she felt him breathe in as if he had not breathed for days. 'God, you smell good,' he said, the warmth of his breath seeping through her hair to her neck and sending a tingle down her spine.

She leaned away from him, looking at his face and his chest. 'Are you well? Were you hurt?'

'Not physically,' he answered. 'Not I.'

But there were small cuts on his hands and his face, and a cut that had two thick black thread stitches sealing it together above one eyebrow.

She raised her arms to hold his face – it would have been with a palm on either cheek, but instead a duster rested against one side of his face and the blistered end of her blunt forearm the other.

'Don't do that.' He knocked her right arm down, sharply.

The gesture and the pitch in his voice punched her straight in the stomach, but she ignored the feeling. He had come home from a war, of course he was going to be a bit tetchy and tired.

Stepping back, she said, 'Come on,' beckoning him with the hand that wasn't there. 'Mama is in the kitchen.'

He looked at her moving arm, shook his head, swallowed and looked at her face.

Her right arm instinctively reached to take his hand, she then reached her left hand towards him instead. The one that held the duster. She dropped that on the hall table and held his hand. He wasn't wearing a coat or cap, just his uniform. The same khaki uniform she had seen thousands of men wearing over the last few days. It was clean, though, and it smelt newly washed.

'When did you get home?' she asked as she drew him along the hall.

'Late yesterday.'

'Where did you come from? I mean, where were you evacuated from? I helped out at a camp they were moving men to, so I heard a few stories. I met Alfred there, what were the chances of that? But it was lovely to see him.' She stopped in front of the closed kitchen door, realising she very much needed to kiss him, and she could not do that in front of her mother. She faced him, lifting to her toes and reaching her lips towards his.

His free hand came to the back of her head and he held her there as he dominated the kiss.

He tasted of tobacco and whisky.

Her right arm lifted and embraced his neck.

He broke the kiss and stepped back. Swallowing as though his throat were dry.

'You do not have to go into the kitchen and talk to anyone else if you would rather we went for a walk,' she said, recalling all those weary, shocked, grieving men in the camp. If he was one of the last to be evacuated... Most of the men had still been asleep this many hours after their return. Perhaps he had come to her because he could not sleep and needed distraction, not a conversation with her mother. 'We have house guests, a friend's aunt and uncle.'

'It's alright,' he answered. 'Do you have any actual tea, not mint or rose petals or some other concoction?'

'We do.' Her right hand reached for the door handle. She let go of him and opened it with her left. 'Mama, Mrs Fletcher, look who is here.'

He waited for her to enter before him. The women, including Maggie's aunt, were leaning over recipe books at the table, planning what could be made with the food products they'd found left in the shops.

'Charles!' Her mother stood, her chair scraping back on the kitchen tiles. She rushed about the table and wrapped her arms around his shoulders. They did not normally hug one another but today was exceptional.

His skin reddened.

She let him go and wiped tears from her cheeks. 'It is good to see you.'

'Thank you.'

'Mrs Richardson,' Catherine said to Maggie's aunt. 'This is my fiancé, Charles.' She looked at him. 'Mrs and Mr Richardson are staying here for a while, they've been evacuated from the coast.'

He nodded towards Mrs Richardson. 'Hello.'

'Hello,' she replied with a smile.

'Mrs Fletcher, Charles would like us to treat ourselves to a proper cup of tea. Would you mind putting the kettle on?'

'It's good to have you home safely, Mr Clifford,' the housekeeper said as she rose from the chair at the table.

'Do you mind if I smoke?' Charles asked the women. 'It has become a very bad habit of mine, I'm afraid.'

'Of course not,' Catherine's mother answered.

'I'll fetch you an ashtray,' Catherine said.

When she brought him the ashtray, Catherine sat next to him at the table, remaining as close as she could.

When he struck the match on the box to light his cigarette, Catherine watched his hands shaking. The kettle's whistle blew and he jumped and dropped the match. He picked it up instantly, blew out the flame and rubbed a finger over the black mark it had burned in the wooden table. 'Sorry.'

'Not to worry, dear,' her mother answered.

Catherine watched his expression as he smoked, while her mother and Mrs Fletcher and Mrs Richardson talked to each other. His mind seemed to drift off to somewhere miles away. His eyes were red with the weariness she'd seen in all the men, and his expression... She could only describe it as hollow. It was the shock. She had seen that look in many men's faces too. Her mother did not know what to say to him. Catherine had been speaking to soldiers for days, but this was Charles.

What had he seen and done?

'Did you arrive in Dover yesterday?' she asked. 'Were you one of the last off the beach at Dunkirk?'

His head spun and he looked at her, seemingly surprised by her voice. 'Yes.'

'I heard there were only stragglers left yesterday. Mostly French and Belgian soldiers. And the small boats were the only ones able to reach the beach because of all the wrecks.'

'Yes.' He nodded.

'Why were you one of the last...?' She dared to ask.

He took a long tug on his cigarette, drawing on it so hard the end glowed red. Then he breathed the smoke out upwards so he would not blow it in her face, and tapped the ash from the end into the ashtray. 'A man in my regiment was severely wounded, I could not leave him behind.' He looked at the ashtray as he spoke. 'The Germans had blown off his leg. I stayed back to get him to the beach. We made it, but by then most of the men had been withdrawn and there was no one to defend us as we crossed the beach. I held him up and ran towards the small boats, and a German's bullet shot him in the head. And that was that. I did not save his life. I could have stayed with him until he died and died myself, or let him go. I let him go, ran into the sea and swam out to a fishing boat that waited for me.'

'I'm sorry...' She could add *how awful or I am glad you came home to me.* But she said nothing else. Nothing would undo what he and all the other men had lived through. Nothing would bring back the men who died.

She reached out with her left hand and lay her palm over his arm. He did not look at her left hand though, he looked at the blunt, reddened and blistered, ugly end of her right arm in such a way that she moved that arm off the table. It was a judgemental look. A look of... Was it disgust?

'Did you see the paper today?' her mother asked, choosing to change the subject entirely. 'Queen Mary bought shirts and socks in Jolly's department store in Bath and took them to one of the camps for the evacuated men.'

'I did see.' Charles tore his gaze away from Catherine and looked at her mother. 'I read the paper this morning. Mother showed me all the headlines last night too. She has been keeping the newspapers for the last couple of weeks because she wanted me to know how proud the nation is of its fighting men.' There was an empty, emotionless sound in his voice.

Catherine glanced at the clock on the kitchen wall. It was ten past eleven. 'My friends are getting married at twelve thirty, at St Mark's, in the Railway Village. I was going to go, but I won't unless you'll come with me. Would you like to come? It might take your mind off things.'

He looked back at her. 'Nothing will take my mind off things, Catherine.'

Again, she didn't know how to answer.

'But I will come and meet these new friends of yours. Will they all be there?'

'Yes. I think so.'

28

LILY FRANKLIN

Lily thought it was impossible to organise a wedding in a day, but Lenny and his mother proved her wrong.

Lenny had acquired a Common Marriage Licence that morning, and his mother had loaned Lily her wedding dress. She had been sewing all evening yesterday, taking up the hem and taking in the side seams so it would fit. The wedding ring was his grandmother's. It was a little loose on Lily's finger, but they had agreed that could be fixed after the wedding.

So, there she was, walking up the aisle towards Lenny who waited at the altar rail, looking back towards her with the warmest smile on his face.

She held a bouquet his father had made from sprigs of lavender, mint and the sage that was flowering at the edges of the vegetable beds. The bouquet smelt heavenly.

Her father was walking beside her. He had not offered to hold her arm and she was glad. She didn't even want him here. He just had to be here to consent. Her friends stood in the choir stalls, Catherine beside the fiancé Lily had met for the first time today. Lily's lips parted in the broadest smile she'd felt them form for weeks as she looked at Polly, who was closest to the altar rail.

Lenny's father stood beside him, as his best man, and on his side of the church his mother sat closest to the rail and beside her, Dietrich, because he was Lenny's friend. They'd been close when they worked together before Lenny joined the army.

All their friends were in working clothes. They'd come from the factory, this was their lunch period and Lenny and Lily had ten minutes to be wed, as another couple and their witnesses were waiting outside the church.

Lenny had told her he had been in a queue of twenty men all organising their marriage licences, so they were not the only ones grasping this brief opportunity.

She didn't care that the people in the choir stalls should be her bridesmaids, that she hadn't been able to have her other brothers and sisters here, that there would be no big wedding breakfast or honeymoon. She just wanted to marry Lenny.

'Ello,' she said when she reached him.

'Who gives this woman to be married?' Father Arnold said immediately.

'I do,' her father answered. He would have taken her hand and given it to Lenny; she moved it away and gave Lenny her hand herself, she didn't need her father to do it.

He stepped away.

Her stepmother wasn't here either. He had not let her come. But Lily didn't care, she didn't want her here; she had never been kind to Lily or stopped her dad hitting her.

The only person who was missing was Art. No one had heard a word from him yet.

'Hello,' Lenny whispered as his thumb stroked over the back of her hand.

The service was a whirlwind, she would not remember a single word Father Arnold said, or she said, or Lenny said. Other than, 'I will.'

They signed the register and certificate, then left the church holding hands, man and wife, only fifteen minutes after she had walked in.

A photographer had volunteered to take pictures of every couple outside the church's side door. They let him take a picture of the two of them, then one with their friends, and one with Mr and Mrs Faraday. Her father had already left and taken Polly with him.

Lily embraced Naomi, Violet, Maggie and Dietrich before they left to walk back to the factory. Then she, Lenny, his parents, and Catherine and her fiancé walked back to Park Lodge. Mrs Faraday had made a nice meal and they sat in the proper dining room rather than the kitchen, with Lily still dressed in her wedding dress, though she had removed the short veil.

As they ate and talked, she tried to get to know Catherine's fiancé. Charles was a bit odd, not very talkative, and he left the table three times to smoke cigarettes. He couldn't sit still when he was there either. And his hands shook as he lifted his glass of wine.

Mr Faraday had opened a bottle of red wine. *I've been keeping this for a celebration.*

Lily remembered Lionel, who had the nightmare in the camp. She kept thinking about him and the other men she had seen shouting in their sleep. And the men who had seemed nervous of every sound and unable to settle. The men who were struggling to cope with their experiences.

The anxiety she'd felt just worrying about Lenny seemed so pathetic in comparison.

When Catherine and Charles said they had to leave, Lenny and Lily said they would walk to the park gate with them. When they said goodbye, Lily held Catherine tight. 'Thank you for comin.' Catherine was still the friend she was closest to, because of the months Catherine had lived in the Faradays' house.

The sound of an engine lifted her gaze to the sky, and she released Catherine.

Charles made the oddest sound, and raised a hand over his head, ducking and turning away.

'It's just the RAF,' Lenny said to him. 'They fly over here all the time.' Lenny looked up. 'Spitfires,' he announced, watching the formation of planes pass overhead.

Charles straightened up, his hand lowering. 'Bloody bombers.'

He had looked so terrified for a moment, Lily felt like hugging him.

Catherine's damaged arm reached towards him, offering that hug. He knocked her arm aside.

A frown pulled at Lily's brow; it seemed a mean thing to do.

'Goodbye, then,' Catherine said.

Lenny nodded. 'Thank you for coming, Cath, it meant a lot to have you here.' He looked at Charles. 'I am sure you had better things to do with your time, sir.'

Charles shook his head. 'I wanted to meet Catherine's friends, and this was important to her.'

'Thank you,' Lily repeated, smiling. Charles didn't look well enough to be here, physically perhaps, yes, but not mentally. Catherine had whispered to her earlier that Charles had only left France yesterday.

More engines roared above them, but this time the sound was different, and for the first time in many months the factory's hooters burst into life. They all looked at the sky. Even from the ground Lily could see the German swastika painted on the side of the aircraft.

'Germans!' Catherine screamed out.

They were actually here. Lily's heart leapt with a desire to run, but she was disorientated by panic and didn't know where to run to.

The factory hooters continued to call out the warning.

'Let's get into the air raid shelters,' Lenny ordered, sounding calm, as though air raids were an everyday occurrence and he knew exactly what to do. But this was the first sight of the Germans here in Swindon. *There were Germans in Swindon!*

Catherine reached for Charles with her left hand, as Lenny grasped Lily's hand.

Lily lifted the long skirt of the wedding dress and together they ran towards the domed, long, narrow air raid shelters at the church end of the park.

Charles stumbled but stayed on his feet. His skin was yellowish, the colour of a scrubbed potato, he looked sickly.

Mr and Mrs Faraday came outside, saw them and hurried in the same direction, towards the rows of previously unused air raid shelters.

Sirens roared into life on the other side of the town. A circular sound. High-pitched then low-pitched.

Lily's heart hammered out its beat as they ran.

The aeroplanes were not overhead now but they could hear them, and the sound was different to any aircraft engine she knew.

Other people were running towards the shelters, from the Railway Village, and Faringdon and Rodbourne roads.

Now Hitler had won France, had he come for Britain already?

Lenny opened the door of the shelter, pulled Lily in and held the door for Catherine and Charles to enter. Charles sat on the bench on the far side and immediately clasped his head in his hands. He rocked slightly. Catherine's eyes watched his reaction with concern.

Lenny stroked a hand along Lily's arm, as other people ran through the door.

'Don't worry,' he said. 'It didn't sound like they were loaded with bombs. I think it must be a reconnaissance flight. They're looking at what we're doing to decide what they do next.'

They sat on a bench on the near side of the shelter, separated from Catherine and Charles by others entering. She felt sick. 'I'm sorry. I'm not brave,' she whispered for his ears only. 'I was scared for you, before you came ome. Terrified. It made me sick. I feel sick now.'

His warm hand wrapped about hers. The callouses, a sign of hard labour, on his palm were rough on the softer skin on the back of her hand. 'I'd be surprised if you didn't feel sick. My stomach is upside down and inside out right now. I can't explain any of this, Lily. I'm just fighting to stop it. But the one thing I do know is that it's normal to be scared. Every single man was scared in France. What we do next is the important thing, and you went to the camp to help. You didn't let the fear stop you. Courage – isn't that what the King said? We will all need courage.'

She nodded and rested her head on his shoulder. Then remembered – *she was his wife!* Her heart filled with happiness. It did not matter what went on outside, for a few hours more she had Lenny with her, and she was his wife.

Charles was sitting bent forward, with his elbows on his knees and his hands covering the back of his head, as if he were hiding from the aircraft, and protecting himself from being hit. She didn't imagine a human in the open could do anything to prevent a bomb from hurting them.

'Charles,' Lenny called to him through the other people entering the shelter. 'They're just scouting. I'm sure. They don't sound loaded.'

Charles's hands fell and he straightened up in a quick movement as if he had only just realised what he was doing, and his hands instead searched his jacket pockets.

His left hand pulled out a box of matches, his right, a packet of cigarettes.

The tip of the cigarette quivered as he put it between his lips so he could light it. He struck the match and held the flame to the end. Then shook the match to extinguish it, crossed one leg over the other and leaned back against the wall of the shelter. He sucked on the cigarette and blew out the smoke.

Catherine watched him. He did not seem to notice her.

Others in the shelter lit cigarettes.

When the factory's hooters fell silent, everyone looked at each other, unsure what that meant.

Had the German aeroplanes gone?

No one else came through the door. No one talked. Everyone listened. Waiting... For the sound of an aircraft or bombs.

Lily coughed. The increasing amount of cigarette smoke trapped in the small shelter was like a smog.

The factory hooters sounded again. A short sharp blast of sound.

'That's the all-clear,' someone said.

'Are you sure?'

'It's so bloody long since this war began and they told us about the air raids, I don't remember what's what.'

'Nor me. I didn't think this would ever happen, even a month ago.'

No one had their gas masks with them. No one carried them any more. Like everyone else, Lily would have to carry hers now, in case the Germans tried to poison them.

'It's definitely the all-clear,' someone else confirmed, as they climbed over outstretched legs, past Lenny, Charles, Lily and Catherine, to reach the door. They walked out and did not come back. More people went outside.

'There's no aircraft,' they shouted back into the shelter.

'Come on,' Lenny said to Lily. 'Let's get out of here. This isn't where I want to spend my wedding day.'

29

MAGGIE ABBOT

A quick knock struck the back door. Maggie glanced up at the clock on the kitchen wall, it was nearly half past seven. It was late for callers, although the evening was still light.

Perhaps it was Ron, she hadn't seen him since he had returned from stoking steam engines.

She rose from her seat, leaving her sisters and Mr and Mrs Faraday at the table. Everyone apart from Lily and Lenny was in the kitchen, no one had left the room after dinner. Maggie presumed for the same reason she had stayed downstairs, because there was a couple enjoying the few hours of their honeymoon in Lily's bedroom upstairs. The bride and groom had not bothered to come and eat dinner.

Maggie didn't blame them. The train Lenny had to catch left at nine o'clock tomorrow morning.

Maggie turned the handle and opened the door smiling.

Her smile dropped. 'Polly. Hello.' Lily's sister stood there, with tearstains on grubby cheeks and red puffy eyes. 'Come in. What's wrong?'

Chair legs around the table scraped the stone flags, as everyone got up.

Polly sobbed and burst into tears, her shoulders shaking.

Maggie wrapped her arms around her. She was thin, Maggie could feel every bone in her body. Polly stepped back, freeing herself, and choked in a breath.

'I'll fetch Lily,' Mrs Faraday said and left the room.

'Is it your father?' Mr Faraday asked.

She shook her head.

'Can you tell us?'

She opened her mouth, but any words were strangled by another sob and a flood of tears rolling down her cheeks.

Maggie's instinct was to hold her again, but she had stepped away.

She wiped the tears from her cheeks with a wrist.

'Come and sit down.' Dot took charge. 'Have you eaten? Would you like anything to eat or drink?'

'No, thank you. I'll stand.'

'Lily might be a little while,' Maggie told her carefully, without explanation.

Polly nodded, accepting she would have to wait.

The ceiling creaked. Lily's room was above the kitchen. Maggie imagined Lily or Lenny getting out of bed to answer his mother's knock, opening the door a crack to see who it was and finding out why they were being disturbed.

The sounds upstairs became more urgent, hurried, heavy steps on the floorboards.

A couple of minutes later, quick footsteps ran down the stairs and then the door between the kitchen and the hall opened sharply and Lily rushed in.

Lenny followed her, in front of Mrs Faraday.

'Pol.' She rushed to her sister.

Polly accepted her embrace and sobbed into the crook of Lily's neck.

'What is it?' Lily's black curls were wilder than usual, and her lips were swollen and reddened by kisses.

Something instinctual stirred a feeling low in Maggie's stomach, a longing, a hunger. Jealousy. But she was not jealous that Lily had Lenny, it was only that she looked so... loved.

Maggie thought of that horrible kiss from the man on the train, then shook the memory out of her thoughts.

'Art's missin in action...' Polly managed to say. 'They think ee's dead. The telegram said they couldn't bring any more men ome, an ee isn't ere. They think ee died at Dunkirk but they don't av is body.'

It wasn't Maggie's relative, she knew Art by sight only. She hadn't ever spoken to him. But her stomach rolled over, the sick taste of bile rising in the back of her throat.

Lily wailed, the sound was like a noise Mr Tabs might make in a catfight. 'No.' Lily shook her head, looking at her sister as though Polly had lied.

Lenny held them both, Polly and Lily, braced tight in his arms, in a way that seemed to hold them on their feet as much as hug them.

He was barefoot, dressed in his shirt and trousers, his braces hanging down.

Lily broke free from his hold. 'I need to go ome,' she said.

'You can't,' Polly replied. 'Dad's mad. Ee's drinkin. Ee's blamin everyone.'

'What about Betsy?' Lily asked.

Polly didn't answer, her voice too strangled by emotions again.

Betsy would be left an unmarried mother now.

Maggie shared a brief look with Dot. Her sister had realised the same thing. Poor Betsy's fate was the one that might have been Dot's.

'I need to go,' Lily said.

Lenny caught hold of Lily's wrist. 'No, don't. You'll only end up hurt. I can go and bring Betsy here if you want to see her?'

'She's shut erself in er room with the baby, so Dad can't get in,' Polly told Lily. 'She as moved the chest of drawers in front of the door. She won't come out until Dad's gone. There's no point goin there.'

Lily seemed to collapse onto one of the kitchen chairs, as if her legs could no longer hold her up. Her palms rested flat on the table and she stared at the back of her hands. On her left hand, her new wedding ring glittered alongside her engagement ring.

Lily and Lenny would not enjoy any more of their wedding day.

'I'm sorry,' Maggie said, walking forward and resting a hand on Lily's shoulder. Then she leaned and hugged Lily's shoulders. Lily was stiff and cold.

'Come along, Polly. You should have a cup of milk with a spoonful or two of honey,' Mrs Faraday said – as ever, the guardian angel, mother to them all.

Maggie thanked God for the Faradays every night in her prayers, for their kindness and generosity. She knew how different her life might have been now if her family had not been taken in by them.

'And I'll add a dash of brandy for the shock,' Mr Faraday said.

'Would you make Lily one too?' Lenny asked.

30

LILY FARADAY

Lily and Lenny were making love when Lenny's mother had tapped the door and called quietly, *'I'm sorry, Lily, your sister's here. She'd like to talk to you.'*

Lenny had withdrawn from her body with a whispered curse and a twisted smile, then walked over to the door, opened it a crack and peered around it. 'Lily will be down in a minute,' he had said.

'It's urgent, Leonard. Polly is in a real tiswas.'

Lily had heard the words and known something was horrifically wrong. Polly wouldn't normally come out at this hour...

She'd thought it was something to do with their dad. She'd forgotten about Art. She hadn't thought about him for at least three or four hours. Not since she and Lenny had gone to bed. She had forgotten to think of him and pray for him and now he was dead.

The heels of her bare feet tapped in a jittery motion on the cold stone flags, as Polly sat down next to her. Lily reached out and held Polly's hand.

Art was so much older than the younger ones that they had not spent much time with him. But he had given them more attention, kindness and love than their dad and her stepmother had, and she knew the children loved him regardless. He was an idol to the boys.

The tears diminished, the pain did not.

Lenny's fingers rested on her shoulder and squeezed gently.

Yesterday she had compared the men's return to some sort of grotesque lottery. She and Catherine had won. Betsy had lost.

But what about Catherine's other brothers? And Naomi's brothers...

Lily's heartbeat skipped out of its regular time. She wanted to run and do something. But there was nothing she could do. She couldn't go to Art... She didn't even have his body to hold.

A knock sounded on the back door, one sharp, hard strike of knuckles.

Everyone looked over, and Lily's heart leapt with hope. She stared at the door as though Art would walk through it. As Marjorie turned to open it, she pictured Art standing there, with his arms open wide, waiting to embrace her. 'Ey, our kid,' she heard him say in her mind. 'They were wrong, I just got back. Nothin is gonna kill me...'

It was Violet who entered.

Lily's heart sank to the soles of her feet, with such a weight it felt as heavy as the iron implements she moved around in the works.

'Lily.' Violet rushed in. 'I just heard. I am so sorry. I know you and your brother were close.' She leaned down and wrapped her arms around Lily. 'The post office received dozens of telegrams for the factory workers. The messenger boys have been taking them out all over. Ron was in the Glue Pot when your father came in, he came home and told me. He knew I would want to come and see you. I'm sorry,' she said again.

Lily was sorry too, but the last thing Art had said to her when she begged him not to volunteer for any dangerous action, was, *'You know me, Lily. I won't be able to old my feet back. But if the worst appens, you'll know I died doin my best to make sure those bastards don't get this far...'*

He had died to save others. He had died fighting against Hitler. He had known he might die and still chosen to go, he was one of the first to go, a volunteer.

She wiped the tears from her eyes and looked at Lenny, her lips downturned. Her heart was broken in half. She had lost Art forever. It was hard to believe it, but at least Lenny had lived. She reached out a hand towards him, as her other hand held Polly's. She was not alone. She had this family and these friends. Art would be proud of her. She must continue to make him proud, and...

'We must do all we can to win this war,' she told everyone. 'Otherwise, is death an the deaths of everyone else who died will be in vain. To onour is life, we must keep fightin...'

'You don't need to worry about that, Lily, we will,' Mr Faraday said as he walked forward and rested a hand on Lily's shoulder, in the same way he might rest a hand on Lenny's. It was a fatherly touch that gently squeezed her shoulder. She looked up, he was looking at Polly.

'And you, young Polly, and all your brothers and sisters are welcome here anytime. You must consider yourself a part of this family, and our house another home.'

'Thank you, Mr Faraday,' Lily said, wiping the tears from her cheeks, only to cry some more as she saw his eyes welling up.

Her father would probably never shed a tear for Art. Emotion like that wasn't in her father.

'I think it's a good time to stop calling me Mr Faraday, don't you, Lily? Use Dad or Father, or whatever you would like to call me.' He smiled and nodded slightly, encouraging her to agree.

He had asked her to call him Hector previously, but she'd told him it would be too odd when she'd called him Mr Faraday all her life. But she would be glad of a proper father. 'Thank you, Dad,' she answered.

31

LILY FARADAY

Wednesday 5 June

Lily lay still on the single bed she shared with her husband. Mr Tabs had curled himself up beneath the covers like a furry hot water bottle beside her feet, tickling her toes.

She was doing her best not to wake Lenny. He needed his rest. He would be working day and night again from tomorrow. They'd told him before he'd been given leave to build up his strength because they would be building Britain's defences when they reported back for duty.

Her mind was too full of Art to sleep. Memories. Imaginings – she couldn't help wondering how he'd died. If he'd been afraid. Alone. Lain in pain for long. How long had it taken him to die? One second or hours? One single deadly bullet or a bomb strike? Or days... with a festering wound? She had to stop asking herself about these things. She may never know the answers, and imagining the answers would not help her or him or anyone.

She would work as many hours as it was humanly possible to from the day Lenny left. Hitler was not going to get away with murdering Art. Christian or not, she hoped it was a bomb she helped make that killed the man who'd killed Art.

Lenny's foot lashed out suddenly and Mr Tabs meowed with a startled, disgruntled note as he was kicked. The sounds that came from Lenny's throat made Lily think he was shouting in a dream, although he didn't actually say any recognisable words. His arms thrashed, fighting the covers, only tying himself up in them. She didn't know if she should wake him or leave him to wake himself.

Her imagination travelled again, to the beach where Art had died and where Lenny might be in his dreams. She couldn't leave him there among the bodies and bombs.

She turned, facing him. 'Lenny,' she whispered. The room was pitch-black, the sky beyond the curtains had clouded over and she couldn't see him, only feel his movements and hear his distress. She touched his face, her fingers finding his forehead that was damp with sweat.

She touched his cheek, where sharp stubble protruded.

'Lenny,' she said more loudly.

He fought harder, trying to free his arms from the sheet.

'Lenny.' She rose up onto her elbow. 'Lenny,' she said much louder, concerned for him.

He growled, his hand breaking free, and it swung around in a punch, struck her shoulder, knocked her off balance and sent her flying onto the floor with a bump.

The sound of her hitting the floor and her yelp woke him.

He scrabbled off the bed. 'What happened? Are you alright?'

'I think so, apart from a bruised bum. You were dreamin, I was tryin to wake you, an you it out.'

'I'm sorry.'

'It's not your fault.'

Mr Tabs meowed, from somewhere in the room.

Lenny's hand found Lily's in the dark and pulled, hauling her onto her feet.

A different sound. A click.

Lily stood silent in the dark, listening. So did Lenny.

There was no other sound. 'Was that a mouse?' she suggested. 'Mr Tabs, your untin skills are needed.'

Click. There it was again.

'That's something hitting the windowpane.' Lenny's voice turned away from her.

She reached out a hand, searching through the darkness for the edge of the bed, and used that as a guide to walk towards the window.

Click.

'Lenny?' Her voice searched for him. She could hear his bare feet on the carpet.

'It's alright,' he whispered. His voice did not sound as though everything was alright. He sounded nervous.

He reached the window first. The curtains swished along the rail as he pulled them open quickly, as if he expected to find something or someone on the other side, even though they were on the first floor.

She could see his silhouette now, darker than the dark outside.

'What is it?' she asked.

'There's someone out there.' He reached for the window latch.

'Be careful,' Lily said, imagining a Nazi spy with a gun, ready to shoot Lenny and take him from her too. But she knew that was ridiculous. She hurried the last few feet and leaned to look past her husband.

She was wearing her nightdress, Lenny was naked. He didn't seem to care, though, as he pushed the window wide open. They both looked down.

'Lily,' a voice called, not shouting, but trying to make herself heard from the ground below.

'Betsy?' Lily called back. 'What are you doin ere?'

'I need to speak to you.'

Betsy must have thrown pieces of gravel at the window with the hand that was free, her other held a bundle of what might be rags. But Lily knew it was her nephew.

'I'll come down,' Lily called, as quietly as possible, hoping not to wake anyone else.

'She must av snuck out, now Dad's asleep,' she said to Lenny as he shut the window. 'Ee's probably flat out drunk. Come on. I bet she's lookin for somewhere to stay.'

Lenny held back to put his trousers on and pull a shirt over his head, but Lily hurried out of the room and down the stairs as quickly and quietly as she could, racing to the front door.

She slid back the bolts and reached for the key to unlock the door. As she opened it, Lenny walked down the stairs.

Betsy stood on the doorstep. 'You av to take im, Lily' she said, holding out the baby wrapped in a blanket in her arms. His feet kicked within the blanket.

Lily didn't take the child.

'We can't stay with your family any more. Your dad doesn't want us there. Ee was fine with it when Art was sendin money. But now Art's dead an we weren't married, I'll get nothin. We can't live on nothin. And because I aint married, no one will give me work, an ee will always be a bastard. You're married now, ee as your colourin, if you raise im as yours, people will forget ee was mine. You can say you're is mother. Is life will be better with you, an I'll go away an find work somewhere no one knows me.'

Lily didn't even raise her hands. She didn't know what to say.

'Please. Ee'll have a decent life with you.' Betsy looked beyond Lily. Those words were said to Lenny.

Lily glanced over her shoulder and saw Lenny standing close behind her.

'Please,' Betsy said to him. 'I know you'll both be kind to im. Ee would be safe with you.' She looked back at Lily. 'And ee'd be loved. Take im. Please.'

A touch brushed Lily's waist. Lenny had stepped closer and put his arm around her. 'It's up to you, Lily,' he said quietly. 'She doesn't want children, Betsy. We don't plan to have them.'

'If we don't take im,' Lily said, 'what will you do?'

'I'll leave im at the police station, on the step. I can't keep im. I don't av any money. I don't av an ome.'

'Where will you go?'

'I don't know, somewhere there's work. Somewhere away from ere where I can work an no one will know I've ad a baby. I was just goin to get on the first train that stops at the station in the mornin.'

Lily stared at her, unsure. Then glanced at Lenny.

'It is up to you,' he said again.

'I don't want im to go to just anyone. Art wouldn't want that either. But what can I do...?' She bit her lip.

'If you want to raise him, Lily, we'll raise him and we'll love him, and do everything we can for him,' Lenny said.

The baby made a mewling sound. Not a cry, a whimper, perhaps to say he was cold or just to say he wanted to be held tighter.

Lily reached out and took him from Betsy's arms. She expected him to be heavier than he was. She brought him to her chest, and with one hand moved the blanket away from his face. Dark inquisitive eyes looked at her, and a hand escaped the blanket and caught hold of her finger.

She couldn't let him go to anyone else. He wouldn't know who his father was. And what if they didn't love him?

Her gaze lifted to Betsy. 'We'll look after im. But I'll tell im the truth that is father was Art, an is mother is Betsy Lloyd.'

'Then you won't be doin im a favour. Ee'll always be a bastard.'

Lily breathed in and out and didn't answer. She couldn't think of the future. 'Ow will I feed im?'

'I was givin im formula. I av it in a basket. I brought it with me, with is bottle an nappies. I didn't think you'd av anythin.'

Lily shook her head. There was nothing in the Faradays' home for a baby.

'Ee'll want a feed soon. Ee'll be ungry.' Betsy looked down at the baby, now in Lily's arms. Her fingertip stroked his cheek, and his eyes turned to her. 'I'll miss you, little Arthur. I aint givin you up because I don't love you, it's because I do.' Even in the darkness, the tears on Betsy's cheeks sparkled – like ice, Lily thought.

'You'll av a better life ere,' Betsy told him. 'I promise. Your Auntie Lily is goin to love you with all er eart an you'll av everythin you need. If you came with me, we'd never av nothin. You'd be ungry an cold.'

'You don't have to let him go,' Lenny said. 'I'd give you some money, or whatever you need.'

Betsy's gaze lifted to him sharply. 'I'd still be an unmarried mother, no one would give me an ome or a job, an...' She looked back down at little Arthur. 'Ee'd always be a bastard.

'I love you.' She leaned and kissed his cheek. Then she smelt the crown of his head, in a way that said she was trying to remember the smell forever. One of her tears dripped onto his forehead. She wiped it off his skin with her thumb. 'Goodbye, my darlin.' She turned away quickly, as though she were tearing herself free from him and walked a few paces to a shadowed area, where she picked up a basket woven from hazel branches. She brought it to them.

Lenny reached around Lily and accepted it. 'Thank you.'

'No, thank you,' she said. Then she sniffed, looked down at the baby for one last time, then turned away.

Lily stood in the open doorway, watching until she couldn't see Betsy in the dark any more.

She turned and looked at Lenny, with her nephew in her arms. The nephew that she'd just agreed to raise.

32

MAGGIE ABBOT

Most mornings, Maggie walked downstairs with aching heavy limbs, her body complaining about being forced to rise and work again. Her heart heavy. Today she felt... determined was the word. Determined to carry on, to make as many bombs as she could produce, and win this war. Hitler and his horrible Nazis had to go.

She heard someone on the stairs behind her, glanced back and saw Marjorie and Dot.

'Good morning,' Marjorie said.

Dot smiled.

'Morning,' Maggie answered, and carried on to the bottom of the stairs. She waited for her sisters there and walked to the kitchen beside them.

'Did you sleep?' Marjorie asked Maggie.

'Not very much.'

'Nor me. I kept thinking about the men left in France.'

'And me,' Dot answered. 'And the sailors who are still out on the sea.'

Maggie nodded, her mind had turned to the men left behind now too. The euphoria of welcoming all the rescued men home was long gone already.

She reached out and opened the kitchen door, then stood stock-still. Staring. Her hand lifted and rubbed her right eye, as if she might be half asleep and dreaming.

Lily was sitting at the kitchen table feeding a baby from a banana-shaped glass bottle. The child was coloured, so it must be Maggie's brother's. The boy sucked greedily, noisily, on a rubber teat. Lenny stood behind Lily, clothed in his full uniform, leaning back against the kitchen sink, with his hands behind him.

'Blimey, I didn't know you could have them that quick,' Marjorie joked.

Lenny looked at her as a low chuckle broke from his throat.

Lily looked up from the child. 'Betsy brought im ere last night. She's gone. She didn't wanna keep im.'

Maggie glanced over her shoulder towards Dot.

Dot didn't look at her, she walked to the kettle, picked it up and took it to the tap to fill it.

'Are you his mum and dad now then?' Marjorie asked, heading for the bread bin.

'It seems so,' Lenny answered.

Lily glanced at him, her expression saying she was trying to judge the tone of his voice.

Unlike Maggie or Lenny, Lily had plenty of experience of looking after babies in her house, but she'd always said she didn't want one herself.

'Wife and mother all in one day,' Maggie said. She didn't know what to say, really. It was a big step.

'Yes.' Lily's voice was a little breathless. A note that implied she felt overwhelmed by the notion of it.

'How will you work?' Marjorie asked her, as she opened a drawer and found the bread knife.

Lily looked at her blankly. Her eyes saying she had not had chance to think about anything like that.

'You won't be able to work now, anyway,' Maggie said. 'GWR don't let married women work.'

Lily's mouth dropped open. In the rush of these huge changes, Maggie could see Lily had not considered the results of the decisions she had made.

Dot turned quickly, leaving the kettle on the gas stove to heat. 'I wouldn't worry. They need the women even more now. They won't ask you to leave.'

'The newspaper certainly does indicate that.' Lenny leaned forward and picked it up from the top of the pine table. He tossed it in Maggie's direction. 'Britain lost thirty thousand men in France, but the Navy rescued three hundred and thirty-five thousand of us. We haven't lost, but if we're going to win, production is key. We still have soldiers, but we soldiers, and the pilots and sailors, need equipment. GWR can't let the women who have married go now, this country needs you women in the factories as much as it needs all of us to fight.'

'What's that?' Maggie reached out and picked up the paper, having spotted a headline. She read the article on the front page, then said, 'Churchill was deploying his oratory skills in Parliament yesterday. I quote' – she did an impression of his voice – '"Even though large tracts of Europe and many old and famous states have fallen or may fall into the grip of the Gestapo and all the odious apparatus of Nazi rule, we shall not flag or fail.

'"We shall go on to the end, we shall fight in France, we shall fight on the seas and oceans, we shall fight with growing confidence and growing strength in the air, we shall defend our island, whatever the cost may be.

'"We shall fight on the beaches, we shall fight on the landing grounds, we shall fight in the fields and in the streets, we shall fight in the hills; we shall never surrender, and even if, which I do not for a moment believe, this island or a large part of it were subjugated and starving, then our Empire beyond the seas, armed and guarded by the British fleet, would carry on the struggle, until, in God's good time, the new world, with all its power and might, steps forth to the rescue and the liberation of the old…"'

Her voice had silenced everyone.

She folded the paper and put it back on the table.

'Lenny's right,' Dot said. 'They've been pushing us to speed up production for months, they can't lose skilled workers, Lily.'

'But who will look after little Arthur while I work?' Lily said, in the same moment that Mrs Faraday walked through the door.

All their eyes turned to the older woman and Lenny smiled towards his mother, his smile lifting to a grin as her lips parted in an O of surprise when she saw the baby.

'We've adopted,' Lenny said. 'Betsy brought him to us in the night.'

'I'm sorry,' Lily apologised. 'Dad won't support er any longer, an as they weren't married, she didn't know what else to do.'

'Lily, dear, do not apologise for taking in a poor baby. I approve. What a hard decision for his mother. Poor woman. She could have lived with us.'

'She wouldn't,' Lenny answered. 'She didn't want to face the stigma of being a single mother, and...' He looked down at the baby still greedily drinking his formula. '...she didn't want Arthur to face the stigma of being a bastard. She wants us to register him as ours.'

'Will you?' Maggie asked.

'We haven't decided,' Lenny answered with a one-shouldered shrug. 'Lily wants him to know who his father is.'

'Who wants some toast?' Marjorie called out.

'Me.'

'Yes, please.'

'I would love some, thank you, Marjorie,' Mrs Faraday said as she walked across to Lily, settled a hand on Lily's shoulder and leaned forward to look at the baby.

'He's charming. What a lovely little fellow. Arthur, did you say?'

Lily nodded. 'Arthur, after is father.'

'Arthur. Hello to you.' She rubbed his arm. 'I will be your grandmother.'

'We were just wondering who could look after him while Lily works, Mum,' Lenny said in a tone that encouraged a response. 'We had no chance to think about things like that last night and GWR need Lily at the factory.'

'Well, apart from the committee meetings, I am at home...' It was the offer Maggie knew Lenny had hoped for.

'You wouldn't mind?' Lily asked her.

'I would love to look after him,' she answered.

The child's lips released the bottle. It was empty. Lily lifted him to her shoulder and began rubbing his back with the flat of her palm. She did it so confidently it was obvious she knew how to care for babies.

'May I get to know him?' Mrs Faraday reached out her hands. Lily lifted him and passed him over, in the same moment that Mr Faraday walked in.

'Who is this little fellow?'

'This is Arthur,' Mrs Faraday said. 'We are grandparents. Lily and Lenny are going to adopt him and bring him up.'

Mr Faraday's eyebrows slid up then down. 'Oh.'

'Do you mind?' Lenny asked him.

'No, son... Of course not. Of course not,' he repeated as if his mind was adjusting to the idea as he spoke. 'Hello, young man.' He stepped forward and introduced himself to Arthur. One of the baby's tiny hands reached out and touched Mr Faraday's nose.

Maggie watched Dot. She was staring at Arthur, her attention transfixed and her eyes were swimming. She would give herself away, anyone looking at her would see the craving in her eyes, and it was far beyond a broody look.

'Dot…' Maggie said quietly, to capture her sister's attention, as the Faradays, the whole family, including Lenny and Lily now, fussed over the child. 'I would love a cup of tea before I leave for work.'

Dot's gaze spun to her, perhaps realising she was behaving oddly. She turned to the teapot and kettle.

'Are you meant to be working today, Lily?' Maggie asked.

'No, I aven't spoken to the foreman since I came ome, an I wanna see Lenny off at the station. I'll come in afterwards an agree my shifts.' The look on Lily's face said she suddenly remembered the baby. 'If that's fine with you, Mrs— Mum. Are there shifts you'd prefer I don't do?'

'You work the hours that suit you, Lily. Hector and I can manage looking after Arthur around those times between the two of us.'

'And we can help,' Dot offered. 'There are plenty of us in the house to help care for him.'

'Thank you,' Lily said to Dot, then she shared a smile with Mr and Mrs Faraday that also said, *thank you*. 'I am grateful for all the elp you're givin me.'

Perhaps it was wrong, the child had no connection to Dot, yet a rush of relief raced through Maggie. This opportunity to look after a child might help relieve Dot's grief and guilt – it was a better idea than becoming a nun.

'I'm not working today, I have a night shift,' Dot said, looking at the group clustered around the baby. 'I could look after him while you say goodbye to Lenny.' The offer was made to the whole of Lenny's family, not just Lily.

Lily nodded. 'Yes, please. Thank you. That platform will be like a cattle market, so many of the men will be boardin.'

'Yes, please, thank you, Dot,' Mrs Faraday confirmed.

Maggie ate her breakfast in a world that continued to be distorted by oddities. In this home that still felt strange, with a hole in her heart that belonged to her father, the noises of a baby whom everyone cooed at as they ate, and with Lenny here, but about to go again…

And meanwhile, Nazis ran all over France like ants, working out ways to cross the sea.

A need for Ron clutched at Maggie's stomach, a fist gripping at the nerves right in the middle of her belly. Her desire was to be walking beside him, and to just have someone to talk to about nothing in particular. Just to talk about something that wasn't war, or anything sad.

33

CATHERINE PEARCE

Catherine climbed the steps to the platform of the train station, her left hand held tightly by Charles. His parents climbed the steps behind them.

He was pale.

He'd been silent this morning. She had walked to his house and eaten breakfast with his family.

They'd sat alone in her parents' parlour last evening, side by side on the sofa. The door had stood slightly ajar, but her parents and Maggie's aunt and uncle had let them be. He'd kissed her, in a desperate fashion, leaned her back and lain over her. His hand had cupped her breast, then released the buttons of her blouse and stroked her breast and nipple through the silk of her slip. She wasn't wearing a bra because she hadn't been able to do up the hooks and eyes. His warm hand had found her skin. His palm was rough, calloused. She'd let him lift her skirt and touch her there. She hadn't stopped him until he was going to undo his trousers.

'We can't, Charles.'

He had turned to his side, moving off her, squeezed into the space against the back of the sofa, giving her room to right her clothes. He had breathed heavily, but he had gallantly accepted her request to stop.

'Next time I'm home,' he'd said. 'I want to marry you.' His fingers had stroked the hair from her cheek and he'd kissed her lips.

'I'd like that. I'd love that, Charles. I don't want to wait any longer.' Not when you might die...

Her last silent thought hovered over them for the rest of the evening, a dark looming storm cloud. It was still there when they ate breakfast this morning. And now, neither of them was sure if they were about to say goodbye for the last time.

When she walked through the barrier onto the platform, her penny platform ticket in her skirt pocket, she spotted Lily with Lenny and his parents. Lily and Lenny were locked in an embrace, their lips firmly pressed together. She and Charles should have married too.

She did not speak to them. She did not like to disturb their kiss.

Charles let her hand go.

She looked at him. He pulled the cigarette packet from his pocket and started searching for a match. He had smoked constantly since he came home.

'Charles, do you have to?' his mother complained as he put the cigarette between his lips and struck the match. 'You'll be leaving in a moment.'

His eyebrows reached towards the peak of his cap, and he shook his head slightly.

In her mind Catherine heard him saying, *'Mother...'* dismissing her complaint.

Catherine had not complained about his smoking. She'd seen hundreds of other men facing the same memories, shock and grief, using cigarettes to fill their hands and absorb their thoughts, it hardly mattered. If it helped him, she did not care how often he smoked.

Several of the other men on the platform were smoking too.

After he put the matches away, she reached her right hand towards his. Then realised and turned to hold him with her left hand. He hadn't become accustomed to her wooden hand. Both the false hand and the stub of her forearm disturbed him. He frequently stared at her right arm, and he hated it when she touched him with it.

Lily stepped back from Lenny, letting him speak to his parents, and looked across the platform.

Catherine's gaze collided with hers. She lifted a hand and waved. Lily beckoned.

'Can we speak to Lily and Lenny?' she asked Charles. She did not want to leave him.

'Yes. Alright.'

Charles trailed after her, exhaling smoke into the air above her head. His parents followed.

'Hello,' she said in a rush to Lily.

'Av you eard about your other brothers?' Lily asked.

Catherine shook her head. 'No. Not yet. But they would have gone to their wives, as would any telegrams if they have not made it home.'

'My brother died,' Lily told her, her voice oddly blunt, as though she had not absorbed it. 'Is girlfriend gave me is child last night.'

'I'm sorry.' Catherine embraced her. 'That's awful.'

Lily drew back. 'We must be strong. All of us. Only one of Naomi's brothers as come back. Asher told Violet. Samuel is a prisoner.'

'He's Jewish,' Catherine stated the obvious, horrified, her mind racing through images of how the Germans might treat a Jewish prisoner of war.

Lily didn't respond to Catherine's statement – the truth might be unthinkable.

Catherine's stomach rolled a somersault, she had not been thinking about her brothers, her mind had been too full of Charles. But surely her parents would have heard if they had come home. She should cycle out to see their wives this week, before she returned to work.

The stationmaster's whistle blew. 'The train is approaching! Ladies and gentlemen, please step back from the edge of the platform!'

Catherine turned to Charles.

He dropped the rest of his cigarette and extinguished it beneath his boot.

She grasped their last moment, wrapping her arms around his neck to kiss him. But her right arm had encircled him first.

He reared back, almost in an expression of shock as the leather glove she had put over the wood must have brushed the back of his neck. Then he realised how inappropriate his reaction was and his hands held her waist and brought her close again and he kissed her.

She let her right arm fall and hang by her side as she kissed him back urgently.

The engine passed them, the steam and smoke embracing them, and then they broke apart. The tip of his nose brushed across hers and she breathed in his tobacco-scented breath. 'I love you,' he said over her lips.

'I love you too.'

He released her and turned to say goodbye to his parents, briefly embracing his father and mother. The coaches stopped beside them. The uniformed men on the platform crowded around the doors. Charles's expression stiffened as he looked towards the carriage door and his whole body seemed to tense.

'Shall we travel in the same carriage?' Lenny suggested.

Catherine was glad. She was terrified for Charles. Mentally, he did not seem ready to go back. But he was not physically unwell, there was no reason for him to deny being called back.

Charles's thoughts returned from somewhere else – Catherine imagined it was Dunkirk. He looked at Lenny, and smiled, in a way he had not smiled at her in all the time he'd been here. It was not broad, just one that seemed to transmit some shared understanding.

He nodded. 'Good idea. Come along then.' Charles turned to the train door.

Of course, Lenny was a private, a soldier, and Charles an officer. That didn't appear to bother Charles, though. Together, they joined the end of the group of men boarding the carriage.

Catherine felt a hand on her right elbow. She glanced across her shoulder and faced Lily. Lily's hand wrapped around Catherine's elbow as they stepped forward, following their men. Because Charles and Lenny had waited to be the last to board, there was a chance for them to turn and share one last embrace.

Charles's parents were close, but they allowed Catherine the last goodbye without interruption.

The stationmaster's whistle chased the men aboard.

Lenny stepped onto the train, then Charles. Charles pulled the door closed.

The window was already pushed down. Charles leaned out and pressed one last quick kiss on Catherine's lips, as Lenny reached around him and caught hold of Lily's hand. A third man reached out around them and waved at his relatives too.

The train whistle blew, and the engine's pistons chuffed as the train built up steam and rolled away. Lily ran a few steps, clinging onto Lenny's hand. Charles waved. The other man waved and then Lenny was waving too. Hands reached out all along the train waving as almost everyone on the platform raised an arm and waved back.

Teardrops trailed down Catherine's cheeks.
She turned and saw that Lily was weeping too.
They embraced each other, not attempting to hold back their emotions.
At least they had each other.
At least Catherine had her friends, the sisters she had dreamt of as a child.

34

NAOMI ISAACS

Tuesday 18 June

Dietrich's boot heels struck heavily on the hall's floorboards. Naomi knew it was him coming, his marching footsteps were unmistakable. He'd joined the Scouts. He'd volunteered to join the new Home Guard but they'd told him fifteen years of age was too young. He hoped as a Scout he could do something to help anyway. The Scouts were growing vegetables on waste ground, and helping evacuees and refugees. He said the Home Guard would accept him when he turned sixteen.

The evacuation of France and the news of Samuel's capture had jolted Dietrich. The war, the Nazis, had come into the house he thought was safe.

Naomi, like everyone else, expected France to yield and announce her surrender at any hour. And then what would happen? That is what everyone wondered.

'Look.' Dietrich entered the parlour, waving the leaflet Naomi must have heard being posted through the door.

He turned it so Naomi and her mother could see its title.

If the INVADER comes.

'What does it say?' Her mother set down her sewing. She was altering a dress for a neighbour who was expecting her first child.

'They must believe the Germans will come,' Dietrich said.

'We know this,' her mother said in a calm voice, holding out a hand to take the leaflet.

Naomi's stomach rolled, she was terrified of the German army arriving here. It was the speed with which they'd invaded France from border to coast that scared her. The invasion had begun the second week of May and here they were in the third week of June and France had no hope of victory.

'You must not be taken by surprise...' Her mother read aloud from the leaflet, her eyebrows lifting, then she read on silently.

At the beginning of the war, the newspapers had all talked of the threat of Hitler's favoured blitzkrieg approach – a sudden assault with bombing from the air and the ground in a constant and sustained attack. If Britain was unprepared, they had no hope of fighting back against this. It had happened to Poland, and now France.

Naomi leaned over and read the leaflet as her mother held it. Dietrich leaned across her mother's shoulder to read it too.

> When Holland and Belgium were invaded, the civilian population fled from their homes. They crowded on the roads, in cars, in carts, on bicycles and on foot, and so helped the enemy by preventing their own armies from advancing against the invaders. You must not allow this to happen here...
> STAY PUT.

The leaflet shouted at them.

The bold capital letters went on to describe more things they must do, and probably more importantly not do, to stop the German army winning Britain. It made it clear how true the Government thought it was that Hitler would try.

The twins ran into the room, playing a game of tag, oblivious to the danger. Naomi hoped they lived their lives here as happy as any childhood could be. Her family tried to protect them from news of the war; even when the family heard that Samuel was missing, her mother had taken the telegram and her misery up to her room.

The twins missed their parents, of course, but their mother and father had travelled from London to see them twice since the girls had returned.

Naomi's mother turned the page of the leaflet. The back contained more dos and don'ts and ended with a final warning.

THINK BEFORE YOU ACT. BUT THINK ALWAYS OF YOUR COUNTRY BEFORE YOU THINK OF YOURSELF.

35

CATHERINE PEARCE

The hinges of the letterbox creaked stiffly, then the internal flap rattled back down and post of some description flopped down on the doormat. Catherine was sitting in the leather armchair in her father's study, reading an Agatha Christie novel. She had begun reading more often to relieve her mind from thoughts of the war and her fears for Charles, and as everyone else was in the kitchen while she waited until it was time to leave for work, she'd sought the quiet of the study and her book.

The sound of the arrival of post had her rising so quickly she missed the table when her wooden hand put the book down. The book fell on the floor. She left it there and raced to see what letters had arrived. She immediately spotted Charles's handwriting addressing one of the letters to her. But there was something that wasn't in an envelope too. A large, printed leaflet. She picked that up, along with all of the post. *'If the INVADER comes,'* she read the title aloud. The Government really thought the Nazis were coming, then.

Her heart beat faster and faster as she read instructions on the need to damage your own car so the enemy couldn't use it, to dispose of food, petrol and maps and anything that might help the German soldiers progress from where they were to anywhere else. This leaflet, from the Ministry of Information, made the prospect of invasion real.

As she carried the leaflet and the post through to the kitchen, her mind visualised German tanks driving through Swindon – having seen the German aircraft, it was no longer unimaginable.

Her mother was standing at the table, kneading bread, working alongside Mrs Fletcher who was shelling peas, and Mrs Richardson who was sewing a shirt.

Her mother worked all the time now, on household chores, or sewing for the military cause, meeting with the Helping Hand Fund committee to help the women who had lost men, or packing gift boxes for the GWR men in the Army, Navy and Air Force.

'Look.' Catherine held out the leaflet for her mother to see. 'This is a government leaflet telling us how to fight the Nazis if they invade.'

Her mother wiped her floury hands on a tea towel. Then took the leaflet and the rest of the post, apart from the one from Charles that Catherine kept hold of.

Her mother put the leaflet on the table and looked through the other letters, looking for news of Harold or Roger. Graham had come home. Like Charles, he had been one of the last to leave the beaches of France. Roger was missing, no one knew if he had died, or been taken prisoner, or perhaps had somehow found a place to hide and someone to help him.

Catherine prayed nightly that he had not been captured, and was not dead, but being cared for by someone kind.

Harold, her eldest brother, was a prisoner of war. Captured by the Germans like Naomi's brother Samuel. They had no idea where the captured men had been taken to. The newspapers had talked about the Geneva Convention of 1929. It was the agreement made after the Great War. It meant, if the Germans treated British men well, the British would do likewise with the German prisoners in camps here.

There was nothing in the post to ease her mother's mind. She put down the letters and picked up the leaflet. 'Oh dear. Oh. Is this what we must expect?'

Catherine tore open the envelope from Charles, it contained a single thin sheet of paper, with writing on either side. He wrote with a shorter style now to fit more on a page.

He had not been allowed to tell her where he was, but she knew he was somewhere in the country building defences. Men were erecting pill boxes in strategic places along all the rivers and canals, where guns and soldiers would be housed to prevent the German army spreading through the country via water. They would not overtake Britain as easily as they had swarmed through France.

Mr Richardson had received a letter the other day from a friend who told them about the soldiers in the coastal towns. The army had lain mines beneath the sand on the beaches, stretched rolls of barbed wire across the whole length, and put in tall wooden criss-crossed posts to prevent landing craft from being able to unload tanks or any wheeled vehicles onto the beaches.

Charles wrote about missing her more often than he had before the evacuation.

She thought what he missed most was their life before the war. She folded his letter and slipped it into the pocket of her overalls. She would read it again at lunchtime.

'It is time I left,' she said. 'Goodbye, Mama. Mrs Fletcher. Mrs Richardson.' Her mother turned her cheek, so Catherine could kiss her there.

As Catherine left the room, her right arm lifted, as though her hand would wave.

When she worked, Catherine now cycled to and from the Railway Village with Naomi. Naomi left her bicycle at Violet's, so she had an opportunity to see Asher, while Catherine left hers at Park Lodge so she could walk to work with Lily and Maggie.

She took her bicycle out of the shed, thinking about the leaflet and wondering whether, if the Germans came, she would have to puncture the tyres on her bike too. But an army wouldn't get very far on one bike.

She yawned as she climbed onto the bicycle and cycled towards Naomi's house. Even one-handed work was exhausting. Mostly because of the long hours. But pressing buttons at the right time so she didn't injure anyone also needed constant concentration. She had tried working a lathe once but the skill in her left hand wasn't good enough. She was getting better with it though, she was improving the dexterity of her left hand by forcing it to hold a pen and write.

She did not have to knock. Naomi was waiting on the pavement for her, holding her bike. She waved as Catherine cycled about the corner of her street.

When Catherine rode closer, she saw that Naomi was not her normal smiling self.

A year ago, to think it was strange that someone was unusually glum when their brother was a prisoner of war would have been an odd thought. But now, everyone was enduring this and carrying on, everyone looked haggard and wan but still smiled.

Catherine didn't say anything, because she knew why Naomi's lips were downturned. That leaflet would have worried her. The war, the worry for her brother and of an invasion, must have got into Naomi's soul today.

When Catherine reached Park Lodge and knocked on the door, she saw that Lily was not herself either. As they walked to work, Lily's steps were slower. If she were a child, Catherine would say she was dragging her feet. Though she smiled as she spoke about little Arthur. She had told Catherine she had promised Lenny she would keep laughing and smiling, because that is what he was fighting for.

Then there was Maggie, who was trying to cheerfully carry on with life while she grieved for her dad and her old home.

Life was more challenging today, but, as Naomi had said when they went to the swimming baths, they would always have each other, they would survive together, no matter what happened next.

On the other side of the tunnel, Catherine threaded her left arm around Naomi's and her right around Maggie's, so they were linked by their elbows, in a chain. Maggie glanced sideways and smiled. She knew what Catherine intended, for her to continue the pattern. She threaded her arm through Lily's, and Lily threaded hers through Violet's. Then they walked on, in their line of five, unbreakable – Catherine's rally of Great Western Railway machine shop sisters.

They would never be separated, not by life, by marriages, by accidents or by war.

36

LILY FARADAY

Sunday 23 June

Lily stayed in the pew after the sung Mass service finished, with Mr and— with Hector and Valerie, her new mother and father. She was struggling with calling them Mum and Dad but at least trying to use their first names.

Maggie and her sisters, and Ron and Violet stayed in the pews too with Catherine and Joe Marsh, who had attended the service in St Mark's solely so they could be with Lily and little Arthur for his christening.

When everyone else had left they stood and walked across to the church font, Lily with Arthur in her arms.

Farther Arnold took Arthur, leaning him back so his head was above the font. He poured holy water over his forehead and hair, washing his sins away, as though a baby might have any. 'Arthur Faraday, I baptise you in the name of the Father, the Son and the Holy Spirit...' Then, with the water on his forefinger, he made the sign of the cross on Arthur's forehead.

Catherine, Maggie and Violet were Arthur's godmothers, and Ron and Joe his godfathers. Lily and Lenny had agreed on Ron and Joe in their exchange of letters.

The choice about Arthur's surname had not been theirs in the end. Only parents could register a birth, and his birth had to be registered if they wanted to claim rations for him, and when he was older, if he was going to have a place at school. So, little Arthur was now theirs, according to the government administration. She made Lenny promise in a letter to tell Arthur about his mother and father when he was older, if she couldn't.

Lenny's regiment had been building the coastal defences for the last few weeks, and the flow of their letters, back and forth, had been almost daily, with the post travelling via the trains.

As Father Arnold raised Arthur, drips of water ran from Arthur's forehead into his eyes, making the baby cry. Dot reached out in the same moment as Lily, as if she would take him. Father Arnold passed him to Lily. 'There...' he said. He glanced towards Dot and smiled.

Dot was good with Arthur. She would often pick him up if he was grumbling. She was good at settling him too. But like Lily, she had helped raise siblings. He was a lucky boy, it was as though he had five mothers with Lily, Maggie and all of her sisters in the house, as well as his grandma and grandad.

'You're a very lucky boy,' Lily whispered to him. 'With so many people to love you.' And a boy needed all the love he could get when the world had gone mad.

This morning, she'd been woken by Mr Faraday shouting the newspaper's headline through the house. 'France has signed an armistice!'

All the women had run downstairs in their nightclothes to hear the rest of the news. An armistice was a surrender.

He was reading the article as Lily came downstairs with Arthur in her arms. He looked around at all the women and said, 'The Gestapo made the French sign it in the same place where Germany conceded at the end of the Great War. The bast—'

'Hector!' Valerie had warned him to mind his language.

Lily had felt like cursing too.

Mr Faraday had looked at the newspaper then and read the article aloud for them all to hear. 'The Americans and Germans released the news that the treaty was signed at 5.50 p.m. on 22 June.' He looked back up. 'The French have not said a word about it. No announcement has been made to the French people on their radio broadcasts. And Germany have refused to make public the terms of the French surrender. The only thing the reporters know is that they asked for complete surrender of all the land, sea, air forces and armaments, but the commander in chief of the French forces in the Middle East is defiant. He's said they will fight on, and good for him, I say.'

'Yes, good for him,' Maggie had responded, unusually the vocal one among her sisters.

The French soldiers Lily met at the camp had come to mind as she listened to the news. She knew those men would keep fighting. They'd come to England for that reason.

Mr Faraday had looked back at the newspaper, then at them all. 'God bless the French troops, because they're still fighting in France too despite,' he looked down and read the words in the article, 'the immense difficulties caused by the Germans' deep penetration of the country, where they are disputing the ground inch by inch.' He looked back up, tears in his eyes. 'All the French colonies are fighting on, side by side with the British Empire, under British orders. Our soldiers will support the French defence of Egypt too. Hitler and Mussolini must be fighting to control the Suez Canal.'

Churchill had said they were fighting for civilisation, and Lenny was involved in it. He'd told her in a letter, *'I might be posted to Egypt.'* This morning's paper told her why.

Her heart beat quicker as they walked out of the church in a group. Arthur's hand rose and his fingers wrapped around one of the curls of her hair. His eyes looked into hers, searching for love. Every time she looked into his eyes she saw a future – and hope. Her heart ached for Art, but she had Arthur who needed her now.

When her friends had signed up to make bombshells in the factory, most of them had done so to help the men fight. She had signed up to earn money to escape her father. Today, because they'd killed Art, and for this little boy in her arms and for Lenny, she had reasons to fight, and she would work her fingers to the bone to win this war.

She was fighting to save Britain now, let alone the rest of the world.

EPILOGUE

North Wilts Herald

Friday, 14th June 1940

Trip Arrangements Must Be Cancelled

An official announcement by Mr C. B. Collett, Chief Mechanical Engineer of the G.W.R., states that Swindon Works Annual Holiday is postponed INDEFINITELY, and employees have been advised that any arrangement they have made should be cancelled.

* * *

MORE FROM JANE LARK

The next book in The Great Western Railway Girls series from Jane Lark is available to order now here:
https://mybook.to/GWRGBook3BackAd

ACKNOWLEDGEMENTS

Thank you to my editor Francesca Best and all the fabulous team at Boldwood Books, who are an absolute joy to work with. You are all so committed to finding the readers for the books, and ensuring the books are right for the readers you've already discovered, it's a fabulous connective way to work, and such a pleasure to be writing for you.

So, of course, let me thank you, the readers, too. Books are nothing without readers, and I appreciate every single one of you and especially thank, from the bottom of my heart, all those who take the time to login to sellers' websites to post reviews on the books' webpage, those who follow my author pages on your book sellers website, who recommend my books to their friends and other readers, and who sneakily turn my book to be front-facing in a shop or a library. You are all amazing, and every little thing you do to share how much you enjoyed a book enables me to write more! Thank you.

To the discover real stories and research behind the Great Western Railway Girls series, follow my **Jane Lark** blog at https://janelark.blog

ABOUT THE AUTHOR

Jane Lark is a writer of compelling, passionate and emotionally charged fiction filled with diverse characters. She is an international bestselling author of both historical fiction and psychological thrillers, and a finalist in British Fiction Industry awards.

Can't get enough of Jane Lark's gripping sagas? Sign up for Jane's newsletter to get an exclusive prologue from The Great Western Railway Girls!

Visit Jane's website: www.janelark.co.uk

Follow Jane on social media here:

- x.com/JaneLark
- facebook.com/Janelarkauthor
- instagram.com/jane.lark
- youtube.com/@janelark3537
- bookbub.com/authors/jane-lark

ALSO BY JANE LARK

The Great Western Railway Girls Series
The Great Western Railway Girls
The Great Western Railway Girls Do Their Bit

The Marlow Family Secrets Series
The Dangerous Love of a Rogue
The Seductive Love of a Lady
The Secret Love of a Gentleman
The Reckless Love of an Heir
The Tainted Love of a Captain
The Scandalous Love of a Duke
The Forbidden Love of an Officer

Sixpence Stories

Introducing Sixpence Stories!

Discover page-turning historical novels from your favourite authors, meet new friends and be transported back in time.

Join our book club
Facebook group

https://bit.ly/SixpenceGroup

Sign up to our newsletter

https://bit.ly/SixpenceNews

Boldwood

Boldwood Books is an award-winning fiction publishing company seeking out the best stories from around the world.

Find out more at www.boldwoodbooks.com

Join our reader community for brilliant books, competitions and offers!

Follow us
@BoldwoodBooks
@TheBoldBookClub

Sign up to our weekly deals newsletter

https://bit.ly/BoldwoodBNewsletter

www.ingramcontent.com/pod-product-compliance
Lightning Source LLC
Chambersburg PA
CBHW011404210526
45464CB00009B/3034